In Dublin's Fair City

In Dublin's
Fair City

Rhys Bowen

 St. Martin's Minotaur New York

IN DUBLIN'S FAIR CITY. Copyright © 2007 by Rhys Bowen. All rights reserved.
Printed in the United States of America.
For information, address St. Martin's Press, 175 Fifth Avenue, New York, N.Y. 10010.

ISBN-13: 978-0-312-32819-1

*This book is dedicated to the memory of two wonderful women,
almost Molly's contemporaries, who died within a week of each other.
Marie McCormack and Alice Stinchcomb were smart, feisty, enthusiastic, like Molly.
They were both university graduates at a time when it was unfashionable for
young women to pursue education. They devoured books—especially mine.
Their minds remained sharp and witty until the end .
I will miss them terribly.*

❧ One ❧

"B e careful what you wish for."

That was another of my mother's favorite sayings—one of the few in her wealth of warnings that didn't predict a bad end, hell fire, and eternal damnation. It was brought out any time I expressed my childhood ambitions to see Dublin one day, to dance at a ball like a real lady, to own a horse and carriage, or just to free myself from our dreary life in Ballykillin. The end of the sentence was rarely said, but always implied—"or you may get it."

Now it had finally come back to haunt me. My mother would undoubtedly be chuckling her head off in heaven, or wherever she was spending the hereafter. Ever since I'd arrived in New York and met Captain Daniel Sullivan, I suppose I had secretly nourished a hope that we could be together some day. Although I told myself that this would never happen, also that he was unreliable, two-faced, and all around bad news, I had never quite managed to put him out of my thoughts or my heart. And now it seemed I was being offered as much of Daniel Sullivan's company as I ever wanted. More, in fact.

Three weeks had gone by since his release from The Tombs on bail, and he was still charged with taking bribes from a gang member, being in the pay of a gang, and setting up an illegal prize fight. Since then he'd received no news on his future or his fate, although we now knew who had so carefully plotted his downfall. It was a horrible way to be living, to be sure—like walking on eggs—and Daniel wasn't taking it

1

well. He was used to being cock o' the walk, a powerful man who commanded the respect of his colleagues among the New York police and who had connections to the Four Hundred—the highest-born families in town. Those weeks in The Tombs had taxed him physically and mentally so that he was now alternately moping or prowling around like a caged tiger.

And much of his prowling was being done at my house, which is why I was pacing the floor myself one muggy September afternoon. Daniel had finally managed to engage the services of a reputable attorney, who was working on his behalf, and had arranged a meeting today with the police commissioner, Mr. John Partridge. And I was left to pace the floor at home, wondering if he'd return a free man, reinstated at his job. Please let him be freed from this terrible burden, I found myself praying, even though I was not much one for chats with the Almighty. And please let him get his old job back and leave me in peace. I was appalled at myself immediately. Wasn't I supposed to be in love with Daniel Sullivan? Hadn't I seriously considered the prospect of marrying him some day? And yet here I was, dreading the thought of his presence. What about for better or worse, richer, poorer, in sickness or health? This marriage question would require some serious rethinking, provided Daniel was ever in a position to ask for my hand, of course.

While I waited I cleaned the house feverishly, polishing my few pieces of furniture till I could see my face in them and still no Daniel. Surely the interview must be over by now. Surely the commissioner would have no alternative but to declare him a free man. I paced the house, exactly as Daniel had done so often these past days. I pulled back the net curtain, looked down Patchin Place, then let it fall again. Suddenly I could stand it no longer. I needed company, and I needed it now. Pleasant company, amusing company. And I knew exactly where that could be found.

I crossed the street and knocked on the door of the house on the other side of the alleyway. It was opened by an alarming vision with a deathly white face and two green circles where eyes should have been. I gasped as the vision removed one of the green circles.

"Sorry about that," she said. "Cucumber. We're trying out skin

2

remedies. Sid just read an article in *Ladies' Home Journal* on the subject of natural health and beauty from the larder."

The white-faced ghost now revealed itself as my dear friend and neighbor, Augusta Mary Walcott, of the Boston Walcotts, but more usually known by her nickname, Gus.

"*Ladies' Home Journal?*" I had to chuckle. "You two are the last creatures on earth I would have suspected of reading ladies' magazines."

"The cover promised interesting tips for decorating the home in the Japanese style, which we were thinking of doing anyway, so we bought the magazine and there was this delicious article on health and beauty, so of course we had to try it for ourselves. Come on in, you're just in time to try our complexion paste." She ushered me in and set off ahead of me down the hall and into their kitchen. "It's egg whites boiled in rose water with alum and oil of sweet almonds, and a dash of honey, all whipped together into a paste, and then left to dry," she called over her shoulder. "I must say, it feels very strange as it hardens, but you can actually sense all the impurities being drawn from the body."

Sid and Gus had added a conservatory onto the back of their kitchen and the doors between the two were open, as were the doors to the little garden beyond, giving the place a delightfully rural feel. As we approached I could see another white-faced specter lying under a white sheet on a garden chair, looking horribly like a corpse until she started fanning herself furiously.

"These damn flies," she muttered. "I suppose they are attracted to egg white, but they won't leave me alone."

"We have company, Sid darling," Gus called. "Molly has come to share in our experiment."

Elena Goldfarb, usually known as Sid, sat up and peeled the cucumber slices from her eyes. "I wanted to send Gus to fetch you, but she said you wouldn't be able to desert Daniel the Deceiver."

"He's not around at the moment, saints be praised," I said.

"That doesn't sound like the voice of a woman in love." Sid attempted to frown, but her mask would not let her.

"I know. It's terrible of me. I should be delighted that he is gracing me with his constant presence, but frankly I'm not. His gloomy, moody behavior is driving me insane. I've come to the conclusion that I won't make a very good wife."

"I'm sure every person on this earth drives his or her partner insane from time to time," Sid said. "I know we do. Now tie back your hair and let me slather some of this mixture onto your face. Madame Vestris is said to have preserved her beauty with this very concoction until late in life."

I had no idea who Madame Vestris was. "Oh, I really don't think—" I began.

"Don't be a spoil sport, Molly." Gus was already gathering back my unruly mop of hair. "Besides, it's supposed to draw out impurities so you may be more saintly and forgiving the next time Daniel comes to call."

I resigned myself to my fate, and was soon laughing with Sid and Gus as they turned me into a meringue. The laughter felt strange. How long since I had laughed and allowed myself to be silly with friends? The whole summer had been one of tension and heartbreak, to say nothing of the constant worry about money. Now I was recovered from my recent ordeal, both physically and mentally, but there were no new cases on the books for my small detective agency.

"So where is the dreadful Daniel this afternoon?" Sid asked. "Sit still, or the cucumber slices will fall off."

"His new attorney has set up a meeting with the police commissioner and is asking to have all the charges against him dropped."

"Well, that's finally good news, isn't it?" Gus said.

"I do hope so," I said. "Daniel's reputation means so much to him. His fellow officers still think he betrayed them, and I know how deeply that has affected him."

"All's well that ends well," Sid said. "Daniel will be exonerated and go back to work, Molly can get on with her life, and peace will reign in Patchin Place."

She was just finishing the sentence when there came a thunderous knocking on their front door. Gus hurried to open it. We heard an explosive, "What the deuce?"

"Beauty treatments." We heard Gus's calm voice. "And if you're looking for Molly, she's with us."

I hastily removed the cucumber slices from my eyes in time to see Daniel striding down the hallway toward me.

"I went to your house and you weren't there," Daniel said petulantly.

"So being a great detective, you deduced she might be over here with us," Sid said calmly. "Would you like a glass of ice tea, Captain Sullivan, or something stronger?"

"I'm not in the mood for socializing, I'm afraid," Daniel said. "I've just had an infuriating meeting with the police commissioner."

"He wouldn't agree to drop all the charges?" I asked.

"No, he damned well wouldn't." He checked himself. "I apologize for the language, ladies, but my patience has been stretched to its limit this afternoon. Molly, would you please remove that ridiculous concoction from your face and let's go home."

I put my hand up to my cheek. "I think it needs to harden first or it will be impossible to remove," I said. "But what was Mr. Partridge's reason for not declaring you innocent on the spot?"

"Because that snake Quigley refuses to confess to anything. So until he is brought to trial and found guilty, I am still officially charged and will still have to stand trial myself."

"But that's ridiculous," I said, rising from my garden chair with difficulty. "We have the proof that Quigley is guilty."

"Of his part in the murders, yes, but there is nothing to prove that he orchestrated my meeting with the gang member; and I have, of course, admitted to my part in setting up the prize fight."

"But they can't punish you for that. Half the New York Police Department was present at that fight. I saw them with my own eyes."

Daniel sighed. "I know none of it makes sense, but I have the feeling that Partridge wants to make an example of me. The only way that he'll let me off is if I can get the gang member in question or Monk Eastman himself to come forward and categorically deny that I was working with them."

"Then that's what you should do," I said.

Daniel gave a bitter chuckle. "Ask Monk Eastman to speak in my defense? I don't think you understand the adversary, my dear. He would like nothing more than my downfall. He'll not say a good word on my behalf nor let any of his gangsters."

"He might, if I asked him for you," I said.

"Under no circumstances, Molly. And that is an order."

5

"You can't order me around," I said. "I'm not married to you, and even if I were, I'd not take commands like some dog."

He laughed again. "I don't doubt it for a second," he said. "But I'd rather suffer the indignities of a trial than send you to plead with Monk Eastman on my behalf."

"Then send Gentleman Jack to plead for you," I said. "He must be in favor with Monk at the moment. I'm sure he made Monk a good deal of money by winning that prize fight."

"I'm sure he did, but you've met him, Molly. The man is so addlepated that he'd forget his own name if people didn't keep addressing him by it. What good could he do?"

"At least give him a try, Daniel," I said. "Write a letter to Monk and send Jack in a hansom cab to deliver it in person. He could then add his appeal to the letter."

"Molly, I can't go on discussing this in these circumstances," Daniel snapped. "Would you please do as I ask. Remove that ridiculous stuff—it makes you look like an iced cake—and let us continue this conversation in private. I hardly think it appropriate to discuss my current situation in front of those who aren't concerned with it."

"Oh, we are most concerned," Gus said. "It affects us too. If you are unhappy, then Molly is unhappy, and if Molly is unhappy, then we cannot truly enjoy life ourselves. And since it is our aim and pledge to enjoy every moment, the sooner the situation is rectified, the better."

"Hmmph," was all that Daniel could say to that.

"Captain Sullivan, let us pour you a glass of brandy," Gus said in her soothing voice. "I'm sure you have had the most vexing afternoon, and poor Molly was quite distressed when she came to visit. It's not easy for her either, you know."

"I'm sure it's not," Daniel said. He sighed again. "Very well. I accept your kind offer, simply because I refuse to walk across the street until Molly has removed that stuff from her face."

"Replace the cucumber slices, Molly, or your eyes won't feel the true benefit," Gus directed as she disappeared into the drawing room to find the decanter. Feeling stupidly self-conscious with Daniel's eyes on me, I replaced them, then thought better of it.

"I think you should stay for dinner over here, don't you, Sid?" Gus said, returning with a generously full brandy snifter. "We could try something Japanese. I've been dying to do things with raw fish."

"I really don't think . . ." Daniel began when there was yet another knock at the front door.

"My, but we are popular this afternoon," Sid said, attempting to rise.

"Perhaps I should answer it," Daniel said. "You ladies present a most alarming appearance."

Almost instantly we heard a man's voice saying in theatrical tones, "What a disappointment. I was expecting to see two lovely ladies. Don't tell me they've hired a butler?"

"The lovely ladies you refer to are unable to receive visitors at this moment," Daniel said. "And I am not the butler."

"Unable? Don't tell me they have succumbed to the horrible grippe that is felling everyone. Oh God, tell me it's not bad news. You're not the doctor, are you?"

"No, I'm not, and may I ask who you are so that I can convey a message?"

"Moi? I thought everyone knew me. Tell them that Ryan is pining for them and has to see them immediately. You wouldn't happen to know where the divine Miss Molly is, would you? She's the one I am especially seeking tonight."

"Miss Molly is with the other ladies at the back of the house, but they are in no condition—"

Before he could utter another word there was the sound of some kind of scuffle or commotion, a yell from Daniel, and wicked Irish playwright Ryan O'Hare came flying down the hallway toward us. He was wearing a white peasant shirt, a royal blue cape, and I must say he made a most dramatic entrance.

He stopped short when he saw us then gave a delighted gasp. "It's the complexion paste from *Ladies' Home Journal*. What fun. I'm dying to try it."

"We used up the last on Molly," Sid said.

"Molly, my angel, is that you under there? Yes, it is. I'd know that delicate white hand anywhere. Let me give it a kiss."

"I'm sorry about this, ladies," Daniel said in a tight voice. "I presume you know this gentleman?"

"Oh dear. You two gentlemen obviously haven't been introduced. Ryan O'Hare, playwright extraordinaire. Captain Daniel Sullivan of the New York police."

"Not Daniel the Deceiver?" Ryan exclaimed. "We meet at last. I have heard much about you. We're all so proud that our dear Molly managed to rescue you from prison."

"Well, actually I'm only out on bail," Daniel said dryly. "Of course I'm grateful for what Molly tried to do."

Then it hit me. He didn't know the truth. I had never managed to speak of that night on Coney Island, so he didn't know what I'd been through. And would never know, I decided. That chapter of my life was firmly sealed.

"I think the paste has hardened enough," Sid said, and began to peel it off. We followed suit. Ryan danced between us, stroking our cheeks. "Wonderful," he exclaimed, "deliciously soft, like a baby's bottom."

"Really, Ryan, you'll go too far one day," Gus scolded. "You know you only do it to shock."

"One just wants to have one's little fun," Ryan said, pouting.

"Molly, can we please leave now?" Daniel came over to me and took my arm.

"You haven't drunk your brandy," Sid pointed out.

"Thank you, but in the circumstances—" Daniel said.

"You can't possibly take Molly away. I forbid it," Ryan said. "It was to seek her out that I trudged all this way through the heat and the flies and the dust." Ryan took hold of my other arm. "I'm whisking you away, Molly dearest. I've been instructed to escort you to a party tonight. Someone is dying to meet you."

I glanced at Daniel. His face was like granite.

"I'm afraid that I can't go to a party tonight, Ryan," I said, then my curiosity got the better of me. "Who is dying to meet me?"

"None other than Tommy Burke."

"I'm afraid I don't know Tommy Burke," I said.

"Never heard of Tommy Burke?" Ryan sounded shocked. "My dear girl, he is only the leading theatrical impresario in the city. If Tommy Burke puts on a play, it is always a sensation. Did you not see his version of *Uncle Tom's Cabin*? Not a dry eye in the house. But that's beside the point. Tommy Burke is hosting a fabulous party tonight at the roof cabaret at Madison Square. Now tell me you can't resist that, can you?"

"My, that does sound glamorous," Sid said. "But you're only inviting Molly so we understand. Gus and I are mortally wounded that we're not to be included."

"Of course you two are included. Our bold police captain too, if he so wishes," Ryan said. "It just happened that Tommy Burke expressed a desire to meet Molly."

"Why?" I asked. "How could he have heard of me?"

"I can't exactly say. Something to do with your detective work, I understand. Anyway, all will be made clear tonight at the roof garden cabaret of Madison Square Garden, while sipping the most delightful champagne. I'll return to escort you at eight. Wear something devastating." He glanced at the clock on the kitchen wall. "Horrors. Is that the time? I'm late for my fitting. Must fly."

And he was gone.

❧ TWO ❧

D aniel and I crossed the cobbled alleyway in stony silence.

"You can't seriously be contemplating going to a party with that dreadful creature?" Daniel said, as I closed the front door behind us.

"He's not a dreadful creature. He's actually quite delightful and very talented."

"He's a freak, Molly," Daniel said, "an outcast from civilized society."

"As for that," I said, "you are also an outcast from civilized society at the moment, are you not? A jailbird, only out on bail? Dear me, what must Miss Van Woekem and her set be saying about you now?"

His face flushed with anger. "It's not the same thing at all and you damned well know it," he said. "You let him paw you all over. Is that the way you behave when I'm not around?"

"Paw me all over? Daniel, he took hold of my arm. He patted my cheek, if I remember correctly. That hardly constitutes pawing. And for another thing, Ryan sees me as a sister, nothing more. His interests lie elsewhere."

"Another Oscar Wilde, you mean? I suspected as much. Molly, I utterly forbid you to go to this party tonight or to go on mixing with people like that."

Like many of my fellow countrymen, I've never been known to back down from a good fight or a challenge.

11

"You utterly forbid me?" I demanded. "And who are you to be laying down the law, I'd like to know? Until a couple of weeks ago you were promised to another woman, and I don't recall you getting down on one knee and proposing to me since then. And if you had, then this kind of talk would cause me to rip the ring right off my finger."

"Then maybe it is lucky that we have made no such promises," Daniel said stiffly.

"How right you are. Nobody owns me, Daniel Sullivan. I am my own person, and I mix with whom I choose. If you can't trust me enough to have good judgment in my friends and my actions, then I see no future for us together."

Daniel picked up his straw boater. "In that case there is little point in my remaining here any longer. Good day to you, Miss Murphy."

He gave a polite little bow and left. I stood there staring at that front door. I was so tempted to run after him and make everything all right again, but I forced myself to stay where I was. For the first time in my life I'd had a glimpse of what being married might mean: having a man dictate to me how I should think, with whom I should associate, surrendering my own identity and my freedom. Why did so many women opt for this so readily? Love, I supposed. Did I love Daniel Sullivan enough to marry him and subordinate my will to his for the rest of my life? In the first flush of romance with Daniel I'd have willingly said yes to any proposal. And then there's security, of course. How many women can provide for themselves? Even professional women find it hard to overcome the prejudices of society. Those with private incomes like Gus and Sid do just fine, but I wasn't making too good a job of keeping J. P. Riley and Associates afloat.

Which brought me back to the invitation for this evening. Something to do with your detective work, Ryan had said. Did that mean that Tommy Burke, impresario, was interested in hiring me for an assignment? Wild horses would not keep me away from the party tonight.

I half expected that Daniel might come back to apologize for getting upset over nothing, but he didn't, leaving me feeling uneasy and hollow inside. Maybe I felt a little guilty too, because I did realize that Daniel was on edge at the moment and it was not a good time to confront him. But it didn't bode well for any hope of a future relationship if we both flew off the handle so easily and had such different views of what we wanted from life.

By eight o'clock I was dressed in my finest attire, a sea green taffeta dinner dress, cast-off from Gus's days as a society debutante. The leg-o'-mutton sleeves were now old-fashioned, but the color contrasted well with my red hair. Besides, it was either that or a muslin. After much struggling I managed to tame my hair and hold it in place with tortoise-shell combs. The complexion paste had certainly made my face feel smooth, but it was glowing like a setting sun and I had to calm it down with some corn starch. Still, the final result, as I glanced in the mirror, was not too terrible; and I felt a wave of excitement surge through me. Fancy parties at a roof cabaret with a famous theater impresario were not something that happened often in my life.

Sid and Gus emerged at the same moment as I, looking stunning in emerald green and peacock blue. Sid's short dark hair was styled in a sleek, smooth cap, and I noticed that under her emerald green theater cape, she was wearing trousers. Normally such attire would cause a stir, but I suspected that at a theatrical party, she would feel right at home. I supposed that Daniel did have a point when he saw that such friends would be frowned upon in polite society. But then we didn't live in polite society.

Ryan was waiting for us at the entrance to Patchin Place, having already secured a cab, and we all piled in. He was still wearing the royal blue cape over a frilled lace shirt tonight and looked ridiculously like Hamlet.

"No Daniel, I notice," Ryan said. "Not his cup of tea, does one surmise?"

"Daniel walked out in a huff after forbidding me to attend this party," I said.

"And you didn't allow yourself to be browbeaten. Splendid. Well done," Sid said.

"Have you ever known me to be browbeaten?" I asked.

"No, but women have been known to act quite ridiculously when it comes to pleasing a man."

"For your information," I said, "I don't ever intend to take orders from a man, not even Daniel Sullivan. If he doesn't trust me to choose my own friends, then he'd make a poor sort of husband."

"Ah, so we were to blame for the upset," Sid said. "Daniel doesn't approve of your mixing with people like us."

"Then I pity Daniel and his lack of judgment," I said. "And we will talk no more about him."

We were making our way up Sixth Avenue and I stared out at the pageant of New York life unfolding on the sidewalks, as it did every warm evening: mothers sitting on stoops with babies on their laps, small boys playing kick the can, small girls jumping rope. As always I was conscious that I was in a great city, teeming with life, full of exuberance and promise, and I tried to put aside my dark mood.

"Tell me, Ryan," Gus said, steering the conversation onto a new topic, "what has happened to the good Dr. Birnbaum these days?"

"We've parted company, alas," Ryan said. "I think, like Daniel, he found my company detrimental to his professional standing in the community. Even though I tried so hard to be moderate in all things and actually wore an ordinary dinner jacket in the evenings, I fear my reputation had preceded me. We parted amicably."

"I'm sorry," Sid said.

"Don't be," Ryan said. "The world is full of wonderful new opportunities, I always find."

I looked at him with affection. These were my friends who sailed through life determined to wring every ounce of pleasure and excitement from it. Nothing about them was ordinary or plain or boring.

The cab came to a halt outside an imposing brick building. I'd glanced up at it from the outside before, admiring the Moorish colonnades and the tower that seemed to go up into the sky, but I'd never been inside. Never dreamed I'd have the chance to go inside.

Fashionably dressed theater crowds were milling around on the sidewalk. Beggars and hawkers hovered in the gutters, swarming up to each carriage or cab as it came to a halt. Flowers were thrust at us. Hands reached up imploringly, but Ryan whisked us successfully in through an archway and up a flight of steps. As we entered the rooftop cabaret I was definitely overawed and hung back as Ryan forged his way into the room. The room was decorated with statues in archways, tall palm trees around the walls, and Moorish style chandeliers. The floor space was packed with an absolute throng of people, through which waiters with trays of food and champagne dodged and darted, trays held high above their heads. On the stage at the far end a Negro band was playing some kind of modern syncopated music to which several brave couples were attempting to dance with strange, jerky movements. The noise level in the crowd almost drowned out the band. Jewels glittered and sparkled in the gleam of the electric lightbulbs that festooned the chandeliers. Handsome men in tails, glamorous women, sporting ostrich plumes in their coiffures, mingled with theater folk as outrageously dressed as Ryan.

Ryan swept ahead of us into the fray, arms open wide, greeting, embracing, beaming. He seemed to know everybody. Gus and Sid also seemed to have their share of acquaintances, and I felt like Cinderella. I stood there while the crowd pressed around me, feeling dowdy and out of place and wishing I hadn't come. A tray of champagne appeared. I accepted a glass when offered, reminding myself an affair like this had been beyond my wildest dreams just two years ago. I was here in the liveliest city in the world, mingling with its most fashionable residents. Not bad for a girl from a peasant cottage in Ballykillin. I resolved to have a good time no matter what and drained my glass.

"Oh, there you are, Molly. Your champagne glass is empty. Let me get you another," Ryan said, returning to my side.

"The champagne certainly seems to be flowing tonight, doesn't it?" I commented.

"Literally," he answered. "Have you seen the fountain yet?" He dragged me across the room. And there in one corner was a fountain, flowing, if my eyes didn't deceive me, with champagne. "Holy mother, what will they think of next?" I muttered and Ryan laughed. "Tommy Burke has a reputation to live up to," he said. "If his parties are not the talk of the town, then he feels he has failed. Come on, let's try to find him."

We fought our way through the crowd. It was a warm, muggy night to start with. In that confined space it was stiflingly hot, and the smells of competing perfumes, cigars, and perspiring bodies made me feel as if

I might faint. I was relieved when Ryan came to a halt next to a large man in tails. He was middle aged with a good head of wiry gray hair, big boned, beefy, round faced, red cheeked, like an Irish peasant. He had a glass in one hand and a cigar in the other, and he was talking with animation to a gorgeous auburn-haired woman in a stunning white silk gown with a train that she carried over one white-gloved wrist.

For once even Ryan appeared to be overawed. He waited for a lull in the conversation before he tapped the man on the arm. "Here she is, Tommy. Miss Molly Murphy. I promised I'd produce her and I have."

The man turned and his shrewd little black boot-button eyes looked me up and down appraisingly.

"Miss Molly Murphy, eh?" he said, and stuck out a beefy hand. "I'm delighted to meet you, young woman."

"Delighted to meet you too, sir," I said, "but I'm intrigued as to why you wanted to meet me, Mr. Burke. You're not thinking of offering me a part in your next play, are you?"

At this he threw back his head and laughed. "Offer you the lead instead of Oona here? Now there's a thought." And I realized that I had seen pictures of the woman in white gracing posters and newsstands. Oona Sheehan, one of the darlings of the Broadway stage.

"We know you are notoriously fickle, Tommy dear," Oona said in a deep, melodious voice. "If you found someone sufficiently younger and prettier, you'd drop me in a second. I know my days are numbered." She turned to look at me and winked.

"Never," Tommy exclaimed. "You'll still be the darling of the public when you're sixty, just like the divine Madame Sarah."

"And one hopes I'll keep my looks longer than she has," Oona said. "We live in the same building, you know. We each keep a suite of rooms in Hoffman House, and I nod to her from time to time. I fear she has become quite plain and ordinary looking."

"But she can still act," Tommy said. "By God, she can still act."

"Are you a fellow Thespian, Molly?" Oona asked. "I don't recall seeing you—"

"Indeed no, Miss Sheehan. I've no aspirations to go on the stage."

"You might do well for yourself," Tommy said. "I'll wager a good pair of legs extends up from those trim little ankles."

"Tommy, you are incorrigible. Now you've made her blush," Oona said.

"Surely not. Don't lady detectives have to be as tough as nails?"

"She's a lady detective?" Oona asked.

"So Ryan tells me. Although I never expected a lady detective to look so young and winsome. So are you really and truly a lady detective, my dear?"

"I am."

"And Irish too, by the sound of it?" Tommy asked.

"I am that too."

"A perfect combination for my needs. I think you might do very well."

"Do what?"

Tommy Burke leaned closer to me. "I've a little job for you, my dear," he muttered into my ear. "We won't speak of it in public. Come to the Casino Theater tomorrow, where I'm rehearsing a new play. It's on the corner of Broadway and West Thirty-ninth." Tell them to bring you straight to me, and we'll have a little talk. Any time you like. I'll be in the theater all day."

"Hiring a detective, how exciting," Oona said. "He can't want you to shadow his wife to start divorce proceedings because he isn't married any longer. I'm bursting with curiosity, Tommy darling."

"Then you'll just have to burst, Oona, because I'm not saying another thing," Tommy Burke said, with a grin in my direction. "You just enjoy yourself tonight, Miss Molly Murphy, and we'll continue our conversation in private tomorrow."

❧ Three ❧

I'm a self-made man, Miss Murphy," Tommy Burke said, turning to me.

We were sitting side by side in the darkness of an empty theater. On the dimly lit stage actors were reading through lines, but here at the back of the stalls, we were in a private world, and I was conscious of the intimacy of his big shoulder touching mine, of his warm, slightly beery breath on my cheek.

"I've done very well for a boy who came to America with nothing, and who was close to starving several times in his childhood."

He looked at me and I nodded approval. "We came over during the famine, you know," he went on. "Driven out of our homes like so many families. The landowner's thugs actually knocked down the cottage as my parents struggled to save our few possessions. I was only about four years old at the time, but I can still remember it clearly. They broke my mother's one good pudding basin, and she would have killed them if my father hadn't held her back. Then we had the chance to come to America on a famine ship. You've heard about the famine ships, have you? Back and forth across the Atlantic, crammed full of poor wretched souls like ourselves."

He was still looking at me as if he wanted me to say something, but I couldn't think of anything to say. "It was a terrible time," I said at last. "My own family almost died out in the famine."

"What part of Ireland are you from, my dear?"

"County Mayo."

"Ah, the wild, wild west. Never been there myself, but I understand it's very beautiful, all mountains and lakes and rugged seacoast."

"That it is," I said. "Beautiful and remote. You feel like you're at the end of the earth. I couldn't wait to escape from it myself."

"We came from the south ourselves. Near Cork. I don't remember anything of it, but I do remember that ship. No steam in those days, you know. Twelve days under sail, and most of us sicker than dogs. Packed in like sardines, we were. People were already weak from the famine, you know, and they were dying like flies all around us."

"Why are you telling me this, Mr. Burke?" I asked.

"I'm coming to that." He put a beefy hand over mine, making me wonder for a moment whether he had invited me here with baser motives. I'd certainly heard about old men like him preying on young women. But he cleared his throat. "Like I said, I started with nothing, and I've done pretty well for myself, wouldn't you say? Only problem is that I'm not getting any younger, and I've nobody to leave it to."

"No children?" I asked.

"No children," he said sadly. "I was married once, but she couldn't take my sort of life. You're either married to a woman or to the theater. You can't have both. I chose the theater, and she found someone who could devote the time and attention to her that she deserved. I decided not to make the same mistake twice." He gave me a brief, wicked glance and patted my hand, "Oh, don't get me wrong. There have been women since, but nobody I cared about enough to make it permanent. And now it's only me. My sister and brother are both gone. My parents too. I've one nephew and I've done enough for him already—put him through Harvard, paid off his debts, not to mention paying off the young woman he got into trouble. No, I'm averse to leaving my fortune to him, Miss Murphy. This is where you come in."

Now, for one wild moment I wondered if he was hinting that he'd like to adopt me and make me his heir. I always did have wild, improbable fantasies, as my mother would tell you. I looked up at him. "I want you to try and find my sister," he said.

"Your sister? But I thought you said she was already dead?"

He nodded. "That was my older sister, Bridget, I was talking about. My nephew Harvey's mother."

"You had more than one sister, then?"

"That's the strange thing, Miss Murphy." He stared out into the darkness. Someone on stage was crying. I couldn't tell if it was part of the play or if they were genuinely upset. It sounded real enough. "My ma died a few months ago," he said. "God, I worshipped that woman. What a tower of strength she was. I was with her a lot during her final weeks. She wasted away to a skeleton, you know. Like a stick figure, she was. Pitiful to see. And in the last weeks, when they started giving her morphine for the pain, she started rambling. One day she said she hoped God would forgive her for what she had done, leaving her baby behind in Ireland. I was shocked, I can tell you, but I didn't know if it was fantasy or reality. They say morphine gives you dreams and delusions. So I prodded her about it. She wasn't quite lucid anymore; but from what I could gather, I had a baby sister called Mary Ann. When we were about to sail for America she fell sick with a bad fever and was not expected to live. My parents didn't want to give up the chance for the rest of us to sail to a new life. Who knows if they'd have secured passage on another ship? And God knows enough babies die in Ireland all the time. So they left her behind."

"Holy Mother of God. Abandoned her, you mean?" I asked, horrified. "Just left her to die?"

"No, it wasn't like that. I gather they left her with a local parish priest, who promised to find someone to take care of her. But apparently it had been preying on my mother's mind all these years, although she never said a word about it to me."

"And you think your sister might be still alive?" I asked. "Do you have any reason to believe this?"

"None at all. It's just that I won't rest until I know, one way or the other. I'm a busy man, Miss Murphy. As you can see, I've a new play opening at the Casino here in two months. I'm also planning a grand production of *Babes in Toyland* for the new year—lots of good songs and a cast of thousands. It's going to make me a fortune. So I'm tied to New York myself. That's why I'm hiring you. I want you to go over to Ireland and see if you can trace my little sister."

"To Ireland?" I can't tell you what mixed emotions coursed through me at that word. The chance to go home again! There had been times during this tumultuous summer when I had been consumed with homesickness. But no sooner had I thought of going home, than I remembered the reason I had fled in the first place. The man I thought I had killed was still alive, it was true, but he was vindictive and would delight in finding me delivered to his doorstep, like a lamb to the slaughter.

"That's right," Tommy Burke said. "To Ireland."

"Wouldn't it be simpler just to place an advertisement in the *Irish Times* and see what comes of it?"

"What, and have every confidence trickster in Ireland coming out of the woodwork for a handout? I'm known on both sides of the Atlantic to be a rich man, Miss Murphy. That's why I'm hiring you. An Irishwoman like yourself can be discreet. Portray yourself as a cousin, coming home from America and wanting to look up family members, if you like. You don't even need to say you were sent from me."

"You'd pay my expenses?" I asked, weakening.

"All your expenses and a hundred-dollar retainer—and a healthy bonus if you actually find her alive. What do you say, Miss Murphy? Will you take the case?"

I had no other assignments on the books. Funds were dwindling fast, and New York was not the happiest of places for me at the moment. I nodded and held out my hand. "Very well, Mr. Burke. I'll take the case."

❧ Four ❧

The minute I came out of the theater into the bright sunlight of a crisp September morning I realized what I had done. Going back to Ireland? Was I quite mad? For all I knew there was still a warrant out for my arrest in that country. I should go right back into that theater and tell Mr. Burke to find someone else. Then I thought of the nice fat fee, of the chance to travel home to Ireland in a cabin on a luxury liner, to stay at good hotels, to see Dublin at last. And I reasoned that Justin Hartley, the man who would love to see me arrested, was not even in Ireland at the moment, but touring the western states of America. Besides, Molly Murphy is a common enough name. I should be quite safe.

I left the Sixth Avenue el at Greenwich Avenue Station and hurried toward Patchin Place to tell Sid and Gus my news. It was a lovely fall day, the first hint that the heat and humidity of summer was finally breaking. It had been a long, hot summer this year, a terrible season for all the diseases that heat and overcrowding bring with them. But today was just splendid. The leaves on the trees were showing just a hint of yellow in them. The breeze from the Hudson was fresh. Jefferson Market was in the process of shutting down for the day, but I went inside and, on impulse, bought a big bunch of crysanthamums and some bright red apples.

Thus armed, I knocked on the door of Number Nine and waited with a smile on my face, but nobody appeared. Absurdly disappointed,

I turned away only to find myself staring straight into the face of Daniel Sullivan.

"What a charming picture you make," he said. "Those flowers almost match the copper color of your hair. If I were a painter I'd whip out a brush and canvas and paint you as you stand there. Venus with the bounty of the harvest."

"Anyone can tell you are Irish. You're full of blarney," I said, eyeing him stonily. "What do you want? Come back to check if I've made more undesirable friends since yesterday?"

"No, I came back to apologize," he said. "You are right. I have no claim on you and no right to judge the company you keep. I am also mindful of the debt that I owe you—you put your own safety at risk to find the truth behind my betrayal and arrest."

He paused.

"Apology accepted," I said coldly. "Now, if you will excuse me, I have to put these flowers in water."

He stepped between me and my front door. "I realize that the very qualities I admire in you make you different from other women, Molly. Aren't you going to invite me inside?"

"You insulted my dearest friends," I said. "You have apologized for judging me but not for insulting them."

His face flushed. "Oh, come now, Molly. You do have to admit that—"

"That what?"

"That O'Hare man is quite outside the pale."

"On the contrary, he is welcome at the most fashionable salons in the city. That party last night had as many Astors and Vanderbilts in attendance as it did theater folk. And they all seemed to know Ryan. Oh, I agree he is outlandish in his dress and his behavior, but I find him enchanting and never boring."

"So you went to the party last night," Daniel said.

"I did. And I had a marvelous time."

"I see. And this Mr. Burke who wanted to meet you?"

"A powerful theatrical impresario. You go to the theater. You must have heard of him."

"I might have."

"He wanted me to star in his next play—Salome and the Seven Veils."

I watched Daniel's face, then burst out laughing. "I'm just pulling your leg," I said. "He wanted to hire my detective services, if you must know."

"He did? What, a divorce case?"

"You know I'm not allowed to discuss confidential business, Daniel," I said. "Oh well, I suppose you had better come in, before I drop these apples."

I let him open the front door for me and preceded him inside. "You can put the kettle on while I find a jar to put these flowers in," I called over my shoulder.

"So you'll be out working on a case," he said. "I won't be seeing much of you."

"You'll be seeing nothing of me for a while. The assignment is in Ireland."

"Ireland?" He stared at me in horror. "Are you mad? I thought you said you could never go back home again because of what you had done. I thought there was a price on your head."

"I'm willing to risk it," I said.

"Molly, this is absurd. How many risks do you think you can take in your life before the odds are against you?" He was yelling now.

"There's really not much of a risk, Daniel, so calm down." I had found a glass jar on the scullery shelf and now filled it with water, my back to him. "It turns out things weren't as bad as I had feared; and besides, I'll be going nowhere near my home, and how many people are called Molly Murphy, for heaven's sake? It must be one of the most common names in Ireland. You really don't have to worry about me."

This speech was braver than I was actually feeling, but I wasn't having Daniel forbidding me to go to Ireland now.

"What is this Mr. Burke wanting you to do in Ireland, I'd like to know?" he went on.

"I told you I can't discuss a client's business. Let's just say it's a family matter."

Daniel scowled. "I smell a rat here. A rich impresario can cable Ireland and hire someone on the spot to do the investigating. He doesn't need to send an unproven girl from New York."

"In the first case, he wants a complete stranger to do the poking around; and in the second, I'm no longer a girl but a woman."

"So you are," he said, looking at me frankly. "So you are."

There was a long pause and then he said, "How long will you be gone?"

"I couldn't say. Until I've finished the job."

"So you won't be here for my trial?" He tried to sound disinterested, but his face gave him away. He looked like a lost schoolboy. I weakened. "Daniel, I have to take the job. The fee is good and I need the money. It's a wonderful chance for me. If I do well, Mr. Burke is a powerful man. He may well refer me to his friends. Besides," I added, noting his desolate face, "There's not going to be a trial. Now your fellow officers know who was really to blame, they'll be speaking up for you. They'll want you reinstated, won't they? The commissioner will have to let you go free."

"I wish I could believe that," Daniel said. "That certainly wasn't the impression I got when I spoke with him yesterday."

"All he can actually pin on you is the prize fight," I said. "And that would merit a slap on the wrist and a fine, nothing more."

"I admire your optimism," Daniel said. "I have none myself. Those weeks in jail have crushed my fighting spirit, Molly."

"Not enough to stop you trying to lay down the law with me," I said, and couldn't resist a smile. He looked at me and smiled back. Those alarming blue eyes flashed for the first time since I'd seen him in that jail cell. He reached out his hands and took mine. "Don't go, Molly. I need you here."

I could feel myself about to weaken. It was a fault I had when I was around Daniel Sullivan. That electricity sparking between us whenever he touched me hadn't dimmed with time. "I have to go, Daniel," I said, trying to pull away from him. "But I shouldn't be away for long. And you have others you can turn to now. It's time you told your family the truth. They'd want to know, I'm sure. Don't they have powerful friends and connections who'd put in a good word for you? I seem to remember that they were pals with the governor. Have him step in on your behalf."

"You know my reason for not contacting my family is that I'm concerned for my father's health problems," he said. "I'd still rather he wasn't involved in this."

"Then your other alternative is to stall," I said. "Find excuses to have the trial delayed until the end of the year. Then we'll have a new police commissioner and ten to one he'll be a friend of Tammany Hall."

He squeezed my hands tightly. "I'm sure everything you say makes sense," he said, "but this has all been like a nightmare to me. I never believed I could be arrested in the first place. And when I was arrested I never believed I'd be put in jail. Nothing seems secure anymore, Molly. Only you. Stick with me, won't you? One day maybe we'll be able to look back on this and laugh."

"One day," I said.

❧ Five ❧

A few days later a packet of instructions arrived for me, along with a second-class ticket on the White Star Liner *Majestic,* sailing out of New York on September Twenty-fourth bound for Queenstown and Liverpool. The irony of this was not lost on me. It was on this very ship that I had fled from Liverpool less than two years ago. Only that time I had been down in the hold, battened down and crammed in with all those poor wretches in steerage. This time I was to have a second-class cabin to myself. I was moving up in the world.

Now that the trip was actually becoming a reality, I couldn't help feeling excited as well as apprehensive. Going home, the words whispered in my head. And not going home a failure, but as a successful businesswoman on an assignment. I'd have dearly liked to travel out to county Mayo to visit my family and let them see that I hadn't come to a bad end after all, but that would have been tempting providence too much.

Sid and Gus came over to help me pack, offering to lend me everything from clothes to reading matter for the journey.

"You two have already given me more than enough," I said. "I'll do just fine with the clothes I already have. Besides—" I added, trying to think of a tactful way of putting things, "I don't want to stand out over there. It's important that I look like one of the locals. And your lovely clothes—"

Sid threw back her head and laughed. "I wasn't suggesting lending you my emerald green smoking jacket, my sweet. Yes, I suppose our clothes would stand out at a provincial Irish market, wouldn't they, Gus dear?"

"What I really meant was that cupboard full of stuff from my former life in Boston society," Gus said. "I'm sure there is a smart, fur-trimmed traveling costume there that would suit you, Molly. And you know I'll never wear it again, I'm sure."

I smiled at them. "Thank you, but I don't think I'll be mingling with the smart set in Ireland. The Burkes were the poorest of peasants when they left. Their child would either have been farmed out to another peasant family or sent to an orphanage. Frankly I think it would be a miracle if she was still alive after all these years; but I'm being paid to search for her, and search for her I will."

"Then at least take my crocodile-skin train case," Gus insisted. "I found it so handy when I did my European tour with my mother. Now it's just languishing on the top shelf on my wardrobe, and we want you to have something of ours with you to remind you of us."

"And to make sure you come back quickly," Sid added.

"We're worried that you'll decide to stay in Ireland," Gus said.

"And why would I want to do that?" I laughed. "I've told you before, and I'll repeat it now—there is nothing for me in Ireland. My life is here now."

"Gus was worried that you'd realize what you'd missed if you go back there," Sid said.

"You were worried too!" Gus tapped her hand.

"All right. I was worried too. And what about Captain Sullivan? I'm surprised he's allowing you to go."

"He's not at all happy about it," I said, "but there's nothing he can do to stop me, is there? And I think it will be good for me to get away from him—give me time to think about what I really want for my future. So don't worry about me. I'll be just fine, and I'll have a grand time and be back before you know it with tales to tell."

"Of course you will." Sid shot a look at Gus and suddenly I felt a shiver run up and down my spine. They were afraid for me. Was I foolish not to be afraid for myself?

• • •

The morning of the twenty-fourth came, bright and breezy, with puffy white clouds racing across the sky. A good day to be sailing, I said to Daniel, Sid, and Gus, who walked beside me to the waiting cab. I had forbidden Daniel to come to the ship to see me off. I didn't think I could handle emotional scenes at the gangplank. And having forbidden Daniel, I could hardly allow Gus and Sid what I had denied him.

"Anyone would think I was journeying to the North Pole or across the Sahara Desert the way you three are looking at me," I exclaimed, looking from Daniel's face to Gus's and Sid's. "Fashionable people go to Europe all the time. They pop back and forth across the Atlantic as if it were a pond. It should take me no more than a week or two at most, and then I'll be back."

I hugged my friends, then I went to hug Daniel.

"Good-bye, Daniel. Take care of yourself, won't you?" I put my hands on his shoulders and brushed his cheek with my lips. His arms came fiercely around me, almost crushing the breath out of me.

"You take care of yourself," he whispered. "No more stupid risks. Remember that I love you."

I climbed into the cab, my heart beating very fast. I think it was the first time he had actually told me that. I looked out and waved jauntily as the cab set off up Sixth Avenue at a lively pace. The White Star Line pier was at the bottom of West Tenth Street, close enough to walk, really, and I could have saved the expense of a cab if we'd all walked together, with Daniel carrying my valise. But I had money for expenses, a letter of credit, and my stupid pride. I didn't want to risk shedding a tear at the dockside.

We emerged from West Tenth to the hustle and bustle of West Street. Porters, seamen, and passengers were scurrying around the great ship, picking their way among stacks of cargo like a lot of ants around a picnic basket. The ship's twin funnels sparkled in the morning sunlight. She cast a great black shadow over the scene below. Truly a majestic sight, and this time I was really able to savor it. When I had departed from Liverpool, not only had I been a bundle of nerves at sailing under an assumed name, but I had two terrified children in tow—Kathleen O'Connor's little ones, en route to their father in New York. I had written to Seamus O'Connor telling him that I was going back to Ireland and would try to visit Kathleen's grave, if I had time, but had received no reply. Seamus wasn't the greatest when it came to penmanship. I felt a pang of regret that those children were no longer part of my life. Maybe they'd come back to New York in the winter, I thought. I didn't allow myself a pang of regret for my own child. No good would come from dwelling on that.

I paid the cabby and assigned my humble luggage to a porter who looked at it with distaste, when compared to the piles of steamer trunks that were going aboard and led me to the second-class gangway. I went aboard without looking back, my heart racing a mile a minute, and showed my ticket to the purser at the top of the gangway.

"This way, miss," I was told pleasantly, and was handed over to a steward who took my train case from me and escorted me along a never-ending corridor to a small cabin. It was hardly big enough to swing a cat, but at least it did have a porthole. The view wasn't the greatest, obscured by a lifeboat hanging out from the deck above, but at least I could see daylight and a glimpse of sky.

"Your bags will be brought up right away, miss," the steward said. "Have a good trip. We're expecting good weather all the way. That's a blessing at this time of year, isn't it? It's no picnic when we have to outrun a hurricane, I can tell you."

I thanked him, wondering if I was expected to give him a tip. Such questions had not been necessary when I traveled steerage. Before I could fumble for a purse, however, he gave me a cheery grin and left me to examine my quarters. Not that the cabin took long to examine. There were two bunk beds along one wall, a chest of drawers, wardrobe and mirror on the other. And just about enough room between them for a slender person to pass. But I didn't have to share it with anybody, and I didn't expect to be inside it much. I intended to make full use of my time on board. I took off my hat and was about to brush my hair when there was a tap at my door. I expected it was my luggage, but instead another steward entered.

"Note for you, miss," he said, in cheerful Cockney tones.

"For me? Are you sure?"

"Miss Molly Murphy, E deck, cabin 231. Is that you?"

"Yes, it is, but—"

He grinned. "Maybe you've already got an admirer on board. Great place for romance, Atlantic liners." He winked, handed me the note, and was gone.

I stared at my name written on the envelope. Not any handwriting that I knew. For one dreadful moment I had thought that it might be from Daniel, begging me to reconsider. I decided it must be some last-minute instructions from Mr. Burke and tore it open.

"Dear Miss Murphy," the note began, "You can't imagine how delighted I was to find that we were to be shipmates. I too am traveling back on the *Majestic* to my homeland. I'd be most grateful if you'd come to my cabin as soon as you read this. I've a small matter I'd like to discuss with you."

It was signed Oona Sheehan.

❧ Six ❧

I tidied my hair and made myself presentable before I made my way back to the main reception area, where I knew I'd find a staircase.

"Can I help you, miss?" a fierce voice echoed after me.

"I'm going up to A deck," I said. "Isn't this the right way?"

"A deck is first-class cabins, miss." His look was inscrutable.

"Precisely," I answered. "I have just received an invitation from a friend in first class to visit her at her cabin right away." I waved the note at him.

"Very good, miss," he said. "Allow me to escort you. What cabin number is it?"

I smirked as he led the way up the stairs. I don't think I'll ever learn to be humble.

The steward knocked on the cabin door, and we were rewarded with "Enter" in those deep melodious tones that had charmed audiences across the globe.

The steward poked his head around the door. "If you please, ma'am, there's a young lady to see you—a Miss Murphy?"

"How delightful. Send her in," Oona said.

I swept into the cabin, past the rather astonished steward, savoring every instant. Then I just stood there and gasped.

Oona Sheehan's cabin was nothing like my own. It was as big as most drawing rooms, with a double bed against one wall, surrounded by white built-in wardrobes and cupboards. Under her porthole there was a daybed, a couple of gilt-edged chairs, and a low table decorated with a big bowl of flowers. There were more flowers on every surface of the room, great displays of them, orchids and roses and every kind of exotic bloom. Oona was lounging on the daybed, looking stunning in a black-and-white striped traveling suit with a matching black-and-white feather ornament in her hair. She didn't attempt to sit up but raised a hand to greet me.

"Molly Murphy. How good of you to come and visit me."

"How did you know I'd be on board?" I asked. "Did Mr. Burke tell you?"

She laughed. "Not at all. Very tight-lipped is our dear Tommy. Pure coincidence, actually. We bumped into each other buying tickets at the White Star office, so he had to confess he was sending you to Ireland. I wormed it out of him actually. I do have a knack of making gentlemen confess things they never intended to." That enchanting smile lingered on her lips before she went on, "Do take a seat. There's a bottle of champagne already on ice. I know it's morning and I don't usually drink before noon, but I always make it a rule to drink champagne when sailing. I find it calms the stomach wonderfully. I am never seasick."

"No champagne for me, thank you. It goes straight to my head," I said.

"Mine too." She chuckled. "It can probably be blamed for a host of wrong decisions in my life." She propped herself up a little higher and reached across to the table. "Chocolate? I do adore them, don't you? My one real weakness, especially when I have to watch my waistline."

She held out a gold-wrapped box to me. This time I didn't refuse.

"Miss Sheehan," I said, "why exactly did you invite me? You hardly know me, and I can't imagine that I'd be the most exciting person on ship. You've only to go out of that door and you'll be surrounded by admirers."

"Exactly," she said. "I've a small proposition to make to you, Molly." She flashed me a challenging smile. "I may call you Molly, may I not? If you are a lady detective, then you must be the kind of woman who craves excitement and likes a challenge."

"I don't know if I crave excitement," I said, "but I don't seem to be able to escape it."

"Splendid. And you wouldn't be averse to earning an extra fee from this trip?"

"Nooo," I said hesitantly.

She sat up now. "I'm going to make you a proposition, Molly Murphy. I don't think you'll turn it down."

I waited. She glanced out of her porthole—one not obscured by a hanging lifeboat. "It's not always easy being me," she said. "As you said, everywhere I go I'm surrounded by admirers. Foolish men who think themselves hopelessly in love with me, follow me like puppy dogs. I can never be alone, never have a chance to be myself. You may think it's wonderful, but it can become very wearing, I assure you. I'm taking this trip home because my doctor has ordered me to rest or face a breakdown. I have a little cottage picked out on the West Coast, where the local inhabitants won't know who I am and care little about my fame. But it is this journey that I dread."

She paused again, one lily white arm raised in dramatic gesture. Truly she was so lovely to look at that I couldn't stop gazing. Those beautiful green eyes, that perfect little nose. I realized that she was also staring at me.

"You said you had a proposition for me," I said.

She nodded. "I want to trade places with you on this voyage."

"You want what?" I blurted out, forgetting that she was one of the world's most famous women, and I was a nobody.

She smiled, revealing the most enchanting dimples. "Exactly what I said. For this voyage I want to become Molly Murphy, and I want you to stay in this cabin and become Oona Sheehan."

"But that's absurd," I said. "For one thing, I'm in a tiny second-class cabin down five decks from here, with the view blocked by a great lifeboat. For another, I'd only have to show my face for one second and anyone would know I'm not Oona Sheehan."

"I've thought it all out," she said. "We'll announce that I am feeling out of sorts, suffering from exhaustion, and am keeping to my cabin, except for brief walks on deck, during which times I'll be bundled in my cape and hood. If anyone tries to talk to you during these sorties, you can hold a handkerchief up to your mouth and complain in a whisper about your sore throat and inability to speak. I think it might be wise if you avoid mealtimes. It might be harder to carry it off when you're seated at the captain's table, and you are liable to run into somebody who actually knows me.

"I've arranged to have my meals delivered to this cabin so you won't have to risk being caught out at the captain's table or accosted in the public rooms. It will make the voyage rather more boring than you intended, I'm sure; but at least you'll be in luxury, and I'll pay you well for the inconvenience. Above all, you'd be doing a fellow Irishwoman a great service. So what do you say?"

"Let me get this right," I said. "You'll take my cabin, down on E deck?"

"And dress simply and be the humble Irishwoman Molly Murphy, returning home to see her family, sitting quietly on the second-class promenade deck, and resting."

"And I'll be Oona Sheehan."

"Who unfortunately is not well enough to receive visitors for the trip. Help yourself to my clothes, and if you want to walk on deck, may I suggest you put on one of my wigs."

"Your wigs?"

She waved her arm imperiously. "Open that hat box, on top of the dresser."

I did so. It was full of wonderful auburn wigs, some with long curls, some piled up in chic styles.

"Jesus, Mary, and Joseph," I muttered.

"I often have to make quick changes on stage," she said. "I find wigs remarkably helpful in changing my appearance quickly. And also if my hairdresser can't visit before I have to go out. Try one on."

Cautiously I picked out one with curls piled high above the head and tucked my own hair inside it. The change was amazing. I stared at myself in the mirror and put a hand to my cheek. "I look quite—"

"Quite like me," she said. "I thought so when I saw you at Tommy's party. I think you'll do remarkably well. So is it a deal, Molly Murphy? Will you promise not to reveal our plan to anybody on board? Say

38

you'll agree, and I'll write you out a check for a hundred dollars for your pains."

An extra hundred dollars. I could certainly use that. I'd have to forgo the fun of shipboard life, but then there would always be the return journey. "I'll do it," I said.

Her face lit up in that wonderful smile. "I knew you would," she said. "Right." She took out a checkbook and wrote out a check. "There," she said. "Let's get to work and make the switch while everyone is still busy with arriving passengers. Let's exchange clothing and I'll make my way down to E deck."

"You want us to exchange clothing?"

"Of course. I have to go down exactly the way you came up, don't I?"

"But someone is bound to notice the difference."

"My dear, I'm an actress. I promise you that nobody will ever know that the Molly Murphy who walked up those stairs is not the same woman who comes down them again. Now take off that costume and choose yourself something from my wardrobe. How lucky that we're around the same size."

I opened the wardrobe and stifled a gasp at the array of dresses, suits, and evening gowns that hung there.

"You might want to select something rather dazzling to start with. It will help to enforce the illusion," Oona said. She came across to the wardrobe and pulled down a burgundy silk two piece, its sleeves and high neck decorated with pearls. "Burgundy is a good color with our hair, I always think," she said. "Can you manage by yourself, or should I summon my maid to dress you?"

"You've brought your maid?" I stammered. "But what will she say?"

Oona laughed. "She's in on the plot, my dear. She's been with me long enough to follow orders, and she's been told to treat you exactly as if you were me. Her name is Rose, by the way. A nice little thing. Not very bright, but willing enough. But let's not waste any more time." She handed me the dress. "Off with your things and on with this."

I performed the task with considerable embarrassment. I was not used to undressing in front of other people and horribly conscious of the shabby state of my two-piece business suit and my undergarments.

Oona hardly seemed to notice, however. She was out of her own robe in a second and slipping herself into my skirt and jacket. This was accomplished in a twinkling. I suppose quick changes of costume are commonplace at the theater where the exposure of the human form is not considered shocking.

I, on the other hand, was so clumsy in putting on her outfit that she had to help me button up the cuffs and neck.

"Put the wig back on and you'll do very well," she said, nodding with satisfaction. "Just a touch of makeup of course. There is rouge and powder on my dressing table, and you'll need more color on your lips. But as for those freckles . . ." she looked at me and sighed. "There's not much we can do about them in a hurry, is there? Did you never think of taking lemon juice to them when you were a girl?"

"I never even noticed them until I came to New York," I said, laughing. "Now I'm afraid I'm stuck with them."

"You'll just have to use a lot of cold cream and powder," she said. "You're supposed to be ailing, remember. Here, let me do it for you."

Before I could protest she was rubbing cold cream into my face, patting cheeks, drawing arches onto my eyebrows and reddening my lips with a brush and palette, just like an artist. When she was done, a stranger looked back at me from the mirror.

"All ashore who is going ashore," was the cry from the hallway, along with raps on every cabin door.

"I'll leave you now," she said. "We won't meet again on the trip. First- and second-class passengers are not permitted to trespass upon each other's domains."

"So shall I wait for you here when we dock in Queenstown?" I asked. "Are you going ashore there or sailing on to Liverpool?"

"Oh, Queenstown," she said. "Definitely Queenstown."

Then she was gone. I stood there, still feeling a little stupified, looking around my new domain. Of all the strange things that had happened to me in my life, this was certainly one of the strangest. Am I never to cross the Atlantic as myself? I wondered. Then I looked in the mirror and started to smile. The smile turned into a laugh. A week in luxury, waited on by a maid and stewards—that wasn't too bad anyway you looked at it.

❦ Seven ❦

Down below there were shouts and cheers, the sounds of gangways clanking as they were withdrawn. A band was playing
"Rule Britannia," White Star being an English line. We were
underway. I opened my porthole and watched the New York skyline
slide past me, until all I could see was ocean. The great ship reacted as
it met the first of the big waves and my stomach reacted equally—not
with queasiness, since I had proved myself an excellent sailor on the
previous crossing, but with a surge of excitement. I was about to start a
great adventure, now made even more thrilling by my new role as Oona
Sheehan. I was off alone to Ireland, leaving behind the complications of
my life. I planned to enjoy every minute of it, especially my newfound
first-class splendor.

I was just settling down when there came a tapping at my door.

"Come in," I called, trying to sound like a famous actress with a bad
case of sore throat.

Instead of the steward a young girl came in, smiled shyly, and
bobbed a curtsey.

"I'm Rose, miss. Miss Sheehan said I'm to look after you well and
give you whatever you need."

She was yet another Irish redhead, but round faced and sturdy.

"I'm pleased to meet you, Rose. I'm—"

She held up a hand. "Please don't tell me your real name or ask me
to call you by it, or I might slip up. The mistress said I've got to think of

you as Oona Sheehan and that's what I'm trying to do. And it's not at all hard, with you looking like that. You'd be taken for her younger sister any day."

"Thank you, Rose," I said, "but it's only because of her clothes, her wig, and her makeup, I'm afraid."

"Oh no, miss. I think you look lovely. Are you in the theater yourself?"

"No, I'm not, I'm afraid."

"You should be glad, miss," she said. "Terrible hard life in the theater. You should see what the mistress has to go through, with all those men following her around, calling her up on her telephone at all hours of the day and night, threatening to kill themselves if she won't dine with them. My, but they're a silly lot. Too many men with too much money and too much time on their hands, if you ask me."

I nodded agreement.

"Is there something you'd like, miss?" she asked. "I think they've sounded the gong for the lunch sitting. Shall I have some lunch brought to you?"

"Lunch would be a grand idea," I said. "You can stay and have some with me, if you'd like."

She looked horrified. "Oh no, miss. That would never do. I know my place. I'll have your steward deliver your lunch then, shall I?"

She curtseyed and was gone. I arranged myself on the daybed in what I hoped was an elegant pose, pretending to be reading a magazine, and waited. Soon thereafter the steward arrived with a lunch tray.

"I understand you're feeling poorly, Miss Sheehan," he said, looking down at me with concern. "That will never do. I've brought some things that might build you up—a good bowl of oxtail soup, some poached sole, some grapes, and a glass of ice cream. They should slip down easily enough, shouldn't they?"

"Thank you, you're very kind," I whispered as he put the tray on the table.

"That throat sounds terrible," he said. "Should I summon the ship's doctor to take a look at it?"

"No, please don't worry," I said. "I just need to be left alone and rest. I'm sure I'll be up and feeling bright again by the time we dock."

"There will be a lot of disappointed young men when they hear that news," he said, giving me a knowing smile. "I've had to direct several of them firmly from your door when the news got out that you were aboard. But don't you worry. I'll make sure you're kept in peace for the whole voyage."

"Thank you. You're most kind," I said, in what I hoped was a gracious and theatrical way. "What is your name again?"

"Frederick, miss," he said.

"Thank you, Frederick." I tried to give the sort of smile Oona Sheehan might have flashed at an adoring male.

The moment he went, I tucked into the tray. Everything was beyond delicious. For a person who grew up eating stew and potatoes, I had certainly learned quickly to appreciate fine food and fine wine. With great daring I went over to the silver ice bucket and poured myself a glass of that champagne.

Rose appeared again after lunch, wanting to know what she could do for me, but I couldn't think of anything and sent her away. I couldn't imagine ever wanting a personal maid hovering over me, and certainly not dressing me, brushing my hair, and fussing around me, even if I became very rich some day—which wasn't likely to happen. At least Rose could enjoy some freedom and have fun with her own kind during the voyage.

By midafternoon I was bored with sitting alone and decided to risk a sortie. I put on Oona's black velvet cape, trimmed with white fur, and raised the hood cautiously over the wig. Then I found a lace handkerchief to hold over my mouth and ventured out. My faithful Frederick was standing guard at the entrance to my hallway. He sprang to attention when he saw me.

"Feeling better, Miss Sheehan? Oh, that is good news."

"I'm afraid not, Frederick," I whispered through the handkerchief, "but I hoped that a turn on deck and a good dose of sea air might be beneficial."

"It certainly might, Miss Sheehan. And you're not likely to run into trouble, if you get my meaning. Most of the first class passengers take a rest after lunch so that they can stay up late for the dancing."

I felt a pang of regret that I would have to forego the dancing. For a second I pictured myself in one of those silk evening gowns being whisked across the floor under glittering chandeliers. Then, of course, I reminded myself that I didn't know how to dance any of the latest dances anyway and certainly not as elegantly as Oona Sheehan would have done.

"If you like to find yourself a deck chair, miss," Frederick said, "I'll arrange for a rug to be sent out to you and a cup of beef broth."

"I think I'll just take a little walk this time," I said. I pulled the hood even farther forward and stepped out on deck. I was unprepared for the force of the wind, as it nearly lifted hood and wig in one go. I clung onto both, turned my back on the wind and walked in an anticlockwise direction around the promenade deck until I was out of the gale.

It was a bright, sparkling day with enough of a swell to let you know you were at sea, but not enough to make you seasick. I stood at the rail and stared out at the horizon. There was no land, no birds, no sign of other ships, just myself alone on a vast ocean. It was a sobering thought. Exciting too—after the crowds of New York City.

The sound of wind and waves must have masked other noises because I didn't hear the man coming until he spoke, close to my ear.

"Miss Sheehan?" he asked.

I whipped the handkerchief up to my mouth and drew the hood half across my face as I looked up at him. He was young, good looking, with the dark, windswept hair and blue eyes of the Black Irish—not unlike Daniel or Ryan—and he was dressed in fitting shipboard style in blue blazer and striped ascot.

"It is Miss Oona Sheehan, isn't it?" he asked again.

"It is," I whispered, "but you must excuse me. I am suffering from a throat complaint and my doctor has forbidden me to talk."

"I see," he said. "I hope it's nothing serious?"

"It should clear up in a few days if I rest and don't use my voice. Please excuse me, Mr—"

"Fitzpatrick," he said. "I'm sorry to hear you are not yourself. I too am heading home to Ireland. Maybe we shall run into each other again."

"I'm afraid that's unlikely. I have been ordered to rest."

"Ireland is a small country," he said. "You never know."

With that he bowed and was gone.

I'd handled that one well enough, I told myself. I continued my stroll around the deck, holding the hood in place with one hand. I hadn't progressed far when I heard a voice behind me shouting, "Miss Sheehan, Miss Sheehan!"

I stopped and waited as another young man came running up to me.

"Oh, Miss Sheehan, it is you," he said breathlessly. "I couldn't believe my luck when I heard that you were on board. Do you not remember me? It's Artie. Artie Fortwrangler. I came to every one of your performances when you were in *Captain Jinks of the Horse Marines*. I was there at the stage door every night. Remember the white orchids?"

"Of course, Artie," I breathed through the lace handkerchief. "You must excuse me. I am sick and the doctor has forbidden me to talk. It might be catching," I added, as he was getting too close in his eagerness.

"I do hope you recover quickly enough to dance with me while we're on board, Miss Sheehan," he said, gazing at me with hopeful eyes. "They have ripping dances, you know. It would be a lifetime's dream fulfilled to whisk you around the floor in my arms."

"We'll just have to see," I said. "Now I'm afraid I must go and rest again."

"Here, let me get you a deck chair," he said. "Don't take another step."

"No, really. I must go back to my cabin."

"Then lean on me. Let me carry you. Let me get you some beef broth, or some tea, or maybe a brandy?"

I could see the door leading to the interior of the ship looming ahead of me.

"I'm afraid I just want to be left alone," I said, and fled for that door.

"Don't go, Oona, I love you, I adore you, I worship you," he called after me. "You know how I feel about you. Don't leave me in misery."

I ignored his wails as I pushed my way in through the heavy door. I arrived back at my cabin to find Rose there, straightening the toiletries on the dressing table.

"Poor Miss Sheehan," I said. "I understand now why she wanted to change places with me, and why it's so hard for her to go anywhere. I have just been pestered by a most annoying young man. He hung around me like a puppy dog."

"They do all the time, miss," Rose said. "Every time she opens her front door, at least one of them is standing there with a bunch of flowers for her, and when she leaves the theater, she positively has to fight them off."

"She should get married and have a big fierce husband to drive them away," I said. "Does she have no constant escort?"

"There is always some kind of man wooing her," Rose said, "but not a one she takes seriously."

"Has she never been in love?"

"There has only been one man for her, and he's not available," Rose said.

"Married?"

"Oh no, nothing like that." Rose sounded indignant on her mistress's behalf. "He was one of those Freedom Fighters, the Brotherhood, you know, trying to drive the English out of Ireland. He led some sort of attack on an English barracks, and he's been jailed for life."

"Oh, that's terrible," I said. "How sad for her."

"That was years ago," Rose said. "Since then she's devoted her whole life to the theater and now, of course, she's risen to become a big star. She's a wonderful woman. And the best of mistresses too."

"I wonder how she'll fare in that tiny second-class cabin of mine," I said, with a smile. "Sleeping in that narrow bunk bed?"

"Oh, I think she'll be just fine." Rose looked away, not meeting my eyes.

That evening I could hear music floating out from the ballroom across the smooth dark waters. I was tempted to go out on deck again to take a look for myself, but I didn't want to risk meeting Archie Fortwrangler and his fellow admirers. So I sat at my porthole, gazing wistfully at the moon and wondering about life and happiness in general and Oona Sheehan and my own happiness in particular.

The next few days passed smoothly enough. I soon learned that young men about town like to sleep in late, and I was fairly safe if I took an early stroll around the deck, which was most pleasant if a little chilly. On a couple of occasions I was conscious of an older man in a tweed jacket following me at a distance, but he must have been one of Oona's less brazen admirers, as he never dared approach and speak to me.

Rose brought me a selection of books from the ship's library, and a pack of playing cards, to keep myself amused. Meals were brought to me. There was always champagne to drink, chocolate, and bowls of fruit to eat. Frederick reported that he was constantly intercepting young men trying to find a way to my door, each time he brought me another note, love letter, or more flowers or chocolates or champagne. Sometimes I heard them protesting in the corridor. "But I must see her. I know she'll see me! Did you give her my flowers? Tell her that Artie adores her." Or Teddy, or Bertie, or a never ending stream of admirers. Teddy certainly sent lovely flowers—huge displays of them, while Bertie sent a dozen red roses and a box of chocolates every day. I wondered what they looked like and was tempted to invite them in as boredom overtook me. I began to feel like a prisoner in a very exclusive jail. I soon grew weary of wearing a wig all the time. It was devilishly hot and itched horribly, but I couldn't risk not wearing it and being surprised by Frederick as he delivered the latest offering of sweets or flowers.

This was quickly turning into another case of "be careful what you wish for." Growing up in Ballykillin I'd have given anything to be a lady, living the life of ease and not having to work from morning until night. Now I was living in the lap of luxury, had absolutely nothing to do but enjoy myself, and I was going mad with boredom.

After a couple of days, I was sorely tempted to go against our bargain, wash off the makeup, take off the wig, and go out as myself for a while. What would be the harm in it, I reasoned with myself. But of course I had promised. We'd made a bargain, and I was in possession of that check for a hundred dollars. So I stuck it out for six long days. Often during those days my thoughts turned to Daniel. I realized now, with a pang of guilt, that I had been treating him badly when he needed my support. Of course he was bad tempered because he was scared. His whole future hung in the balance. I suppose if I analyzed it, I hadn't forgiven him for what he had put me through, even though he didn't know the half of it and would never know. They say absence makes the heart grow fonder, and it must be true because I found myself missing him and remembering only the good things. I wrote him a cheerful little note, to be posted as soon as we set foot ashore, assuring him that all would soon be well and promising to return home to him as quickly as possible.

"There's to be a fancy dress party tonight, Miss Sheehan," Frederick reported to me on our last day at sea. "And you seem so much better, I was thinking, if you'd a mind to go, nobody need know it was you."

I looked up from my latest hand of Patience. "A fancy dress party?"

"A costume ball, as they say in America, I believe."

"But I have no costume."

"That's no problem. It's easy enough to hire one. They keep a big selection on board for those passengers who haven't brought their own costumes with them. Your maid could bring some up to your cabin for you to try on."

"That's a splendid idea, Frederick," I said. "To tell you the truth, I have been feeling too cooped up, stuck in here all the time. I'll send for my maid and see if there are any costumes that would disguise me completely."

Rose appeared a little later, red faced with exertion at having carried so many costume boxes up to my cabin. What fun it was to open each of those boxes and to be in turn Maid Marion, Columbine, a Spanish senorita . . . I finally settled on Marie Antoinette and added a stylish black mask for good measure. With that big powdered wig and the mask, I could be anybody.

For once I did need help getting dressed and Rose fussed around me, lacing me into the costume, adjusting the wig, even putting on a fake beauty spot for good measure. "You look lovely, miss," she said wistfully.

"You could come too, if you wanted to," I suggested. "Slip into one of these costumes. Nobody would know who you were."

She looked horrified. "Me, miss? Go to a grand party? Holy Mother of God, I could never do something like that."

"I'm just a plain Irish peasant like you, and I'm planning to go," I said.

"But you don't act like one of us, miss," she said. "You've got—well, more of an air to you. Like you were used to fine things."

I tried not to grin at the compliment. "One thing you learn in New

York is that you are as good as the next person, Rose. So will you come with me? It would be a lark, wouldn't it—them not knowing they were dancing with a couple of peasant girls from the Old Sod?"

She shook her head vehemently. "Oh no, miss. Not me. You go and have a good time and good luck to you."

At last I sallied forth, a little nervously. In truth, the air Rose said I had about me was mostly bravado. Inside I still felt like an interloper. Being a prisoner in my cabin all week, I had had little chance to explore the first-class section of the ship. Now I walked into the gracious public rooms and tried not to stare like a peasant girl. I had been to fancy restaurants and even inside the mansions of New York's high society, but this matched any luxury I had seen so far. Lovely Greek statues, carved pillars, huge potted plants, mirrored walls. On a center table there was even a sculpture of a graceful swan carved out of ice. What would they think of next!

Music was spilling out through a doorway, and I followed the strangest-looking crowd you've ever seen into the grand ballroom— priests and nuns, gorillas and cats, cavemen and courtesans all made their way through that door, laughing with anticipation. The dance-floor was already full of costumed couples. It didn't take me long to re-alize that everyone else was there as part of a group or at least a couple. I suddenly felt like an awful wallflower and almost turned right around to go out again. What on earth had made me think I'd have a good time gate-crashing a party at which I knew nobody?

I was close to the door when a male figure blocked my path. He was dressed head to toe in black, with a frightening black-hooded mask.

"And where might you be trying to escape to, my lady?" he asked in smooth, upper-class English tones. "Her royal majesty Queen Marie An-toinette, if I'm not wrong. We have a confirmed assignation, you and I?"

"We do?" I asked cautiously. "I've no idea who you are, and I made no assignation."

"But can't you see who I am?" he demanded. "I'm your executioner." Then he revealed the axe he had been carrying behind his back.

"Wrong executioner," I said, in what I hoped was a confident voice. "I'm waiting for the guillotine. If you don't have one of those behind your back, then I'm afraid I'm not interested."

I left him standing there and hurried forward as if to join a loud and merry party on the other side of the room. I was relieved to find a seat at a table around the perimeter, where I could observe from behind my black mask. People nodded as they passed me. Some commented on the excellence of my costume, but nobody claimed to recognize me.

After a while I was asked to dance and managed a waltz without disgracing myself too much. Luckily the dance floor was so crowded that a shuffle was all that was required. I danced again and again, made small talk, drank punch, and had a good time. Several young bucks tried to find out who I was, and why they hadn't encountered me before, but I remained mysteriously enigmatic. All I would say was that I was a young Irishwoman going home on family matters. A couple of my partners even tried to extract an address from me so that they could visit me once we were in Ireland, but I declined tactfully.

When the dance ended at midnight, I felt like Cinderella, rushing back before my carriage changed back into a pumpkin. I made my way to my cabin, past happy revelers who had been at the punch bowl more frequently than I. Frederick was off duty by this time. I expected to see Henry, the night steward, sitting in his little cubby, but the small room was empty as I passed. I presumed he was attending to another passenger's needs. I let myself into my cabin, closed the door behind me and gave a sigh of relief. Tomorrow we'd dock in Queenstown. I could stop pretending to be Oona Sheehan and get on with my own work. I was looking forward to being anonymous again. I took off the wig, even warmer and more scratchy than the one I'd been suffering with all week, and went over to the daybed where the costume boxes awaited it. Come to think of it, the whole darned costume had been hugely uncomfortable. I couldn't wait to get out of it. That was when it struck me that I probably couldn't get out of the costume alone. It had taken a lot of lacing to strap me into it in the first place. I wondered whether it would be fair to summon Rose at this late hour.

As I turned back toward the door, I stopped dead in my tracks.

Someone was lying in my bed. The satin coverlet was pulled right up, but I could see red hair on the pillow. Had Oona Sheehan decided that she was fed up with sleeping in a second-class bunk and decided to reclaim her own, seeing that we'd be docking tomorrow?

At least she could have notified me of her intentions, I thought angrily. Was I now supposed to find my way back to my own cabin in the middle of the night? And what about my clothes? I could hardly make my way down to second class dressed as Marie Antoinette, could I?

Then it occurred to me that maybe she was angry at finding I had dared to leave the cabin to go to the costume ball. Maybe she had intended to talk to me tonight or even to change places again, but when I wasn't to be seen, decided to go to bed instead.

I went over and tapped at the shape under the coverlet.

"Miss Sheehan," I said gently, "it's Molly. I'm back. Do you want to wake up and tell me what you'd like me to do now?"

She didn't stir. I prodded her again. She didn't move.

I pulled back the coverlet and stifled a scream. It wasn't Oona Sheehan at all who was lying there. It was a strange woman dressed as a Spanish senorita. Her black lace shawl was partly hiding her face. I lifted it away, recoiling instantly in horror. Rose was staring up at me with dead eyes.

❧ Eight ❧

She can't be dead, was my first thought. She's only asleep, or fainted. Then I touched her bare arm and it was cold. And I had seen enough dead people to know death when I saw it. She couldn't just have climbed into my bed and died, surely. She was young and healthy and I'd been joking with her only a couple of hours ago. I walked around the bed, staring at her, trying to think. There was no sign of any struggle, but somebody must have covered her up and arranged her peacefully. Which meant that somebody had killed her.

My heart was racing so fast I thought I might faint. It occurred to me that whoever had done this might still be in the room, waiting for me to return. I backed cautiously until I was within easy reach of the door, my eyes darting nervously from one side of the room to the other.

"Get help. Get the steward" was my first coherent thought.

I reached for the doorknob, opened the door and peered out into the corridor. It was empty. I ran back to the steward's cubby, but there was no sign of him there either. I was truly terrified now.

I half believed I was suffering from a hallucination. I had read about drugs being slipped into drinks. Somebody had put something in the punch bowl to make me drunk. I forced myself to creep back to my door and peer around it. The figure still lay on the bed. As far as I could see there was nowhere in the cabin to hide, apart from the wardrobe, and that was full of clothes. But I wasn't going to go looking on my own.

Then a hand tapped my shoulder. My heart leaped so wildly I

couldn't even scream. I turned to see Henry, the familiar night steward standing there.

"Where do you think you are going, miss?" he asked.

I realized, of course, as I turned to face him, that I was no longer wearing Oona Sheehan's wig, but my own hair, which had now been flattened under the powdered wig of Marie Antoinette. I put my hand up to my face, and of course I was still wearing the black mask.

"This is my cabin, Henry," I said in my deep Oona Sheehan whisper. "Don't you recognize me?" I pulled off the mask and made some ineffectual pats at my rattaily hair.

"Oh, beg pardon, Miss Sheehan. I got a shock seeing someone creeping up to your cabin door, especially since I'd popped off duty for a couple of minutes when I should have been keeping an eye out here."

"How long have you been away from your post?" I asked.

"Oh, no more than fifteen minutes or so," he said. "There was a bit of shindig downstairs in the staff quarters to celebrate last night at sea, and a steward showed up with yet another floral tribute for you. He offered to deliver it for me and said he'd keep an eye on things for a while so that I could pop down and enjoy myself for a few minutes. It was such good fun down there, I might have stayed away a little longer than I planned."

"Which steward was it?"

"I couldn't rightly say, miss," he said. "That blessed flower display was bigger than he was."

"So you didn't recognize him?"

"I can't say I thought much about it, miss. With a ship this size, you don't know all the crew. I just took in the uniform jacket and those flowers really. Why, is something wrong?"

"Something's very wrong," I said. "You'd better come inside and take a look."

I opened the door and stood aside for him to enter first. He gasped when he saw what I was pointing to.

"Oh, my lawks. Is she—?" he stammered.

"Yes, she's dead," I said. "I came back to find her tucked up in bed."

"Do you know who it is?" he stammered. Beads of sweat were now trickling down his face.

"It's my maid." As I said these words, I realized of course that I was

54

lying. She wasn't my maid at all. She was Oona Sheehan's maid. This could become complicated.

"Your maid?" He examined her more closely. "Why so it is. What the deuce is she doing dressed up in that outfit?"

"It could be possible that her killer dressed her in those clothes," I said, "but I can't think why." Then I came up with a more probable answer, and one that sent chills down my spine. "What if she tried on the costume for a lark, and her killer thought she was me?"

"But how could anyone have got into your cabin, that's what I want to know," Henry said. "I'm always here, on duty—especially late at night when the young men have been drinking and think they are brave enough to pay you a visit."

"But you weren't here tonight, Henry. You just said so yourself. Another steward took your place."

"But only for a few minutes, miss."

"Long enough to kill somebody," I said.

He looked at me, horror struck. "But surely you don't think—"

"That's exactly what I'm thinking. I'm wondering if he really was a steward or if he used the disguise and the flowers to get rid of you and enter this cabin."

"Oh no, miss. Don't say that." Henry put a hand to his mouth. "I'd never live with myself if I thought—"

"You weren't to know, Henry," I said. "Try to remember everything you can about him."

"But I told you. I didn't really take too much notice."

"Was he young or old?"

"He had a good head of dark hair, miss. I can tell you that much."

"Tall?"

"Taller than me."

"And his voice? A young voice or an old voice?"

"Youngish, I'd say. And there was something about it—posher than the average steward."

"There you are, you've already given us something to go on."

"We should start hunting for him right away," Henry said.

"He'll have discarded that steward's uniform long ago. Now he's probably lying safely in his cabin."

"You mean one of the passengers?" He looked horrified.

"It's possible. Somebody killed Rose. That means either a crew member or a passenger."

"Stay where you are, miss," Henry said, regaining his composure. "I'll go and get help, and I'll bring you a brandy."

"No, don't leave me," I said, grabbing at his sleeve. "What if he's still here? Is there anywhere in here he could hide?"

Henry searched patiently around the cabin, opening the wardrobe with great caution, looking under the daybed. But he found nothing.

"I'll be back before you can say Jack Robinson," he said.

As he went out, I caught a glimpse of myself in the dressing table mirror. I presented quite a sight with my white face, my matted hair, the improbable costume. Nobody would possibly take me for Oona Sheehan looking like this. My wig, I thought. I must put on Oona's wig before Henry comes back. They mustn't know. As my clumsy fingers struggled to put on Oona's red wig, I realized that they'd have to know. I had promised Oona that we would trade places for the journey. But surely now I'd have to go back on that promise. Oona would understand that I'd have to come clean. She'd want to know what had happened to Rose. She'd want Rose's killer found and brought to justice.

But I continued to put on the wig. It was mainly vanity at this stage, I suppose. My own hair was so flattened and unattractive, that I didn't want to be seen like that. And I wanted to get my thoughts straight before I let the truth come out. I hadn't finished straightening the wig before there were the sounds of heavy feet in the corridor outside and Henry reappeared with a couple of ship's officers.

"In here, sir. On the bed."

The bearded one went straight over to Rose's body. "I'm the ship's doctor, Miss Sheehan," he said. "I understand that the victim is your maid. This is most distressing for you. Most."

"And I am First Officer Stratton, Miss Sheehan," the other one said. "So you found this young girl dead in your bed?"

I nodded. "And I suspect she's been murdered."

He peered at the body, which indeed did look quite peaceful. "Are you sure we're not jumping to conclusions that foul play was involved here? People do die unexpectedly—heart attacks, fatal asthma, that kind of thing—even young people."

"But they don't take the trouble to arrange themselves neatly in bed and cover themselves up first," I said.

"I see what you mean. The captain has been notified. He was asleep, but he will be with us as soon as he can. Why don't we remove ourselves from here and let the doctor get on with his examination. Henry, will you tell the captain that we'll be in the reading room? We're not likely to be disturbed there at this time of night."

He took my elbow and steered me firmly out of the door, up the stairs to the main promenade deck, and then into a quiet lounge. It had paneled walls, comfortable armchairs, and several writing desks. It was in darkness when we arrived, and Henry went around switching on table lamps that threw a warm glow onto the polished furniture.

"If it's all right with you, sir, I thought I'd fetch Miss Sheehan a brandy," Henry said. "She looks as if she's about to faint."

"By all means. Good idea," First Officer Stratton agreed. He pulled out a leather armchair for me.

I wasn't normally one likely to faint and was about to say so. Then I realized that in truth I didn't feel too steady on my feet. Rose had laced me firmly into my costume, and it felt as if my body was locked into a steel cage at this moment, with breathing virtually impossible. I sank, gratefully, into the chair. Henry returned with the brandy; and I sipped, coughed, and sipped again, feeling the comforting warmth of the liquor spreading through me.

In a few minutes we were joined by the captain, a distinguished-looking man with graying beard, looking none-the-less distinguished in a dressing gown and slippers. He barged into the room, bristling with indignation.

"What's all this about, Stratton?" he asked. "We've a death on board?"

"A suspicious death, sir. The doctor is currently examining the body."

"Do we know who the victim is?"

I opened my mouth, but the words would not come out.

"This lady's maid," Henry said for me.

"And you are?" The captain turned a keen gaze onto me.

"This is Miss Oona Sheehan," Henry said proudly.

"Good God," the captain said. He stared at me for a second. "Bless my soul," he said again. "Saw one of your plays once. Dashed good. The one where you were disguised as a boy. Stupid romantic story, but you were splendid. What was it called again?"

Mercifully I was spared having to answer this question by the arrival of the doctor.

"Captain Hammond, sir," he said. "I've completed a brief preliminary examination."

"And what's your opinion, Doctor? Are we dealing with a death from natural causes, or does it indeed look suspicious to you?"

"I think it's safe to say that she was suffocated, sir," the doctor said. "Probably by the pillow on the bed. There are signs of bruising around the neck where she was held down forcibly. However, she had not—uh—been assaulted or interfered with in any way." He lowered his voice as he said this with a quick glance in my direction.

"Blast it. This is most unfortunate," the captain said. "Right. Well, I suppose I'd better go and take a look for myself. If you don't mind waiting here, Miss Sheehan, I'll have the doctor escort me back to your cabin."

"Make sure you don't touch anything unnecessarily, sir," the first officer called after him. "I'm sure the police will want the crime scene undisturbed when they come aboard."

"I'm not a complete fool, Stratton," the captain barked back. "Besides, I am the law on this ship while we are at sea, and I'll conduct my own inquiry. It only becomes a police matter when we dock, and if I choose to report it. Ideally I'd like to have the whole thing sewn up before we get to Ireland."

"Fat chance of that, I should say," the first officer muttered as the door closed behind the captain and doctor. Henry nodded.

I waited, shivering, even though the room was comfortably warm. This whole voyage had been so unreal, and now had taken on a nightmare quality The first officer, Henry and I waited in uneasy silence. I was conscious of a clock, ticking on one wall, the gentle pitching of the ship as we ran with the waves. After what seemed an age, the captain and doctor returned.

"Horrible business," the captain was muttering as he came in. "Quite horrible. Poor girl. We're going to find the blighter who did this, damn his eyes. Well, I suppose we had better get down to it. The girl was Irish, I take it. I suppose that means notifying the police when we dock in Queenstown."

"We will most certainly have to call in the local police when we dock in Queenstown," the first officer said emphatically.

"We don't have to do anything." The captain stared at him. "I am the law on this ship, as you well know."

"We fly under the British flag, sir. We are subject to British law, and a murder will certainly have to involve the British police."

The captain sighed. "Yes, I know, I know. By God, this will be a nasty business. I hope to heaven they don't keep us delayed in port while they conduct their inquiries. The ship's owners will be tearing out their beards if we can't keep to our schedule. They'll blame me for some blasted woman getting herself killed on my ship." He stared out of the window into the blackness, then slapped his hand on the nearest table. "Right. Let's get on with it. Will you take notes, Doctor? There's writing paper on the desk over there."

"Right you are, sir." The doctor crossed the room and pulled a chair up to a writing desk.

"I've never conducted a murder investigation before in all my years at sea," the captain said. "We've over a thousand people on this vessel and I want this man apprehended as quickly as possible. I don't like the thought of a killer running around loose in our midst."

As he spoke it crossed my mind that we should not leap to the assumption that the killer was male. But for once I wisely kept silent.

The captain was pacing now, hands behind his back. "Stratton, I want the crew made aware of the circumstances as quickly and quietly as possible. Have them keep an eye open for anyone acting suspiciously. I'll do a briefing of the day staff at four bells and I want a full passenger list immediately."

The doctor looked up from his position at the writing table. "Sir, I think we should make every effort to keep the news from the passengers or to cause any kind of alarm, do you agree?"

"Oh, absolutely, sir." Stratton nodded his agreement. "If we had some idea for whom we might be on the lookout, we could take steps to apprehend this man before we dock tomorrow."

"If we knew who we were looking for, the matter would be simple, Stratton," the captain said dryly. "We'd go to his damned cabin and arrest him."

I glanced across at Henry to see if he was going to mention the unknown steward. He stood by the doorway with eyes cast down. I was debating whether to mention it at this stage myself and thus risk getting Henry into trouble, when the captain went on, "Well, nobody's going ashore until the police come on board, that's for certain. Have signals standing at the ready. I want semaphore messages sent as soon we make contact with the Irish coast. I'm not putting this ship hours behind schedule while we wait for their inspectors to arrive from Dublin."

"It is possible they'll keep us in port while a complete investigation is carried out," the first officer said.

"They'd damned well better not," the captain muttered. "They can interrogate those who wish to disembark in Ireland and then conduct the rest of their inquiry as we sail to Liverpool."

"I'm not sure that—" the first officer began.

"Damn it, man, stop blathering there. Off you go to brief the crew then," the captain barked. "I want signals standing by immediately. And remember, mum's the word."

"Aye, aye, sir." The first officer left.

"Right. Where were we?" Captain Hammond turned his keen gaze on me. "Miss Sheehan, this poor girl was your maid, you say. Do you have any ideas who might have wanted her dead? Was this just a random act of violence, do you think, Doctor?"

"I don't think so, sir. Such men would normally look for some sexual gratification as part of their acts." Again he glanced at me as if apologizing for introducing so repugnant a subject.

"So we have to assume that your maid was killed for a reason. Miss Sheehan, did she have an unwanted admirer that you knew of?"

"Tell the truth and get it over with," a voice was screaming in my head, but I didn't know where to begin. Also, as the brandy took effect and calmed my racing nerves, I was beginning to see that I might be in a bit of a pickle.

I shook my head.

"Right, let's start with basics," Captain Hammond said. "The girl's full name."

"Rose," I said. "I—uh—don't know her last name."

"Don't know your maid's last name?" the captain asked incredulously.

I took a deep breath. "Look, there is something you should know before we proceed any further. I am not really Oona Sheehan."

The captain slapped his hands together. "I thought there was something different about you. I sat in the front row of the stalls, you know. Now what the devil is this all about? Out with it."

"I thought there was something a bit strange too, Captain, if I might be so bold," Henry said. "I've served Miss Sheehan before. There was something that made me uneasy all voyage long. So that's it."

"I'm sorry for deceiving you, Henry," I said. "I assure you there was a good reason."

"Then who the devil are you, and what's happened to Miss Sheehan?" the captain barked.

"My name is Molly Murphy," I said. "I had booked a passage to sail to Ireland in a second-class cabin on this ship. When I came on board, I received a note from Miss Sheehan, asking me to come straight to her cabin."

"Do you know Miss Sheehan?"

"We met once recently. She asked me to change places with her."

"Change places, why the devil would she do that?" The captain was now eyeing me most suspiciously.

"She told me she was tired of being pestered by admirers and she needed a rest. She offered me money to pretend to be her until we docked in Queenstown."

"And you agreed?"

"I saw no reason not to."

"Why did she ask you to carry out this unusual assignment if you'd only met her once?"

"Because she thought I looked sufficiently like her to carry it off."

The captain looked at me critically. "And did you carry it off? Did anyone twig to the fact that you weren't Oona?"

"I was instructed to keep to my cabin. I only took the occasional turn about the deck, until tonight, when, as you can see from the costume, I went to the fancy dress ball in disguise, wearing a powdered wig and a mask."

"And what about Miss Sheehan's maid? What did she think?"

"Oh, she was in on the scheme. Miss Sheehan instructed her to treat me as her mistress for the entire trip." The initial fear and shock had worn off, and I was now growing weary of this interrogation. "Look, why don't you send someone down to my cabin in second class and have Miss Sheehan brought up here? Then she'll tell you the truth and maybe you'll believe me."

"That makes sense," the captain said. "Henry, would you go to this young lady's cabin and ask Miss Sheehan if she would kindly join us. Apologize about the ungodly hour but tell her it is a matter of great urgency—only it's probably wise not to mention her maid's death until I can break the news to her."

"Very good, sir. What number is the cabin?"

"Two thirty-one, E deck," I said.

Henry departed.

"Why kill a maid?" The captain stroked his beard. "Possibly someone wanted to get into Miss Sheehan's cabin bent on robbery and found the maid in residence, and the maid raised a ruckus and he suffocated her to keep her quiet? Far-fetched, do you think?"

"If you want my opinion," I said, "I think we have to assume that the intended target of this attack was not the maid, but Miss Sheehan herself. I had ordered some costumes for the ball. I kept the Spanish costume because I couldn't make up my mind at first. When I found the maid lying on my bed, she was wearing this costume. My guess would be that she had been trying it on for a lark when the intruder came in and thought she was me—or rather that she was Miss Sheehan."

Even as I said this, thoughts were jelling in my mind. Perhaps Oona Sheehan had an unwanted admirer, one she had previously rejected and who now had reason to turn violent on her. Perhaps she saw a particular man coming on board, knew what he was like, and panicked—and got me to trade places with her so that she could travel in anonymity. Hence the instructions to keep to my cabin.

Well, that's just lovely, I thought angrily. She paid me to get killed instead of her. Only now the final joke's on her—it was her maid who copped it instead. Not very funny for poor Rose.

The door was pushed open and Henry arrived, breathing hard after running up several flights of steps.

"I've been down to E deck, Captain," he said, "and the cabin number the young lady gave me is empty."

❧ Nine ❧

I stared at the elderly steward as he crossed the reading room, still breathing heavily.

"You mean Miss Sheehan wasn't in the cabin?" I asked.

"No, I mean that nobody's been in the cabin all voyage. It's empty. Unoccupied."

"But what about my things?" I demanded. "I left my belongings down there. What's happened to them?" Looking back on it, I suppose my few meager possessions were of little consequence compared to a murder, but they were all I had and I wasn't about to lose them.

Henry shook his head. "I couldn't say, Miss. There's nothing in that cabin—that's all I can tell you."

"Miss Sheehan has to be somewhere," I said. "Perhaps my cabin proved to be too small for her liking and she found something better. Someone must know where she's hiding out."

"This is most peculiar," Captain Hammond said. "What does the steward down there have to say about it? Do we know who is assigned to that part of the ship?"

"I could look it up for you, sir," Henry said. "Do you want me to go and wake the day steward now?"

"Yes, I think you'd better."

"He won't be pleased," Henry muttered. "The crew had a bit of a shindig tonight, and he'll only just have gone to sleep."

"Extraordinary circumstances, my man. He'll just have to be not pleased. And we'd better have the second-class purser up here too."

Henry looked even less thrilled about the prospect of waking him. "Very good, sir. If you say so," he muttered, and left. I felt the captain's eyes on me. It was clear that he was now highly suspicious of me and something awful suddenly occurred to me—I might well be his number-one suspect at this point. Pretending to be someone else, occupying a first-class cabin under false pretences, and then claiming to find the true occupant's maid dead. It didn't look good, did it? Unless we could produce Oona Sheehan to verify my story, I foresaw trouble ahead.

A few minutes later a rather disheveled and bleary-eyed steward stumbled into the room, still buttoning his white uniform jacket.

"This better be bloody good," he muttered, "waking me up in the middle of the bleedin' night."

"Watch your language, man," the captain barked. "There is a lady present."

Those bleary eyes now noticed the captain sitting there. He stood to attention rather rapidly. "Sorry, sir. I didn't realize. Henry just said I was wanted in a hurry and—" Then he noticed me. I must have presented quite an interesting sight in my Marie Antoinette costume.

"Your name again?" the captain asked him.

"Wally, sir. Wally Henshaw."

"Right, Wally. What can you tell us about cabin 231 and the person who occupies it on this crossing?"

"Two thirty-one, Captain?" the wiry little man wrinkled his forehead. "Ain't nobody been in that cabin this crossing."

"You are saying that the cabin has never been occupied from the time we sailed?"

"That's exactly what I'm saying, sir."

"But I left my belongings in that cabin," I said. "It was booked in my name. I have the ticket to prove it in my handbag."

"I believe there was some luggage delivered to it before we sailed," Wally said, "but then I was told the young lady received some bad news at the last minute and had to disembark again."

The truth was finally dawning on me. It appeared that Oona had never intended to sail in the first place. Not only had she tricked me, but she had walked off with most of my worldly goods. Obviously I had a closet of lovely dresses in their place, but they were not mine and they were far too grand and extravagant for me to wear when I went ashore. I was reminded again that clothes were the least of my troubles when the captain said, "Well, young lady. You'd better give us the full details of who you are and where you were heading on this ship."

"My travel documents are in Oona Sheehan's cabin," I said. "Do you want to send someone to fetch them or are you going to take my word for what I tell you?"

The captain looked at me long and hard. "You give us your version right now. It will be easy enough to verify."

I gave him my particulars. Henry arrived with a white-faced purser in tow. He could only repeat what Wally had told us. The occupant of cabin 231 had received bad news and disembarked at the last minute. As to whether that person was Oona Sheehan, he couldn't say. Everything was chaos in the last moments before sailing—people complaining about their cabins, wanting to change them, not being able to find them. He did verify that the cabin was booked in the name of Molly Murphy.

The captain turned back to me. "And for what reason are you traveling to Ireland?" he asked.

"I'm Irish, isn't that obvious? I've a family I haven't seen for some time, and I've finally saved up enough to go home to see them." The nagging voice of conscience reminded me that this wasn't exactly the truth, but I saw no reason to reveal that I was an investigator on an assignment until I had to do so. That would be opening yet another can of worms.

"And their address would be?"

Holy Mother, I didn't want him looking up my family, announcing to the whole of county Mayo that I was back in the land, just waiting for that warrant to catch up with me.

"I'm planning on going to Cork to start with, where I've been asked to look up the sister of an old friend. After that I expect I'll probably be in Dublin, meeting with friends and relatives there," I said rapidly. "I had no firm plans after that."

The captain was still glaring at me as if he was trying to bore into my mind.

"Look here," I said at last. I was tired, upset, angry now too. "I can't think why you are bent on attacking me like this. Anyone would think you were accusing me of being party to this poor girl's death. Why on earth should I want to kill someone's maid, I'd like to know?"

The captain couldn't answer this one, but Henry leaned toward him. "Maybe she's done in the real Miss Sheehan, Captain, sir," he hissed in an excited stage whisper. "Maybe she shoved her over the side when no one was looking and decided to take her place, only the maid found out and she had to silence her."

I looked at him and had to laugh in spite of everything. "You should be writing penny dreadfuls, Henry, really you should. What on earth could I possibly gain from pretending to be Oona Sheehan?"

"Well, for one thing, sleeping in a first-class cabin. Then maybe you planned on impersonating Miss Sheehan when you landed and taking in the local people."

"Absolute rubbish," I said. "Anyway, this whole thing can be solved as soon as we dock. You'll no doubt be sending a cable telegraph communication to Miss Sheehan to tell her what's happened to her maid. Ask her to verify her little scheme with me at the same time."

I got to my feet. "Look, it's the middle of the night and all this is getting us nowhere. If you want to conduct a proper investigation, you should start with the young man who dressed up as a steward and took Henry's place."

"What's this?" The captain turned to Henry, who blushed.

"It's as she says, sir. A man I took to be another steward showed up with a big display of flowers for Miss Sheehan. This wasn't at all unusual. In fact, it has been happening the whole voyage—flowers, chocolates, champagne—aren't I right, Miss Sheehan—I mean, miss?"

I nodded. "All the time," I echoed. "Miss Sheehan obviously has lots of admirers. I could well understand that she wanted to be free of them for a while."

"Go on about the steward," the captain said.

"Well, he told me he'd cover for me if I wanted to join the party going on in the crew's quarters. You know there's always a bit of a celebration on the last night at sea. I was only gone a few minutes, sir. I meant no harm by it."

"And you didn't recognize this man?" the first officer asked sharply.

"No, sir. His face was hidden behind the flowers."

"We've ascertained that he was taller than Henry, younger, and spoke with a more refined accent," I said. "From which I think we might deduce that he could have been one of the passengers in disguise."

They all looked at me.

"I suppose I should tell you that I am an investigator by profession," I said, and instantly wished that I hadn't. When would I ever learn to keep my mouth shut? It would have been simpler had I remained the simple Irish lass returning home to the bosom of her family. But it was gratifying to see their startled faces, I have to admit.

"Good God," the captain said. "A female investigator. What is the world coming to? Then is it possible that this murder could have something to do with your profession and nothing at all to do with Miss Sheehan? Are you hot on the trail of some criminal?"

I shook my head, smiling. "First, this changing cabins was a last-minute occurrence. Nobody could have known that I was pretending to be Miss Sheehan, except for her maid—"

"Who could have blabbed," Henry pointed out. "They often do."

I shook my head again. "Like I told you, I'm only going to Ireland to look up the sister of a friend. Nothing of a criminal nature, I assure you. No, I'm sure somebody wanted to kill Miss Sheehan—some unbalanced young man, mad with unrequited love, I shouldn't wonder."

The captain turned to the other officers. "Then where the deuce do we start? We can't line up all the younger men on this ship and see if Henry recognizes any of them by their hair or their voices."

"You could find out who ordered a large display of flowers this evening," I said, "although I shouldn't think the murderer would have been stupid enough to order them in his own name."

"Worth a try, I suppose," the captain said.

"If you want my advice, sir," the doctor said, looking up from his seat at the desk, "we should make sure nobody goes ashore and then turn this over to the Irish police. We may well bungle the whole thing if we try to conduct our own investigation. These things have to be done with a great deal of subtlety."

"Are you insinuating that I don't know what the hell I am doing?" the captain demanded.

"You said yourself that you'd never conducted a murder investigation before, sir," the doctor said calmly. "It may be wiser, in the circumstances, to put the whole thing into the hands of trained professional detectives."

"Oh, very well, blast it," the captain grunted. "I don't know how we're going to prevent the passengers from going ashore without a full-scale mutiny on our hands."

"Tell them it's a health scare, sir," the doctor said. "A passenger has come down with a suspected infectious disease and nobody is allowed ashore until they've passed a medical inspection."

"Brilliant, man." For once the captain looked pleased. "That way we can take a good look at all of them. A medical inspection. That's the ticket." He clapped his hands. "Right. Make sure you stand guard outside Miss Sheehan's cabin all night, Henry. Nobody is to go anywhere near it. And the rest of us will try for a couple of hours of shut-eye. We'll all need our wits about us in the morning."

"What about me?" I asked. "Where am I to sleep?"

"In your own cabin on E deck, I suppose," the captain said.

"I'll need to collect my few possessions from Oona Sheehan's cabin first," I said. "I can hardly go to sleep dressed like this, and I have to return the costume to your store."

The captain sighed. "Very well. Go with her, man, and make sure she doesn't touch anything she doesn't have to. They can take fingerprints these days, so I understand."

"My fingerprints would already be all over the cabin, since I've lived in it for a week," I said. "And don't worry, I'll not disturb anything."

With that I left the room.

❧ Ten ❧

Of course I found it impossible to sleep. The narrow bunk was cold and hard and the deep dull thunk, thunk, thunk of the engine noise seemed to resonate through my skull. I suppose that delayed shock was setting in too, because I couldn't get warm. My horror until now had been for poor Rose. Now it was just beginning to sink in that had I returned from the party earlier and dismissed the maid, it might have been me lying covered in that bed, staring out with dead eyes. I pulled the coverlet up around me and hugged my knees to my chest. I didn't like to think what tomorrow might bring. So much for slipping into Ireland quietly without anybody noticing me, I thought, before I finally drifted into an uneasy sleep.

I awoke to loud sounds of clanking and grinding and sat up, with heart pounding, only to hit my head against the upper bunk. This, of course, reminded me where I was and the full horror of the night before came flooding back into my memory. It appeared that we had come into Queenstown harbor during the night and were now docking. I got up and peered out under the lifeboat. It was still early—a gray dawn, streaked with rose in the east, the sort of day we Irish would know meant no good would come of the weather. Seagulls wheeled around mewing plaintively, and with that sound came the realization that I was truly home again. There were seagulls in New York, of course, but somehow they weren't the same. These were the cries that had accompanied my childhood outings into Westport or to meet the fishing boats when they delivered their catch to a dock near our cottage.

Another loud clanking noise, accompanied by shouts from below. I suspected that gangways were being raised to the ship. By tilting my head to one side, I could see the little town beyond the docks, rising in tiers up a steep hillside, with a fine-looking church spire right in the middle. So this was Queenstown, the port from which so many of my countrymen had sailed to a new life during the Great Famine.

If gangplanks had already been raised to the ship, then it was possible that the local police had already come on board. I could be summoned at any moment. I dressed hastily in Oona Sheehan's least flamboyant outfit, one of the few things I had brought down with me from her cabin the night before. It was a black-and-white-striped two-piece costume and a jaunty little black hat with an ostrich feather. I couldn't see myself wearing the hat, however. In fact, I felt strange putting on her clothing, now that I knew the truth of the situation and more disturbing questions entered my head. What if she denied ever making the pact with me? What if she accused me of stealing her clothes, or even worse? Then I remembered something—she had given me a check for a hundred dollars. I had it safely in my traveling case with her signature quite legible on it. At least I could prove she had hired me to do something for her!

Feeling slightly better now, I brushed out my own hair and tied it back, glad that I wasn't going to have to wear that hateful wig again, then went in search of some breakfast. I got strange looks when I had to ask my way to the second-class dining room and then find a place that wasn't assigned to another passenger, but I ate a surprisingly hearty breakfast of eggs and bacon, toast and marmalade, and frankly enjoyed it all the more after a week of dainty invalid delicacies from the first-class kitchen.

As I made my way back to my cabin, I saw Wally, the steward who had been summoned to the meeting last night, standing outside my cabin door talking with a big, stocky man in a tweed overcoat.

"Were you wanting me?" I asked, as I approached.

"Oh, there you are, miss." The steward looked decidedly relieved. "We thought for a moment that you'd done a bunk."

"'Done a bunk'?" I demanded. "And why would I want to do that? And what did you think I'd done—dived out through the porthole?"

I saw just the hint of a smile twitch on the big man's face. He was middle aged, with impressive muttonchop whiskers, a ruddy complexion that hinted at a life in the outdoors, and perhaps the love of a good whisky.

"So you're the young lady, are you? Miss Murphy?" he asked. His accent was English, with a just a touch of an Irish lilt to it. "How do you do." He stuck out a big, meaty hand. "Inspector Harris. I've just got here by train from Dublin, and I gather you're the only one who can throw any light onto this whole strange, sordid business."

"I don't know about that," I said.

"Well, to start with, I've been told you've been impersonating the famous actress, Miss Oona Sheehan, for the entire voyage. Is that correct?"

"It is," I said, and started to tell him how that had come about.

Raised voices could be heard coming in our direction. "Where is the damned purser? I'd like to know. Why aren't we being allowed ashore? The gangways are clearly in place."

Inspector Harris glanced down the hallway then opened my cabin door. "Right. Let's go into your cabin and talk then, shall we?"

"It's not very big," I warned. "I can scarcely turn around in it myself."

I opened the door. He took a look inside and retreated again. "I see what you mean. Not enough room to swing a cat, as they say. Okay, why don't we go up to the cabin you've been occupying all week? I've got men going over it as we speak and maybe you can answer some of their questions. Will you show us the way, my man?"

Wally nodded and led us back along the hall. I followed reluctantly. I had no wish to see Rose's dead face in daylight. Our feet resonated as we climbed the steep steps back to Oona Sheehan's cabin and the opulence of the first-class quarters. A police constable was standing guard at the entrance to Miss Sheehan's passage, and there were two more policemen in the cabin itself.

"We haven't found anything so far, sir." One of them looked up from his hands and knees beside the bed as Inspector Harris stood aside to usher me into the cabin. "No signs of a struggle. I think we should probably call in the police surgeon to verify the ship doctor's diagnosis. Isn't it possible she died of natural causes, and this is all a flap over nothing? She looks peaceful enough."

Rose's body had obviously been covered in a sheet all night, but this had now been pulled back. I stole a hurried look at her in spite of myself. Luckily someone had now closed her eyes so she was no longer staring at me. She looked very peaceful, lying there as if asleep, and I felt tears well up into my eyes.

"People who die of natural causes don't end up with bruises on their throats," the inspector said dryly. "He didn't strangle her enough to kill her but probably enough to make her pass out. Not enough broken blood vessels in her eyes. Then he must have rammed her face into the pillow to finish her off."

I felt a sob rising in my throat, put an embarrassed hand up to my mouth, and managed to turn the sob into a sniff. Inspector Harris touched my arm. "I'm sure this must be most distressing for you, Miss Murphy."

"I'm fine," I said, although I didn't feel that way. "It's just seeing her there. Such a waste of a young life."

The inspector took my arm. "Maybe if we go and sit over there at the porthole—you take that sofa and I'll take the chair. Now, first things first. Let's start with your discovering the body. This happened exactly when?" He took out a notebook and pencil and looked at me expectantly.

"It was after midnight, I know that much. The band had played 'Auld Lang Syne,' and I left the ball with everyone else."

"Go back a bit." He held up his hand. "You had been occupying this cabin the entire voyage, correct? But you left it yesterday evening?"

"That's right, sir. I had been told by Miss Sheehan to keep to my cabin as much as possible. But yesterday the steward told me there was to be a fancy dress ball and suggested I might like to obtain a costume and go to it."

"Which steward was this?"

"Frederick, the day steward for this cabin."

He scribbled down the name. "So you decided to go in spite of being told to keep to your cabin."

"Yes. I'd been cooped up in here throughout the voyage. A costume ball was too much of a temptation, and I felt I could safely join in the fun. So I had some costumes sent down from the ship's rental store, tried them on, and kept a couple of them. One was Marie Antoinette and one was the Spanish senorita's costume that Rose is now wearing. I decided to go as Marie Antoinette because of the big, powdered wig and the mask. I thought there was no chance of my being recognized."

"And were you recognized?"

A picture came into my head of that executioner stepping forward to block my path and saying those alarming things to me. Then I shook my head. He couldn't have known who I was. He was only acting, enjoying playing such a macabre part.

"Absolutely not," I said.

"So you came back here after midnight. Anything unusual happen? Did you pass anybody in the corridors?"

"Of course. Revelers from the ball were all making their way to their cabins. The only strange thing was that there was no steward on duty in his little room at the end of the hall. Later, when I found the regular night attendant, Henry, he told me that a strange steward had shown up with a floral display for this cabin and had offered to take his place while he went down to the crew party." I looked around the room. "It must be that big arrangement of chrysanthamums on the dresser."

"You hear that, Jonesy?" Inspector Harris alerted one of the policemen. "Big display of mums over there. There might be fingerprints on the vase. See what you can do, eh?"

He turned back to me. "Did you know you can identify people by their fingerprints? No two are alike, apparently. And Scotland Yard has now come up with a way to dust objects so that the fingerprints show up. So all we'd have to do is to take the fingerprints of all the men on this ship, and . . ."

"There don't appear to be any fingerprints on the vase, sir," the young policeman called back. "It appears to have been wiped clean."

"Ah, a thoughtful criminal then." He nodded. "Right. Back to square one. So you came in and . . ."

"And saw someone asleep in my bed. I thought it must have been Miss Sheehan herself, come back to her own cabin for the last night at sea, and I was rather annoyed that she hadn't warned me. I went to wake her gently and that's when I found it was Rose."

"What made you think it was Miss Sheehan?"

"They both had red hair and that's all I could see. The coverlet was pulled right up, you see. All nice and smooth. No sign of foul play."

"And what did you do then?"

"Went for help, of course. Henry, the cabin steward came in, and then he went to fetch the first officer and the ship's doctor. That's all I can tell you."

He cocked his head on one side, staring at me. "So who knew you were going to be at this ball?"

"Only Frederick, the day steward, and Henry. And Rose, of course."

"And the people working in the costume rental place?"

"Well, yes, I suppose so."

"So it wouldn't have been too hard to ascertain that you were out of the cabin last night."

"No, probably not. But what would the motive for entering this cabin have been if someone thought it was unoccupied?"

"Robbery, of course. I expect Miss Sheehan was quite a rich woman. She probably had a nice little collection of jewels with her."

"If she had, I can assure you they weren't left in this cabin for my use," I said. "Or if they are here, they are very well hidden. She must have taken them with her, or put them in the ship's safe, or even given them to Rose for safekeeping."

"I'll be taking a look at Rose's cabin in a moment," the inspector said, "and my sergeant can check on whether Miss Sheehan left anything in the ship's safe. In either case, Rose would have known where the jewels were, correct? So the intruder comes in, tries to get the truth out of Rose, wants to frighten her by shoving her face into a pillow, and goes too far. Kills her accidentally, then covers up his crime and flees."

"You think it was as simple as that, do you?" I asked.

"It usually is. Most crimes I've handled are bungled attempts of some sort or another." He chewed on the end of his pencil. "You obviously have other thoughts on the matter. Come on, now. Out with it."

"It struck me that the intended target was Miss Sheehan herself. Rose was dressed up in the other costume I had hired."

"Yes, that was strange, wasn't it? Was she dressed that way when you left her? Was she hoping to sneak into the ball?"

I shook my head. "No. I actually suggested she come to the ball with me, but she was horrified at the thought. I expect she probably put on the costume for a lark when nobody was looking. So my thought was that someone took the chance to be alone with Miss Sheehan and killed Rose by mistake."

"And why would someone want to kill Miss Sheehan, in your opinion?"

"Unrequited love? She had plenty of admirers, some of whom bordered on the fanatic. Maybe she spurned one of them and it was too much for him. You know—if I can't have her then nobody can."

"I see." He cocked his head again, studying me. "These admirers you talk about—did she mention any of them by name?"

"No, but she said she was growing tired of being pestered by them; and when I encountered a couple myself, I could see why."

An eyebrow raised, almost imperceptibly. "You said you were instructed to stay in your cabin throughout the voyage, did you not? So where did you encounter these admirers?"

"I didn't say I was told not to leave my cabin. I was advised keep to it for most of the journey by feigning sickness. But when I tried a turn about the deck, I saw instantly what Miss Sheehan had to go through. I was accosted almost immediately by love-sick young men."

"Any names you can give me?"

I frowned, recreating the times I had been on deck. "One of them had a very silly name—Artie something. Rotweiler? Something Germanic sounding. Fortwrangler, that was it, Artie Fortwrangler; but he seemed like a harmless sort of boy."

"Fortwrangler," the inspector said slowly as he wrote it down. "Did he make threats?"

"Oh no. Exactly the opposite. He professed undying love. He was like a love-sick puppy dog."

"And who else?"

"There was a good-looking young man, spoke with an American accent but he was obviously of Irish heritage. Black Irish, you know. Now what was he called? Fitzwilliam, maybe? No, I think it was Fitzpatrick.

But he didn't act the love-sick oaf like the other one. He was polite. He just said he was sorry to hear I was indisposed and expressed the hope that we'd meet again in Ireland."

Inspector Harris nodded. "And then?"

"He went on his way."

"Anyone else?"

I shook my head. "After that, if I left the cabin at all, I went out early, when fashionable young men are still asleep and there was nobody—except there was an older man who followed me at a distance sometimes. Tweed overcoat. Mustaches rather like your own. But he never approached me. It could have been that we both took our morning constitutional at the same time."

"And that's it? Any young men try to come to the cabin?"

"All the time, but the stewards kept them out. There was someone called Teddy and someone called Bertie, who constantly sent me flowers. Teddy sent big displays like that one and gushing love notes. Bertie sent a dozen red roses every day. And there were others who sent me flowers, champagne, chocolates."

"Do you have any of these notes?"

"I threw most of them away, I'm afraid, after I had a good laugh, but one or two may still be lying around or in the wastebasket."

"Wastepaper basket, Jonesy," the inspector said. He stretched out his legs, leaned back on the chaise, and studied me. "So tell me a little about yourself, Miss Murphy. It's not too often that a second-class passenger gets approached by a famous actress with the offer to trade cabins with her. You knew Miss Sheehan, did you, or was this a random selection on her part?"

"I had met her recently at a theatrical party. I gather she found out that I would be traveling on the same ship."

"Exactly why were you making this voyage?"

I wasn't sure how truthful to be and decided to play it safe. "Apart from visiting friends and relatives at home in Ireland, you mean? I'd been asked to look up the sister of a friend in New York."

"You're not married, I take it."

"No, I'm not."

"So you must have done pretty well for yourself in America if you can afford the passage home, just for a visit."

"I've done well enough," I said, and left it at that.

"And Miss Sheehan just happened to pick you to change cabins with her on the spur of the moment, did she?"

"Yes. Apparently I looked sufficiently like her to be able to carry off the switch."

"Did you?" He sounded skeptical. I realized that after an almost sleepless night and with my hair still looking decidedly rattaily, I hardly looked like a famous actress.

"And this girl Rose was in on the plot?" he went on, before I could tell him about how I'd dressed up to impersonate the actress.

"She was, sir."

"And what did she think of it?"

"I've no idea. She was always pleasant enough to me and respectful too. She said Miss Sheehan had instructed her to act as if I was her real mistress for the whole voyage, and she certainly did act that way."

Inspector Harris leaned toward me. "You strike me as an intelligent young woman, Miss Murphy. Did Miss Sheehan's request ever seem odd to you?"

"To begin with, yes. Why would anyone want to trade this cabin for my little cupboard of a place. But then I saw how much she was pestered by unwanted admirers every time she went out, and I began to understand a little more."

"Did you?" He continued to stare hard at me. "So you hardly left your cabin all week and had your meals brought to you?"

"I did, sir."

"And so why couldn't Miss Sheehan just have stayed in her own cabin all week long and have her food brought to her the way you did? Why was there a need to exchange cabins?"

I put my hand up to my mouth. "I see what you mean. Unless . . ."

"Unless what?"

"Unless she suspected her life might be in danger, so she got me to take her place," I finished in a hushed voice.

"That never struck you before?"

"Only after I found Rose's body last night. Then it did occur to me that the person who killed Rose might have thought he was killing Oona Sheehan. I mean, who would want to take that risk, go to all that trouble just to kill a servant girl?"

"My sentiments exactly." Inspector Harris nodded. "Not a very nice lady then, our Miss Sheehan, duping you into thinking you were getting a few days' luxury and a paycheck for very little, when it was, in fact, in exchange for your life."

"I'm sure she didn't really believe . . ." I started to say.

"She's no longer on board. Then why did she disembark at the last moment? Either she never meant to travel at all and wanted you as a decoy, or she saw someone she didn't trust and made a last-minute decision to put herself out of harm's way."

I was afraid I had to agree with him. Miss Sheehan was definitely not a nice lady.

"I'm sure she'll feel badly when she finds out that it was her maid who was killed and not me," I said.

❧ Eleven ❧

Inspector Harris glanced up as the policemen muttered something to
each other. "Have you found something, Shaw?"

"Under the bed, sir. A piece of broken glass, and a wet patch on
the carpet."

He held up a curved piece of glass, touching it with a clean handkerchief.

"That looks like a piece of the carafe from the bedside table," I said.
"It had water in it."

"Most probably the girl thrashed around and broke it in her struggles then," Inspector Harris said. "See if you can find the other pieces,
lads."

"They're over here in the wastebasket, sir," the other policeman
said. "At least there are several pieces of broken glass in it."

"A very tidy murderer," Inspector Harris said. "I wonder why."

"I think he wanted this room to appear normal for as long as possible," I suggested, "to give himself a chance to get well away from the
crime scene. Had my steward looked inside, he would have thought I
was asleep in bed, and my body wouldn't have been found until morning."

"Right." Inspector Harris nodded.

"And if there's broken glass, it's just possible that the murderer cut
himself. You could look for cuts on the hand when you do your investigations of the passengers."

Inspector Harris cocked his head to one side again. It must have been an unconscious gesture on his part. "You've obviously succeeded in the New World by living on your wits, Miss Murphy. I'm beginning to have second thoughts about this whole business. Now if you were some kind of confidence trickster, and you persuaded Miss Sheehan not to travel for some reason—"

"Hold on a minute," I interrupted. "If I was as canny as you suggest, then I'd never have put myself in harm's way with the possibility of being killed, would I?"

He shrugged. "Plenty of explanations for that—you work as a team with a male criminal. Crooks fall out all the time. He thought he was killing you in the darkness of the room. Or Rose got the wind up about your little scheme as you approached the Irish coast. She threatened to spill the beans. You had to silence her."

"As for that," I said, "I was at the ball all evening. Plenty of witnesses could verify dancing with me and even watching me return to my cabin."

"Actually nobody could do so." He smirked. "What any witness would have seen was a powdered wig and a mask and a costume. I asked you myself if anyone recognized you, and you said that nobody did. You have no alibi as far as I can see, Miss Murphy."

"But that's ridiculous," I said, my voice rising now. It was hard to tell whether he really suspected me or was merely going through various possible motives in his mind.

He clarified this by saying, quite sharply, "Is there anything more you'd like to tell me? The real reason that you switched cabins with Miss Sheehan? The real reason that you wound up in first-class?"

"It's exactly as I told you. I came onboard. Miss Sheehan sent for me and made this request. She offered me money, and I am not so well-heeled that I could turn it down. Besides, it seemed a bit of a lark, living like a grandee for a while."

"And you say you'd only met Miss Sheehan once before at a party, I believe, but she singled you out right away to play this part."

"Supposedly I looked enough like her to be able to get away with the deception. She put one of her wigs on me and made up my face, and there definitely was a likeness."

"I see," he said again, then paused and sucked through his teeth. "Now, if you'd just let Jones take your fingerprints, Miss Murphy."

"My fingerprints?" I tried not to sound startled. Surely he didn't suspect me? "Of course," I said breezily, "my fingerprints will be all over the cabin anyway."

"Naturally." He nodded. "We need to rule them out."

I sat in what I hoped was nonchalant indifference while one of the constables pressed each of my fingers onto a felt ink pad and then onto a sheet of paper. "Look, inspector," I said. "If you want to get to the truth in this matter, then you should be sending a telegraph to Miss Sheehan herself. She can verify my story, and maybe she'll even give you more insights."

"It's already been done, Miss Murphy," he said. "We should hear back from her later today, if we can locate her, that is."

"If you can locate her?"

"We've only your word that she was ever on this ship." He was looking at me innocently enough, but I got the feeling that I was still a very definite suspect in his eyes.

"Of course she was on this ship," I said angrily. "Somebody booked this cabin in Miss Sheehan's name, and it certainly wasn't me. I might have done well in New York, but not well enough to travel first class. She'll tell you the truth, you'll see."

"Let's just hope that she does," he said.

Time to put my own skills to work, I decided.

"You know, I've been thinking," I said carefully, "if Rose and the intruder struggled, thrashing around enough to break that water jug, then isn't it possible that he'll have picked up one or more of her hairs on his clothing. Red hairs should be easy to spot, shouldn't they?"

His eyes narrowed as he stared at me. "How did you say you made your fortune in America?" he asked.

I had to smile. "Actually, I run a private detective agency, but I've certainly not made a fortune."

"Good God," he muttered, then apologized profusely, of course. Somehow men think that swearing in front of a woman is a mortal sin— often the same men who think nothing of ordering a woman around, demanding to be waited on by a woman, or even giving her a good hiding. Not for the first time in my life I considered what a strange world we live in.

"And how would your detective agency go about solving this particular crime?" the inspector asked.

"Oh, I don't take on cases of this magnitude," I said hastily. "I stick to strictly domestic matters." I decided to keep quiet about certain of my cases of a nondomestic nature. "But I do think the red hair might give you a good start."

"You propose to round up all the men on this ship and examine their clothing?"

"It's not my place to tell you how to carry out your investigation," I said.

He was still staring at me. "And may I ask what the nature of your real assignment to Ireland is? I presume it's not just a family visit."

"It's exactly as I told you previously. An old friend asked me to locate his sister for him. He has lost touch with her and wishes to be reunited. Very simple really."

"And the name of this friend?"

I saw the well-chewed pencil poised above his notebook.

"Tommy Burke, the theater producer."

"Heavens above," he said, "You move in pretty exalted circles."

I decided not to contradict him. Things might progress more smoothly for me if he thought I had exalted friends.

There was a tap at the door and a very harried-looking first officer came in.

"Sorry to disturb you, Inspector, but we're being besieged by angry passengers demanding to know when they can go ashore. We've told them that they are being held up for medical reasons, but we can't hold them indefinitely. Also, the captain is worried about falling too far behind schedule. What do I tell them, sir?"

Inspector Harris got to his feet. "We had better continue this discussion ashore later, Miss Murphy." He turned to the first officer. "Do you have the passengers assembled in their respective lounges as I asked you? Good. In which case I'll need passenger lists, and I'll have my boys do a quick search of those cabins occupied by men."

"You need a list of cabins occupied by single men?" the first officer asked.

"Married men have been known to stray occasionally," the inspector said dryly. He turned to me. "You'd better accompany me to the maid's quarters. Maybe you'll be able to identify anything belonging to Miss Sheehan or anything that shouldn't have been there."

"Shouldn't have been there?"

"It wouldn't have been the first time a maid filched stuff from her employer."

"Oh, I'm sure Rose was most loyal," I said, glancing back at the bed. The body had been covered again in a sheet now. I tiptoed past as the inspector escorted me out of the cabin.

We made our way down several flights of stairs, each steeper and more Spartan than the previous one, and were shown to a cabin even less inviting than my own. Great pipes ran across the ceiling. It was smelly and airless. It had obviously been shared by four girls, with two top bunks and two bottom. At a request from the inspector, someone was dispatched to bring back the three other girls.

Someone must have broken the news to them, or they'd picked it up on the grapevine, because they shuffled in looking terrified—all young Irish maids like Rose. They pointed to her bunk and to the drawer containing her belongings but they were too terrified to answer questions in more than a whisper. No, Rose had no gentlemen callers on board, as far as they knew. No man ever came to the cabin. No, Rose never disclosed that the woman she was serving was not really her mistress. She did mention something once about "wouldn't they all be surprised?" and she told some juicy stories about Miss Sheehan's men, but that was it. When asked to name these men, however, they shook their heads blankly. They'd hardly had much time for talk and had spent their days waiting on their own mistresses, up in first class.

Inspector Harris turned back the covers on Rose's bunk, then opened her drawer. I felt a new wave of pity when I saw those few possessions—well-darned stockings; gray-looking underclothing; a clean, well-starched blouse; a single lace handkerchief; her missal with a ribbon bookmarker in it. Her second uniform was hanging in the wardrobe. Not much to show for a life. And certainly no sign of Miss Sheehan's jewel case. Then, among the bags piled on top of the wardrobe, I saw something I recognized. My own valise.

"That's mine," I called, pointing at it, and it was brought down. "I wondered what could have happened to it when it had vanished from my cabin."

"You see what I was saying about filching things?" Inspector Harris smirked again.

"I don't think Rose would have any interest in my few possessions, not when Miss Sheehan had so many lovely things."

"Then what was the bag doing in here?"

I shook my head. "That I can't tell you. Possibly Miss Sheehan had instructed her to remove it from my cabin and keep it hidden. I've no idea why."

The inspector had moved the other pieces of luggage aside and brought down my bag. When I opened it, all of my possessions were there intact and on top of them was a note addressed to me. I opened it, conscious of Inspector Harris's eyes on me.

" 'Dear Miss Murphy. Thank you for carrying out your assignment so splendidly. Owing to an emergency, I am not able to collect my luggage immediately. Would you please have Rose pack up my things and keep them with your own luggage until you receive instructions from me.' "

It was signed Oona Sheehan.

I handed the letter to the inspector. "Now at least you can verify what I've told you. Miss Sheehan planned this. I didn't push her off the ship or dispose of her in any other way. Neither did I harm Rose."

He examined the note, nodded, then handed it back to me.

"Perhaps I'd better go and pack up her things, now that Rose can't do it for her," I said. "Will it be all right to do that, do you think? She has so much clothing that it will be a mammoth task and if I'm not quick, the ship will have left for Liverpool."

"The ship's not going anywhere until I'm done with it," the inspector said bluntly. "and I'll need to keep that cabin the way it is until my photographer arrives and my lads have finished."

"But some of my things are up there," I said. "Am I not permitted to take them with me?"

"Not until I'm done, and since all her possessions are to be shipped under your name, you'll just have to wait and get them all at the same time, I'm afraid. You'll not be going far, anyway. You'll be needed for the inquest."

"I wasn't planning to go far," I said. "My search for the missing woman will begin not far from Cork. I'll probably take a room in that city."

"That will do admirably," he said. "I'm sure the inquest will be held at the Coroner's Court there. You'll let us know where to find you as soon as you've taken lodgings." He glanced up with that half smirk on his face, which I had once found friendly and now found annoying. "Luckily it's not easy to run away when you're on an island and the ports are being watched."

"I have no intention of running away," I said haughtily. "I have no reason to."

As he spoke, he continued to poke around the rest of the cabin, but in the end he shook his head. "Nothing more in here," he said. "Right. Let's go upstairs again." He picked up my valise. "You girls stay put until you've given your statements to my sergeant."

"And our mistresses will be wanting us to finish their packing. We'll get in awful trouble," one of them wailed. "We had nothing to do with poor Rose's death, I swear it, sir, on my mother's grave."

"Of course you didn't." He sounded almost kindly. "Go on with you then. Just make sure we've got your names and addresses."

They gave him grateful smiles and fled. As we made our way back to the first-class deck we were greeted by another plainclothes' officer. "I don't know how we're supposed to search the cabins, sir," he said. "A good number of passengers are disembarking here and all their luggage is already packed up and stacked to go ashore."

The inspector sighed. "Of course it would be. So much for that. Oh well, let's get on with that medical inspection. I'll need you with me, Miss Murphy and let's have those cabin stewards as well. What were their names?"

"Henry and Frederick," I said.

"Henry and Frederick. Got that, Connelly? Where's that blasted first officer? I want to know where we'll be setting up shop."

I followed him reluctantly. The shock of the last night, the lack of sleep, and the knowledge that I might be confronting a killer made me feel positively sick. I touched the inspector's arm.

"Do I have to be there? I really don't feel too well."

"Don't worry," Inspector Harris said, sensing my discomfort. "I'll be putting you and the stewards out of sight, behind a curtain or something. I want you to observe but not be seen. You let me know when you see anyone with whom you had any kind of contact during the voyage, anyone you noticed hanging around you, and we'll have his luggage brought to us."

We were led to the foyer and Henry, Frederick, and I were seated behind a screen of potted palms. Inspector Harris sat with the ship's doctor at a table.

"Right, send the first ones in," the inspector called.

The first passengers were brought through.

"How long is this going to take?" a distinguished-looking man in a frock coat demanded. "I'm expected to preside over a meeting later today."

"You'll be free to go after the doctor has given you a quick examination, sir. We don't want any of our passengers spreading disease now, do we?" the first officer said calmly.

"Spreading disease? Look at me, man. I'm fit as a fiddle. Stuff and nonsense. Well, go on then. Get on with it."

The doctor examined his hands, throat, and eyes, then pronounced him fit to go. "Come, Martha," the man instructed, and a meek little woman scurried after him.

A positive stream of passengers followed. Women with children, elderly couples were whisked through with the wave of a hand. Henry or Frederick singled out men whom they recognized as having attempted an audience with Miss Sheehan. As the inspector had predicted, some of them were indeed married and had their wives in tow. They were not pleased at being detained.

Mr. Fitzpatrick came past. He gave his address as Yonkers, near New York City, visiting Ireland on business. He had not attended the ball last night. He didn't go in for such things and had spent the evening in the bar with a couple of other fellows discussing racing prospects.

I peeped around the potted plant as I heard Miss Sheehan's name mentioned.

"The actress, you mean?" I heard Mr. Fitzpatrick ask. "I believe I did observe her out on deck once. She wasn't looking at all well, I thought. Has she been stricken with this sickness we've been hearing about? I have to tell you that I feel absolutely fine myself and see no reason to be detained any longer. I'm interested in a filly racing this afternoon, y'-know."

I watched a police sergeant taking down details, and Mr. Fitzpatrick left. I tried to go through my conversation with him again in my mind. It had been a casual encounter, nothing threatening, but why say that he had observed me on deck once and not mentioned that he had spoken with me? I wondered whether there was any significance in this and decided that rumors must fly around enclosed communities like ocean liners. Perhaps he had gotten word of Rose's death and wanted to make sure he was not detained in any way.

I looked up with interest as Artie Fortwrangler came onto the scene. He smiled easily and gave his address as New York City and Newport, Rhode Island. He stated that his father was Arthur Fortwrangler III, and that he was destined for the family business when he'd completed his studies at Yale. Yes, he'd been at the ball, in a spiffing costume as Mephistopheles—quite sinister, you know. He answered the medical questions the doctor put to him without hesitation. He was feeling just fine and dandy; no contact, as far as he could remember, with anyone who was sick, apart from Miss Sheehan, who had a sore throat. He admitted to an infatuation with Miss Sheehan; in fact, he claimed to have seen every single performance of *As You Like It*, in which she played Viola—even though he loathed Shakespeare. He also admitted, somewhat sheepishly, that he had taken this ship knowing that Oona Sheehan was to be a traveling companion and hoping to strike up a closer acquaintanceship with her. "They always say romance blossoms on the high seas, don't they?" He grinned hopefully.

He looked puzzled when he was asked to wait in a nearby lounge, but went willingly enough. I heard the inspector sending for his bags and also giving instructions to requisition the Mephistopheles costume. As I watched him go, with his long, boyish stride, I couldn't imagine him killing anybody. He'd probably be the type who fainted at the sight of blood.

More people filed past. Teddy turned out to be the Honorable Edward Mulhane, and Bertie was Albert Everingham-Smythe—both harmless-looking young men who expressed extreme disappointment at not being able to meet Oona Sheehan. And then I stiffened. An older man had come into the room, dressed in shabbier fashion than those who had preceded him. Tweed jacket, impressive side whiskers. I realized with a start that he was the man I had observed watching me on deck.

"That's the older man who was following me," I whispered. The message was passed along the line to the inspector. A low conversation followed. The inspector nodded and glanced in my direction. He shook hands with the other man, who then followed other passengers through the door that led to freedom.

"Wait!" I blurted out the word and stood up behind my potted palm. I saw the inspector glance at me and frown. Hadn't he said himself that it wasn't just young single men who would be under suspicion? Then a chilling thought entered my head—he might not be taking this exercise as seriously as I was. It struck me that he might not be observing the people who passed him as much as watching my reactions to them. I might still be the suspect he was observing, or he might be on the hunt for my accomplice.

Then, as the next passengers were ushered in, a note was passed to me.

"The man you identified is an inspector from Scotland Yard, apparently on the trail of a jewel thief. He will now be helping me with my inquiries."

So there was a jewel thief on board the boat! No wonder robbery was the first motive that Inspector Harris had come up with. And the only person who could have told us if Miss Sheehan had any jewels on board was now lying under a sheet, murdered. I found myself feeling strangely relieved. If the crime had only been an offshoot of a robbery that went wrong, then I myself wasn't in any danger. I could leave this ship and get on with my quest to find Tommy Burke's sister.

❧ Twelve ❧

A s the tide of passengers passing us slowed to a trickle, Inspector Harris rose and came over to us.

"You are free to leave the ship, Miss Murphy. I don't think there's anything more you can do for us today."

The thought did cross my mind to remind them that I was an investigator and maybe there was something more I could do to help. Then I decided that I was still a suspect and might easily have been the victim. Miss Sheehan had deliberately put me in harm's way; and if I were sensible, I'd escape while the going was good.

"So can I collect my belongings from Miss Sheehan's cabin now? It's only a few bits and pieces I have there, but a lady can't be expected to travel without her toiletries, can she?"

He nodded without smiling. "Very well. I'll send a constable up with you. And we'll need an address to forward Miss Sheehan's stuff. Remember, you're to stick around the area for the inquest."

"When will that be, do you think? I can't stay in Ireland indefinitely."

"Within the next week, I'm sure. I haven't yet got in touch with the coroner. We'll let you know the details. I'll be making the main Cork Police Station my headquarters until this matter is sorted out, so you'll know where to find me."

"Thank you." I picked up the bag I had recovered from Rose's cabin, and went ashore wearing Miss Sheehan's smart, striped two-piece costume. After what she had put me through, I felt it was the very least she could do for me. It's wonderful what clothing can do for a person. No sooner had I stepped down the gangway than I was besieged by cab drivers, all wanting to give me a ride to the train station.

"Where's the rest of your luggage, my lady?" one of them asked, attempting to wrestle my small valise from me.

My lady? That was definitely a step up. I smiled graciously and said that it was being sent on to my hotel. Then I allowed him to lead me to a nearby two-seater cart. He helped me to climb up, and we joined the crush of vehicles attempting to leave the port. Once I was seated comfortably, I had a chance to become aware of my surroundings for the first time, and memories came rushing back to me: the tang of seaweed and fish in the air, the fishing nets drying on the quayside, the seagulls wheeling overhead, and from an open window the sound of a fiddle being played. I was quite unprepared for the flood of emotion these produced in me. I hadn't thought much of Ireland since I fled almost two years ago. Frankly, I had been glad to get away from it. I hadn't believed I could ever be homesick, but now I felt tears welling up in my eyes that I was home again and this was my land.

"What did you say?" I asked the driver, aware that he had been talking.

"I was saying it was a grand day to be coming home, my lady. They don't make skies like that in America, I'll be bound."

I looked up at the white puffy clouds scudding across that clear, glass blue sky and agreed with him.

"You'll be taking the train for Dublin, I don't doubt," he went on.

"No, I'm staying in Cork for a while," I said. "I have business to attend to there."

"Then why don't I take you all the way myself," he said. "Dolly is as willing and frisky as a colt, and I'll charge you no more than that smelly old train."

For the first time in ages I laughed. "Do you think I've been away from Ireland so long that I've forgotten what blarney sounds like?" I asked, and he laughed too. But it was a delightful autumn day, and I was in no hurry. What could be the harm in riding those five miles in the fresh air?

"Very well," I said, "only let's agree on a price now."

As it turned out I had been away from Ireland long enough to have forgotten several things, one of them being that the weather never stays constant for more than an hour or so. Dolly proved to be neither frisky nor that willing either and toiled slowly up the long hill out of Queenstown. I enjoyed the view down to the harbor with the great liner dwarfing the freighters and fishing boats around it until troubling thoughts crept to the edge of my conscious mind, reminding me that a girl lay dead on that ship, and that her killer was still at large. If I had decided not to go to that ball . . . If I had sent Rose away and been in the cabin alone, I might have been lying there instead of Rose. There had been other times when I would have wanted to help find her murderer, but I confess that this time I just wanted to get as far away in the least time possible. I shifted uncomfortably in my seat as the horse's head drooped and she went almost into a trance of slowness.

"You said she was as 'frisky as a colt,'" I reminded the driver. "I'd like to make Cork before the weather changes. I glanced up at the sky. A stiff breeze had sprung up from the west, sending those clouds scudding faster across the sky. Bigger and darker clouds raced in to take their place, and we were halfway there when the first raindrops spattered onto us.

"Do you have a hood to this contraption?" I asked.

The driver grinned as he shook his head. "A little bit of rain never hurt anybody," he said. "Don't you ladies always carry an umbrella?"

"My luggage is still on board the ship," I reminded him, "and my umbrella with it."

He did, however, produce an old blanket which I suspect had been used on the horse. I attempted to shield myself from the worst of the rain with it and eventually made him pull up at an inn so I could take shelter until the storm had passed. The gray drizzle persisted, and I arrived in Cork at last, feeling chilled and miserable.

"And where will you be staying?" he asked.

Having been dubbed "my lady," my vanity took over and I didn't want to diminish myself in his eyes by suggesting some clean and simple establishment. Besides, my expenses were being covered, weren't they?

"I've never been in Cork before," I said, "but I'm sure there are some fine hotels here."

"I wouldn't know one from the other myself," he muttered, "not having stayed at a hotel in my entire life, but I'll take you to St. Patrick's Street. The Victoria Hotel is about the best Cork has to offer, so I hear. It's the sort of place where the gentry hobnob."

As we approached St. Patrick's Street, a wide and elegant boulevard with gracious stone buildings on either side, we were treated to another dose of cloudburst, so that I went up the steps of the Victoria Hotel looking less like "your ladyship" than I had hoped.

"Who would have thought the weather would have turned on us so quickly?" was the closest the clerk at the reception desk came to acknowledging that I looked like a drowned rat. I showed him my letters of credit and was taken to a spacious room. I'd have been overwhelmed at the opulence of it had I not spent the last week in a first-class cabin and thus become used to such finery. All the same, it was very nice, and I admired the molded ceiling, the velvet drapes, and the regency-striped wallpaper while I waited for the enormous bathtub to fill with hot water in the white-tiled bathroom. If only I could invite my family to visit me here, I found myself thinking—showing, of course, what a shallow person I really was. Then I reminded myself that I could not contact my family. Nobody in county Mayo must know I was here or the warrant for my arrest might resurface. So far I had been lucky, and I had pushed my luck too many times recently. I was here to perform a simple task. I was going to do it and then go back to America and get on with my life.

Which made my thoughts turn to Daniel. He hadn't entered my head for a day or so. Was that a bad sign? Surely young lovers pined for each other constantly, thought of nothing else, and sighed with deep longing for the moment when they could rush into each other's arms again. I suppose it was because my courtship with Daniel had taken so many strange turns that I had learned to shut him from my mind and not dare hope for a future together. I was still finding it hard to picture that future.

I sat at the writing desk and wrote him a quick note, informing him that I had landed safely and would be based here for the next few days.

I didn't mention Rose's murder or the strange circumstances on the ship. No need to inflict any more worries on him at this moment when he was clearly still in the deepest fear for his own future. I hesitated at signing it "love, Molly" and signed it just with my name instead. Then I repeated the same sentiments in a letter to Sid and Gus and finally a note to Inspector Harris, care of the Cork Police Station, letting him know where he could find me.

The rain had now stopped, so I ventured out to find the police station for myself. Cork was an elegant city with lots of fine buildings, but after New York it felt like a sleepy backwater. Not an automobile to be seen on those broad streets, no electric tram cars, just the occasional horse-drawn cart or carriage. The sidewalks were not crowded with New York's teeming crush of humanity, and it was so quiet that the seagull's cries and clip-clop of horse's hooves were the only sounds over the sigh of the ever-present wind. It was like being in a city that time had forgotten.

At the end of the street I came to a wide river, and I stood on a bridge savoring the feel of the fresh Irish air in my face. And a surge of excitement swept through me—I was back in my homeland, I had money in my pocket, and a straightforward task to fulfil. Free and independent—what more could I wish for?

Then, of course, I was reminded that life wasn't as simple as I was making it out to be. I wondered how the police were getting on with solving Rose's murder. Had their search turned up any suspects? And more to the point, had Miss Sheehan telegraphed from New York to give some explanation for her strange behavior? I wondered if she felt guilty about what had happened to her servant. Maybe servants were as expendable to her as young lady detectives. Had she really tricked me into traveling in her place because she knew her life would be in danger? In which case, why not report her suspicions to the police? Why not hire a bodyguard to look after her? The more I thought about it, the less sense it made.

I turned away from the river and set off again at a brisk pace. I located the police station and handed in the note for Inspector Harris. The young policeman at the counter eyed me with obvious interest, asked me if I was new in town and where I might be staying. I was gratified to notice his expression change when I told him the Victoria Hotel.

After that I made my way back to the hotel in time for afternoon tea, which I ate among the potted palms to the sound of an orchestra composed entirely of elderly men. It was most civilized, to be sure. I was interrupted in the middle of a chocolate éclair to be told that my luggage had now arrived and had been taken up to my room. I went up to see, opened the door, and stopped short: my train case was on a side table and the entire floor was taken up with five huge trunks. Miss Sheehan, it seemed, did not believe in traveling light.

How on earth was I going to deal with that amount of luggage? I sincerely hoped she would arrange to have it collected right away, or I'd be forever clambering over a mountaineering course to reach my bed. I tried to drag one of the trunks into a corner, but it was too heavy for me to move alone. Two of them were locked and I possessed no keys. One was open. I rummaged through it but it contained only clothes. I supposed that those beaded capes and velvet evening dresses must weigh a ton. I stared at them, puzzled. If she had really not planned to travel in the first place, why pack what must have been a good portion of her clothing? Which brought me back to my first theory: she had spotted someone on board who represented danger to her and had decided to remove herself from harm's way.

I decided to go back to the police station and see if there was any news yet. Coming down the steps of the hotel, I bumped into Inspector Harris, on his way to see me.

"I was coming to see you, Inspector," I said. "Is there any news?"

He shook his head. "Nothing that I can tell you at the moment."

"So that medical inspection didn't turn up any suspects? No red hairs on garments or crumpled stewards' uniforms stuffed into luggage?"

He shook his head with a smile. "I'm afraid not. We saw how nicely our man cleaned up after himself in your cabin. And no fingerprints. He's a careful, tidy sort of chap, by the look of it, and we'll have a devil of a time catching him. But we're not about to give up yet." He glanced up at the imposing portico of the hotel. "I take it Mr. Burke is financing this fancy establishment," he said.

"I do have traveling expenses," I agreed, "although I can't see how I pay for my hotels really has anything to do with you."

I really hadn't meant to be so rude, but I was tired and edgy and just a little scared too.

"Oh, but it could be of great interest to me," he said. "A young girl obviously not born with a silver spoon in her mouth, no clear male protector. She has to come up with the money for a top-notch hotel somehow. And various suggestions come to mind." He looked at me, cocking his head on one side in that strange gesture. "Now, if you were in league with that jewel thief, for example . . . or in league with the person who killed Rose, or had quietly done away with Miss Sheehan. . . . Shall I go on?"

"You can go on as long as you like," I said. "I'm none of the above. I've told you who I am and what I am doing in Ireland. I've told you the truth about changing places with Miss Sheehan. If you don't believe me, then you'll just have to wait until Miss Sheehan verifies that switching cabins with her was entirely her idea."

The ghost of a smile twitched on his lips. "We've just heard from Miss Sheehan," he said.

"And?" I felt my heart flutter alarmingly. He's come to arrest me, was the thought that flashed through my mind.

"And she backs up your story. So sorry she had to disembark at the last minute. Even more sorry to hear about Rose. She'd like to come over for Rose's funeral, but unexpectedly has rehearsals starting for a new play." He glanced up at me. "Convenient, don't you think?"

"She didn't venture any suggestions as to who had been threatening her or might have wanted to kill Rose?"

"If she had, she has kept them to herself so far. We're asking the New York police for assistance."

I felt a powerful emotion shoot through me: the New York police! On another occasion it might well have been my own Daniel Sullivan who could have been put in charge of the case. I almost opened my mouth to tell him I knew Captain Sullivan, and then, of course, I remembered that he was Captain Sullivan no longer but plain Mr. Sullivan, still under suspicion. What a lot of loose ends there seemed to be in my life at the moment.

Another thought struck me. "And her luggage?" I asked. "My hotel room is full of her trunks. I won't be keeping on at this hotel. I plan to go tramping all over the countryside, and I certainly can't take them with me."

He fished into his pocket and produced a piece of paper. "This came for you separately," he said.

It was a telegraph, addressed to me, care of the Cork police.

HAVE BAGS SENT SHELBOURNE HOTEL DUBLIN UNDER YOUR NAME. WILL ARRANGE TO HAVE COLLECTED. THANKS. EXTRA FEE. OS.

I looked up at the inspector. "She doesn't express any regret at what happened to Rose or what I had to go through," I said.

"You pay by the word for a telegraph," the inspector said dryly.

"She wants me to send her trunks to Dublin," I said.

"So I observed. Were you planning to go to Dublin yourself?"

"Hoping to. I'll have to see where my search takes me. I was thinking of setting out tomorrow to start searching. I may be away overnight if I can't find transportation. You'll not need me before then, will you?"

He shook his head. "The inquest won't be until the end of the week, I'm sure. It takes time to set up these things, arrange for an autopsy, and to find a court date. If you can tell us where you're going?"

"I wish I knew. I'm looking for someone whose last known address was in a hamlet beyond Clonakilty, at the time of the Great Famine."

"About thirty-five miles from here," he said. "Wild country out there. You'll take the Cork, Bandon and South Coast Railway. Change at Clonakilty Junction after Bandon. The branch line will take you into Clonakilty. Then I suspect you're on your own."

"I'm glad to hear there's a railway line," I said. "I thought I might have to use my own two feet all the way."

"We're not that primitive in Southern Ireland, you know," he said, smiling. "Did you know that fish delivered to those South Coast ports in the afternoon makes it to Billingsgate Fish Market in London next morning? That's what that railway was built for—carrying fish. No doubt you'll get a good whiff of it."

"Nothing worse than the smells I'm used to in New York City," I said. "I'll hope to be back in a few days then. By then I should know my plans, one way or the other."

"I wish you luck," the inspector said. "I think you've got quite a task ahead of you."

I thought so too. I went back into the hotel and made arrangements for someone to pick up those trunks and ship them to the hotel in Dublin, under my name. I hoped that I'd seen the last of them and that I was finally getting Oona Sheehan out of my life.

✵ Thirteen ✵

I started for Clonakilty early next morning. News vendors at the station were hawking their wares, calling out loudly, "Girl murdered on transatlantic liner. Famous actress involved. Read all about it." I glanced at them in horror and hurried past.

There was a quite a group of travelers boarding the jaunty green-and-yellow train with me at the terminus. Most of them seemed to know each other. I thought this boded well for my search—maybe news had traveled when a baby girl was left behind in the care of a priest all those years ago. As we pulled out of the station with much huffing and puffing I listened to the lilting accents of Cork and the discussion about things that seemed so remote to me now—harvests and stolen pigs, fishing boats and men lost in storms, deaths, and babies born. The tapestry of simple life outside of big cities, where nothing changed but the seasons.

Green countryside slipped past us: fields and cows and horses, and now and then a fine house among the trees. This was still the tamed part of Ireland, where nature was at the service of man and the ground yielded good harvest. Out where I came from, it was all peat bogs and mountains, and you'd have been lucky to grow enough potatoes to feed the family at the best of times. Often it wasn't the best of times, and during the famine the entire potato crop had failed.

A road ran alongside the rail, and I wondered if this was the very road that the Burke family took from their croft beyond Clonakilty to the famine ship in Queenstown harbor. I didn't think they'd have taken the train, if the railway was indeed up and working back in 1848. People only left their homes when they had no money and no hope and could only take what they could carry. I pictured the road very different from its current air of prosperity, lined with a ragged column of starving people, some pushing everything they had managed to salvage in a wheelbarrow, some falling along the way and being left behind to die. Had Mary Ann Burke been left to die, or had she recovered and been taken in by a kindly family? Tommy had been told that she had been left in the care of a priest, and I scanned the road, making a note of any churches we passed.

So little to go on: her approximate age and the place where she was born. And all of this happened over fifty years ago. Now that I was here, I had to admit that my chances of finding what happened to her were indeed slim.

Around me the other passengers chatted on in their lilting Cork accent, regarding me, the outsider with the fancy clothing, with obvious interest and suspicion as they passed along juicy pieces of gossip. It was hard to remember that I had lived such a life myself once. They did inquire of my destination, and when I told them the name of the hamlet beyond Clonakilty, they instructed me where I should change trains.

"Are you going to the seashore for your health, miss?" another asked. "I can't think of any good boardinghouses in that area. You'd do better to go to somewhere fashionable like Bantry where I understand they have lovely hotels."

"Actually, I'm looking for someone," I said. "I've come over from America."

This news caused quite a stir and almost everyone present in the carriage chimed in, asking if I knew relatives or acquaintances who had also gone to the New World. When at last I could get a word in edgewise, I told them I was trying to trace a relative who had been left behind when the family sailed in a famine ship. "Her name was Burke, Mary Ann Burke."

They debated among themselves as to Burkes that they knew or had known, but most of them weren't from around Clonakilty. When we reached the junction, they put me off the train as if I was a two-year-old simpleton; and in fact one of them, also bound for Clonakilty, led me like an errant child across to the train waiting on the other side of the platform. During the next portion of the ride, I asked about how to get to a hamlet called Ardfield.

"It's a goodish walk if you're not used to it," one of my fellow passengers said, and I realized suddenly that I was no longer one of them. My clothing, my manner, were now that of a stylish lady, not an Irish peasant. I have to say it did give me a little thrill of pleasure.

Again I explained my mission. Again met with blank stares. Nobody had heard the story of the abandoned baby.

"Likely enough she'd have wound up in the workhouse," one of them said. "That's where most poor wretches wound up in those days. And not many got out alive."

With that depressing news we pulled into Clonakilty station. They set me in the right direction, and I came out to a bustling market square with the market in full swing. I pushed my way between the stalls, bought an apple from a child whose own cheeks were as rosy as his wares, and set off along the road munching it. On one side of the square there was a fine church with a spire. I was tempted to go right away to talk to the priests, but I had resolved to start at the Burke's croft and work my way back.

The town was soon left behind. It was a crisp but chilly day, perfect for walking, and I strode out, remembering how I had walked for miles in my youth with my hair blowing free behind me and usually no shoes on my feet. My current costume prevented me from taking more than dainty steps and the shoes pinched at my toes, but I hitched up the skirts as high as I dared and became less dainty after a few yards. I passed people along the road and asked each of them about the Burkes with no success, until at last I came to an old man, sitting outside his cottage door. He vaguely remembered a family called Burke, but couldn't remember a baby called Mary Ann.

"Is there anyone you know around here who is old enough to remember the famine, besides yourself?"

He thought for a moment then spat down into the dust. "Paddy O'Reilly," he said. "He lives out that way, if he's still alive. Haven't seen him recently, but then he's got a gammy leg. Doesn't get about much any more."

The man's name made me react with a start. Paddy O'Riley had been my employer and mentor in New York. From him I had been learning how to be a detective. If he hadn't been killed just when I was getting started, I might be more use at my profession by now instead of stumbling along blindly most of the time, solving cases more by luck than skill. And now it seemed I was to be in the hands of another Paddy O'Reilly. We Irish are a grand bunch for believing in portents and dreams and that kind of thing, so a shiver went up my spine as I heard the name mentioned. It never occurred to me that Paddy Reilly must be one of the most common of Irish names, with one in every town. Instead I felt the excitement of believing I was finally on the right track.

I set off again. The countryside now was more like the Ireland I had known—wild, rocky with the occasional cottage and a glimpse of the sea in the distance. Along the way I passed the ruin of one cottage after another, with four crumbling walls, some with roofs caved in and some with no roofs at all, but no sign of live inhabitants. At last I came to a cottage with a line of nappies flapping outside and the sounds of children's voices squealing as they played. A woman came to the door, a baby on her hip, another one on the way, by the look of it. She had never heard of the Burkes and confirmed that Paddy O'Reilly would be the only one in the neighborhood who might be able to help me.

I followed the road down toward Clonakilty Bay. A couple of cottages perched on the small quayside, a rowing boat bobbed in the waves, but there was no sign of life. Then I noticed smoke rising from a cottage chimney and savored the familiar sweetness of burning peat. I went to the front door and knocked. A dog barked and an old man appeared from a vegetable plot beside the house. His face was rough and weather beaten, the wrinkles set into a permanent scowl, and indeed the face did seem to mirror his temperament.

"What do you want?" he demanded. "If you're one of those do-gooding church ladies you can turn right around and go home. I'm not coming to your services nor reading your confounded Bible."

"Are you Paddy O'Reilly?" I asked.

"What if I am?" he demanded. He was certainly nothing like the Paddy Riley I had known.

"I'm here because I'm trying to find information on a family called Burke who used to live around here."

"There's no Burkes around here anymore," he said grudgingly. "They're all gone. Those that didn't die in the famine went west across the ocean."

"But you remember them?"

"I do," he said. He glared at me suspiciously. "Are you a relative?"

"A friend of the family. Which was their cottage?" I asked.

He pointed. "Up on the hillside over there. You can scarcely tell it was once a home now. The land agent's men didn't bother to wait for the people to die. Wanted them out in a hurry. They came in and set fire to the thatch and started knocking down the walls. Didn't even wait for folks to get their possessions out first. And those that couldn't get out quick enough burned with the thatch. I still remember the stench of it in my nostrils."

"That's terrible," I agreed. "I gather we had the same sort of thing where I come from in county Mayo."

"That's how they behaved in those days. There were once three hundred or more people living in these parts. A thriving little port it was here. Now there's just a handful of us left, waiting to die."

"So what happened to your family? You didn't go away?"

He grunted. "I didn't say that. I went away all right. My dad was lost at sea when I was a boy. I couldn't wait to get out. I took a job on a merchant ship, sailing to South America, bringing back beef from Argentina. It wasn't a bad life at all. I came back here when I was too old to do the work, and everyone had gone. Not a soul that I remembered from the old days."

"But you do remember the Burkes? Tommy Burke?"

"Tommy Burke—was that one of their children? They had a brood of children like most people around here."

I nodded. "Four children, I believe. An older boy and girl. Tommy would have been about three or four at the time they left. And there was a baby sister too—Mary Ann."

He shook his head. "Can't say I remember clearly now. I heard that the Burkes went to America. The old folks died and the younger generation went. That's how it usually was in those days."

"But the baby didn't go with them," I said. "She was sick. They had to leave her behind. Tommy has sent me to find her."

He looked scornfully at me. "They'd only have left her behind if she wasn't expected to recover, wouldn't they?"

"How would I find out if she died? Where's the nearest churchyard?"

He jerked his head to the right. "There's a churchyard at the old abbey, behind those pine trees on the hill. That's where we bury folks around here, but it won't do you any good looking. During the famine there were too many to bury properly. They just dug big pits and filled them up with bodies. The priest said a prayer over them and that was it. No headstones, no memorials."

"So where would her death have been recorded, do you think?"

He looked at me scornfully. "They didn't bother with recording births, deaths, or marriages in those days. Not for us Catholics. We were like cattle. Not worth much alive; worth even less dead."

I tried another tack. "Tommy Burke believes the baby was left with a priest along the way to Queenstown. Where's the nearest church?"

"The nearest church would be that grand-looking affair in Clonakilty. You'll have passed it. Just as fancy as the ones those Anglicans build."

"So you can't think of an old priest around here—one who might have been around since the famine times?"

He shrugged. "I don't go near the place myself. Already damned to hell, that's me, and not a thing any of them do-gooders can do about it. Off you go then. There's nothing more I can tell you. The Burkes are all long gone."

He stumped back to his garden and I made my way back up the hill to those pine trees. I wanted to take a look at the graveyard for myself. I found Burkes buried there, but no Mary Ann, nobody from the time of the famine. If they'd added her body to a family grave, I had no way of knowing it. As I stood beside the old abbey ruins, listening to the sigh of the wind through those Scotch pines, I felt overwhelmed with the melancholy of the place. Great sorrow lingered here. I couldn't wait to get away.

❧ Fourteen ❧

I found the Burke's old cottage, now just a pile of rubble overgrown with dying weeds. I stood staring down at it for a while, then I turned away and began the long trek back to Clonakilty and called on the priest at the grand-looking church. He was a young man, fresh faced and eager, but he could tell me nothing about older priests who might have been in the area at the time of the famine.

"I must have been the fourth or fifth priest to occupy this post since then," he said.

His parish records only dated from the 1880s.

"You'll not find good records before then anywhere," he said. "They didn't care about recording the births or death of Catholics in Ireland. Took more trouble to note the birth of their cattle."

"So there is nobody by the name of Mary Ann living around here these days?" I asked "She might have grown up and married."

He considered this. "I can think of a couple of Mary Anns," he said, "but they wouldn't be the right age for the woman you are seeking. Have you tried the workhouse? That would have been the logical place to have taken in an abandoned child."

"The workhouse," I said. "In Clonakilty, you mean?"

"Oh indeed, we've a small one still operating here, but there would also probably be one in Bandon and certainly one in Cork city," he said. "Any one of them could have taken in the child, but I doubt most of them kept good records at a time like that. They must have been full to overflowing. And rampant with disease too. No, I think you'll have to assume that it's likely a child left behind did not survive."

I thanked him, and left in a cloud of gloom. Nobody seemed to believe that Mary Ann might still be alive. And if she didn't survive there was not likely to be any record of her death. I went to the workhouse in Clonakilty and a sad, sorry place it was too: a grim brick building, with bars on the windows like a jail. Inside, it was dark and dank. Someone was coughing. And the news was equally depressing—there had been no proper records kept from that chaotic time. People arrived and died every day and were buried in mass graves.

I made a few more half-hearted inquiries around the town and then began my return journey. This time I could not take the train, which I could hear puffing merrily in the station. I had to follow the route the Burke family would have taken. There were a couple of older people who had seen the famine processions pass and pointed me in the right direction. By now it was past midday and I was hungry, tired, and dispirited. My legs, no longer used to walking five miles over rough terrain, were feeling the strain. I was on a hopeless quest, no way of finding if the little girl had lived or died. Most likely she was in one of those unmarked mass graves in a local cemetery, and Tommy Burke would never know what happened to her.

But I wasn't about to give up yet. I hadn't really expected to find Mary Ann on my first day of searching, had I? I was going to see it through to the end, one way or another. I bought a meat pie in a bakery and stared walking again, this time in the direction of Bandon, the nearest big town on the main highway. I managed another three miles before my legs refused to go on, so I was forced to spend the night at the Nag's Head Inn, part of a cluster of houses beside the road. And an uncomfortable night it was too—lumpy bed, wind whistling through the cracks around the window. I couldn't wait to be up and out in the morning.

I set out at first light, stopping to ask anyone I met along the way. But most people were too young to remember the famine, and nobody recalled a family taking in a girl child called Mary Ann. Older people were noticeably absent from the scene. They probably went first in the famine, sacrificing their share of the food to the young. Those few old women I met shook their heads sadly.

"A sick child left behind on the way to the famine ships?" one asked. "There were so many of them, my dear. You'd seldom pass along a road in those days without seeing a funeral procession, or a body, just lying there. We had a man employed full time by the government, just driving around with his cart and picking up bodies. Children fared the worst. The poor little souls didn't have a sporting chance at life. I lost two of my own, you know. Watched them slip away and couldn't do a blessed thing about it."

She sighed and wrapped her shawl around herself.

And so it was all the way back. I asked in every village, at every workhouse, general store, in every church and heard the same story. So many people had passed through on their way to the ships. So many had died along the way.

I had to spend another night on the road. I met no old priests and only blank stares at the various churches in response to my questions. One priest suggested that I contact the bishop's palace and take a look at the diocesan records. But any priest in 1850 would now be seventy or eighty at least. Likely not still working.

Thus I arrived back in Cork on the third day, my shoes much the worse for wear, and my legs not much better. I was unsure what to do next. I had retraced the route that the family probably took to Queenstown, but it was possible they had followed the coast along byways instead of the most direct route along the road. If I was going to do the job properly, I should now go back and visit every hamlet between Cork and Clonakilty. Not an enviable task.

I walked into Cork longing for a hot bath, a change of clothing, a comfortable bed. I arrived back at the hotel to find a note from Inspector Harris informing me that the inquest had been arranged for the very next day. Lucky that I hadn't lingered any longer along the way then. I washed, changed, and enjoyed a good cup of tea with warm scones and cream. Thus fortified I decided I should make use of the remaining hours of daylight by visiting the cathedral and asking questions at the diocese headquarters.

As I turned a corner, I saw a neat procession of little girls, dressed in somber black uniforms, marching two by two under the stern gaze of two black-robed sisters. The sisters looked like two large black birds, wings flapping menacingly, and one called out, "No dawdling, Adeline, and don't drag your feet."

And a sudden flash of inspiration came to me. What would a kindly priest have done with a child—the obvious thing, of course. Handed her over to the nearest nuns as quickly as possible, who would most likely have placed her in the nearest orphanage. I darted across the street.

"Excuse me," I asked the good sisters, "but are you the sisters from an orphanage?"

A look of horror crossed the nuns' faces. "The orphanage? Holy Mother, we are not. These are the pupils at St. Catherines, where we educate girls of good family from all over Ireland and the continent too."

The other one muttered, "Orphanage indeed. The very idea of it."

"I'm sorry for my mistake," I said, observing the little girls' giggles and trying not to smile myself, "but is there not an orphanage to be found around here?"

"There is. St Vincent's, run by the Sisters of Charity. On the other side of the river. Cross by that bridge, go about half a mile, and you can't miss it."

The two sisters followed me with disapproving glances, obviously wondering what I'd be doing poking around in an orphanage, then set their little charges off at a marching pace again. I set off at a marching pace myself, in the opposite direction and crossed the bridge out of the city. The sound of children's voices at play directed me to a stern brick building. The orphans sounded as if they had a better time of it than those girls from St. Catherine's, I thought, until I met the Mother Superior. What a severe-looking woman she was too, with a face looking as if it was carved out of marble under that white wimple.

"I wonder if you might have been here at that time," I asked, after I had explained the purpose of my visit.

The look was withering. "I did not arrive here as a young postulant until 1875," she said.

"I'm sorry," I said. "I've always found it impossible to tell a nun's age. You all look ageless to me."

A ghost of a smile rewarded that obvious attempt at flattery. "Let us hope that is because we live pure lives, unaffected by the corruption of the outside world," she said.

"So would any of your sisters have been alive then?"

"A couple in the infirmary, but it won't be necessary to disturb them, since we have always kept meticulous records. If the child came here, her name will be in our ledgers."

"That's wonderful. Would it be possible to take a look then?"

"Of course. May I ask why, after all this time, her brother wishes to contact her?"

"He has only just discovered her existence, and he wants to make sure she is provided for. He's a very rich man."

"I see. Well, that's good news, isn't it? Very well. Follow me, please." She set off at a brisk pace down a hallway that smelled of disinfectant. As she pushed opened a frosted glass door, she turned back to me. "I should warn you, if the child had been very sick, I'm sure she would not have been accepted here. We have the health of a hundred children to consider. She'd most likely have been sent to the charity hospital wards where she'd most likely have died."

Children passed me, walking two by two, not speaking but glancing up shyly under the direction of more sisters.

One little boy gave me a cheeky grin, reminding me of my own brothers at the same age. I wondered what they'd look like now. Joseph and Liam would be almost young men, and young Malachy would also likely be shooting up. A wave of homesickness came over me quite unexpectedly. When I had left Ireland I had never thought I would long for my family again. And here I was ready to leap on the next train to county Mayo. I had to remind myself that when I last saw them, they had been an ungrateful, lazy bunch, and I was well rid of them.

In a dark and musty storeroom, the Mother Superior brought down boxes of ledgers. "This would have been the time period you wanted," she said.

I started to turn through the pages. For the years starting in 1845 there had been a huge number of children coming to the orphanage, coinciding with the outbreak of the famine. Several Mary Anns. Several "baby girl, no name. Parents unknown." If the Burkes had abandoned her, would they have told the priest their names? Would he necessarily have remembered them?

And there, at last, it was. Mary Ann Burke. Aged about two years. Transferred from St. Vincent's Hospital. May 1849.

"It's her," I said excitedly. Then my gaze moved along the line of the ledger. More details were written across the double pages. Date of first Holy Communion. Conduct Satisfactory. Health Satisfactory and finally, "Placed in service, Ormond Hall, county Waterford. September Third, 1861."

I looked up at the Mother. "She was sent into service. It has the name of the house."

The Mother nodded. "Most of our girls are placed in service. We educate them to be of use in the domestic arts, and we prefer to see them in the care of a good family rather than working in a factory where they can meet with undesirables."

The picture flashed into my mind of that son of a good family, Justin Hartley, regarding me with greedy arrogance as he tried to rape me in my cottage kitchen. I didn't think that Mary Ann Burke would have necessarily been any safer in service, but for once I wisely kept my mouth shut. I took out my notebook and tried to hold the pencil steady as I wrote. "I must copy this down," I said. "This is encouraging. It means that she survived her childhood and might well still be alive."

She nodded. "One would sincerely hope so."

Suddenly the feeling of being trapped in that dusty room with its shelves of ledgers was overwhelming. I had to escape. Mother Superior had softened a little and was muttering how happy she would be if Mary Ann was found and had come into a fortune at last. I think she was hinting at a bequest to the convent that raised her. I was even offered tea with the sisters, but I made hurried expressions of gratitude and fled as quickly as I could.

❦ Fifteen ❦

The inquest into Rose's murder was held at the Coroner's Court, in a somber, wood-paneled room with bottle-glass-paned windows through which light filtered dimly. It was a sunny morning and dust motes floated in sunbeams, giving the scene an air of unreality. In truth I had put the whole thought of the inquest out of my mind while I was searching for traces of Mary Ann, but as I came in and saw a jury seated in a dark oak box, the fear came rushing back.

I had told myself I wasn't a suspect. Nobody could believe I was a suspect. And yet when Inspector Harris gave his testimony, I could see the faces of those jurors staring in my direction. The body of a young girl had been found in a cabin booked by the famous actress, Miss Oona Sheehan on the night before the *Majestic* docked in Queenstown. The cabin had, in fact, been occupied, not by Miss Sheehan, but by a young woman called Molly Murphy, posing as Miss Sheehan. She, along with the girl's cabinmates and the third-class steward, identified the body as that of Rose McCreedy, Miss Sheehan's personal maid.

Medical details were given. The ship's doctor's statement was read.

The coroner was a wizened little man with a receding hairline and beaky nose. In his black robes he looked like a perched raven. "And why isn't the medical man present to give testimony?" he demanded and was told that the ship had not been detained in port as the shipping company would have suffered considerable hardship by deviating from their scheduled Atlantic crossings. "Should the matter come to trial," Inspector Harris said, with a glance at me, "the shipping company has expressed itself willing to put any of its officers at our disposal."

An autopsy report was given by a local doctor. He confirmed the ship's doctor's original findings. The large amount of carbon dioxide in the blood suggested that the girl had died by suffocation. The bruise marks around her neck were not severe enough to have resulted in strangulation. There was no damage to the windpipe. Therefore it was surmised that the girl's face had been pressed into the pillow with a good deal of force.

I was called to the stand. I was asked to describe how I found the body. I was asked why I was occupying a cabin booked in the name of Miss Sheehan. I gave my explanation. As I was speaking, I heard a slight commotion at the back of the courtroom and I looked up to see the door closing behind the hastily retreating silhouette of a tall man. A reporter, no doubt on his way to dig up juicy dirt about Miss Sheehan. Now my name would be in the papers as well, which was the last thing I wanted.

I expected to be cross-questioned by the coroner, but he merely stared at me with those hawklike eyes and said, "It is not the business of this court to delve into why you were posing as another woman. Should a murder trial later come from the results of this inquest, I should imagine such facts may well be relevant." He glanced across at the jury, who were still staring at me in fascination. I was released from the stand. The statements of various stewards and ships officers were read. I expected that Inspector Harris would say something about our suspicions and mention the various young men who had tried to make contact with Oona, not to mention the one who posed as a steward, but nothing more was said. The coroner summed up, and the jury brought in a verdict of unlawful killing by person or persons unknown.

We were dismissed and came out into a bright breezy morning. I only stood for a second or two, breathing in the fresh air before I was aware of an approaching clamor. I looked up to see a throng of young men with notepads and cameras heading toward me.

"Miss Murphy? A word or two if you please."

"Miss Murphy—is it true you were asked to impersonate Oona

Sheehan? Can you tell us why? Can you tell us where Miss Sheehan is now? What are your own thoughts on who killed her maid?"

I put my hand up to my face as a camera was pointed at me. I turned to flee, but they came after me like a pack of wolves.

"My paper will pay for an exclusive, Miss Murphy. Where are you staying?"

I saw a passing cab, waved to the driver, made a sudden dash across the street, and climbed up with the wolf pack on my heels. As we took off at a lively trot, I found I was shaking. I had hoped to come to Ireland unnoticed, do my work, and then go back to New York. But now it seemed every paper in the land would be broadcasting the fact that I was here. I was no longer safe. The most sensible thing to do would be to book a passage on the next ship home, but I was now part of a murder inquiry and wouldn't be allowed to leave. Failing that, the most obvious course of action would be to start using an alias.

I made it back to the hotel, half expecting to hear the clatter of hooves on our tail. But the hotel still stood quiet and serene. I should make my escape before those reporters discovered where I was staying. I asked the cabby to wait and ran upstairs to pack up my things. I paid my bill with one ear listening for approaching feet then I was off again in the cab, with relief and excitement flowing through me. I'd be out of Cork before they knew it!

"The train station, as fast as you can," I shouted to the cabby.

The station clock was striking twelve as we pulled up. I would still have plenty of time to go to Waterford that day. Presumably I'd find somewhere to spend the night in that city, if necessary. I realized as I hurried down the platform that I should have told Inspector Harris of my plan to leave the city, but I decided that it was his fault he hadn't provided adequate protection for me at the court building. I'd drop him a note when I knew where I'd be staying.

The train that took me to Waterford was not a merry little yellow-and-green puffing affair, but a big main-line engine and we sped along at a rapid pace, frightening horses and cows as we roared past their meadows. I arrived in Waterford and asked about Ormond Hall. I learned that it was about eight miles out of town, near the village of

Dunhill. I inquired if another train went in that direction and learned that none did, however the Royal Mail had a coach going out that way every morning and took on extra passengers. I had no wish to walk eight miles that afternoon and risk arriving at a great house looking like something dragged through a hedgerow, so I found a modest boarding-house on the waterfront. Probably not a good choice of location, as I was kept awake by rowdy singing, raised voices, and what sounded like blows.

In the morning I went to pick up the coach. It was a misty, chilly day, and we passengers huddled together with a rug over us as we were quite exposed to the elements. The mail, one gathered, stayed dry. From my fellow passengers I learned that the hall had been in the Con-roy family for generations. Old Sir Henry Conroy had died a couple of years ago, and the new Lord of the Manor was Sir Toby Conroy. They didn't say, but I got the feeling that the change in masters had not been for the better. Young Sir Toby had been in the army until he inherited the estates and had run up some enormous debts during his time with the Irish Guards—debts from which his father had had to bail him out, so one gathered. And no, he wasn't married yet. Maybe he'd settle down when he finally chose a wife.

They were obviously curious about why I was planning a visit there. In my current dress, I was probably not going into service there, and yet I was clearly not posh enough to be making a social call. I put their minds at rest by saying I was inquiring about an aunt of mine who had been in service there once and with whom the family in America had lost touch.

"Oh really?" one of the ladies asked. "And who was your aunt? I was in service there myself for a while."

"Her name was Mary Anne Burke," I said.

"Mary Ann—no, the name doesn't ring a bell. What position did she hold?"

"I'm not even sure of that," I said. "It would have been quite a while ago. I think she went there in 1869."

The woman started laughing. "Eighteen sixty-nine? I was only a child of five then, so I'm afraid our paths never would have crossed."

The coach stopped at the bottom of a long driveway, lined with poplar trees.

"Here we are then, me darlin'," the driver said cheekily. "Watch out for that one, won't you? They say he's a terrible one for the ladies."

The coach drove off and I stood facing an imposing gateway, the two gateposts crowned with stone lions, each one resting a paw on a stone ball. I took a deep breath before entering. The driveway was made of fine gravel and continued for a while before it swung to the right and the house came into view. And what a fine house it was, almost a castle with its battlements and turrets, and with an ornamental lake before it. Mary Ann must have thought she'd died and gone to heaven when she went from the orphanage to this place, I decided.

A flight of duck rose from the lake, and from the trees behind the house came the cawing of rooks. I watched the smoke curl from those tall chimneys and something stirred in my memory. Then I realized what memory it had rekindled, and I froze on the driveway. The Hartleys had lived in a house not quite as grand as this one, but with the same air about it, and as a young child I had always been fascinated that a family could afford more than one fire and more than one fireplace lit at the same time. I remembered walking to that house every day of my girlhood to do my lessons with Miss Henrietta and Miss Vanessa after their mother was impressed with my youthful eloquence when the land agent tried to evict my family from our cottage. To me it had been both a joy and a torment: the joy of all those books, all that knowledge, a governess who said I was a delight to teach and shared with me her travels around the continent and her love of music, art, and literature. And the torment, of course, in knowing that none of it could ever really be mine. The Hartley daughters always made very sure I knew I was an outsider, only being included in their lessons through charity. And then there was Justin, who was the reason for my fleeing from Ireland.

I glanced back at the gateway, now hidden behind the row of poplars. I had reassured Daniel and my friends that I was in no danger going back to Ireland, and yet here I was walking into a lion's den. These great Anglo-Irish families all intermarried and knew each other.

Even though we were many miles from county Mayo, it was highly possible that Toby Conroy knew the Hartleys. He may have heard of Justin's "accident," and the name Molly Murphy may even have come into the conversation. From now on I reminded myself that I would be using an alias, just in case.

I straightened my hat, brushed the travel dust from my two-piece, and strode out for the front door.

"Yes? May I help you?" The maid who answered it wasn't quite sure what to make of me. She peeped past me but saw no carriage.

"I have come from New York to inquire about a woman who was once in service here," I said. "May I speak to someone in charge? My name is Miss Delaney." It was a name I had used before during investigations so I wasn't as likely to slip up.

The girl glanced down the front hall. "Mr. Phipps is butler here, miss. You'd better speak with him. Come this way, please."

I was led across the front hall, through the baize door, and then down a flight of steps to that semisubterranean area always inhabited by servants. The maid tapped on a closed door, and I was admitted to a cubicle. As soon as I saw Mr. Phipps, I knew that he'd be of little use. He was a relatively young man. I gave him my name and told him that I had been sent by the family from America to find out if Mary Ann Burke was still alive. He regarded me with a haughty stare, also trying to place my class and background, thus to decide whether he needed to be polite to me or not. I'm sure he took in the cut of Miss Sheehan's silk two-piece and her jaunty burgundy hat.

"You're sure she was a servant here, are you?"

"I was told by the orphanage in Cork that she had been placed here at fourteen, but I have no idea how long she stayed. It would have been many years ago, in the sixties."

He frowned. "We have no servants currently employed who go back that far, Miss Delaney. We do have the house books, of course. They should indicate when she came and when and how she left us. Let us take a look. He searched among dusty ledgers and finally extracted one. His finger searched down columns of faded ink, names and dates written in a meticulous script.

"Ah, here we are," he said at last. "Mary Ann Burke. You are correct.

She was a servant here. And I have a date too: left employment July Eighteenth, 1873. No references requested or provided."

"Does it say where she went?"

He shook his head. "I'm afraid not. There is no mention of her having left in disgrace. Possibly she left to get married, which was why she did not request a reference."

"And there is nobody here from those days?"

"I regret that there isn't," he said. "It's not like it used to be, is it? Young people become dissatisfied with their lot and try their luck at the factories in the big cities. I understand that the Jacobs Biscuit Factory in Dublin employs thousands of young girls. I can't personally see that such a life would be preferable to good food and fresh air, but to each his own, I suppose. I'm sorry I can't be of more help, Miss Delaney. Allow me to escort you back upstairs."

He had just opened the baize door for me to pass through when I heard the crisp sound of boots on the marble floor and a young man came in through the front door. There was no mistaking the master of the house. He carried himself with the air of arrogance and authority of one brought up to privilege. He was dressed in riding gear, with a crop tucked under his arm, and mud from his boots left a trail across the white marble. He was halfway across the floor when he noticed us.

"I have a visitor, Phipps?" he asked, his eyes doing a swift examination of my person.

"No, sir. This is a young lady from America, a Miss Delaney, trying to trace a relative who was in service here once."

"I see. And have you succeeded in locating her?" He looked me rather than Phipps.

"She is listed in your ledger but there is no indication as to where she went on leaving your service," I said. "It was all such a long time ago, I'm afraid. She left in 1873."

"I was only a small boy then," he said. "I suppose we don't have any servants who were employed here in those days, do we, Phipps?"

"I regret that we don't, sir," Phipps said.

"That's too bad. All the way from America, and we're not able to help you," he said, looking at me in a way that made me slightly uncomfortable. "Was this a close relative?"

"No, not very close. I was merely looking her up as a favor to an uncle," I said. "Her name was Mary Ann Burke."

His face lit up. "Mary Ann. I do remember a Mary Ann. She helped nanny in the nursery. I was very cross when she went away because she was much better at playing with me than Nanny was."

"You don't happen to remember anything about her departure?" I asked.

"Nanny said I wasn't to speak of her anymore, so I got the feeling that she'd left in some kind of disgrace," he said. "My sister would remember more than I. She was six years my senior and very fond of Mary Ann."

"Your sister? Does she live nearby?"

"Good lord, no. She's married and very much the grande dame these days. Caught up in the social whirl. Divides her time between London and Paris and Dublin, so one hears. Very much the society lady. Patroness of the arts and all that bosh. Lady Ashburton. If she's in Dublin when you're there, she may be able to help you—if you can track her down between her numerous committees and charities, that is."

He gave what was intended to be a gracious smile, I suspect, but came across as a smirk.

"Thank you. I'll try to do that," I said.

Phipps coughed discretely. "Pardon me, sir, but shouldn't you be getting changed? I understood that Miss Henrietta would be arriving for luncheon."

"What? Oh yes, you're right, Phipps. I had better go and change."

"Miss Henrietta?" I couldn't resist asking, although it was incredibly rude of me.

"My fiancée," he said. "She's meeting her brother from the ship. He's been in America too. You'll excuse me if I beat a hasty retreat, won't you, Miss Delaney?"

I managed to control my voice as I said, "Certainly, sir. I thank you for your time."

I bobbed a poor attempt at a curtsey. I saw interest flicker in his eyes as I straightened up. Lucky that his fiancée was about to arrive, I decided. His fiancée whose name was Henrietta and whose brother was arriving home from America. I attempted to walk toward the front door with measured step and much dignity. I had taken a few steps when Toby Conroy called after me, "I've just thought of one thing, Miss Delaney. Old Harry. He lives on the estate. Used to be the head groom. He's been with the family all his life. He might remember where Mary Ann went. Phipps will direct you to his cottage."

With that he bounded up the stairs, two at a time. And I only half listened to the directions that Phipps gave me on locating Old Harry's cottage. In truth I couldn't wait to distance myself from that house. I told myself I was being silly and worried over nothing. It was surely too much of a coincidence that Sir Toby's fiancée's name was Henrietta and that her brother was arriving back from America. In any case, I wasn't planning to linger around long enough to find out.

❧ Sixteen ❧

The result of not listening properly to Phipps's directions meant that I got hopelessly lost among the farm buildings and ended up with my shoes caked in mud and worse. At last I passed a farm laborer who escorted me to old Harry's place. The old man was sitting in front of his fire and was very deaf, but at last he understood my question and nodded vigorously.

"I remember that well enough. Master was quite put out. So was mistress too. Rory was a good groom, you see. Great with the horses."

"Rory?" I asked.

"The man she went off with," Old Harry said, with a toothless grin.

"They ran away together to get married?"

"So we heard. Never asked for permission or nothing. Just upped and left."

"You don't know where they went, by any chance?" I asked.

He leaned forward, confidentially. "I heard tell that Rory opened a blacksmith's shop in Tramore, down on the coast. But that was more than twenty years ago now. Whether he's still there, I couldn't say."

"Thank you," I said. "You've been most helpful."

He looked at me expectantly, and it suddenly occurred to me that he might be waiting for a tip. I fished in my purse and came out with a shilling. But when I handed it to him he closed my own fingers around it. "I don't need your money, me darlin'," he said. "You keep it for your trousseau. I don't drink much no more. Don't eat much either. I have no needs except for a good fire to keep me warm and that's provided from the estate. No, I'm quite content, thank you."

He was still holding my hand, his gnarled old fingers over mine. Impulsively I leaned forward and planted a kiss on his forehead. That made him chuckle.

"Now that kind of payment I'll take anytime you like," he said.

I came out smiling too, but as I started down the long drive, I found I was walking very fast, not wishing to encounter an arriving carriage maybe.

"This is ridiculous," I told myself. "I can't always be living in fear like this. What on earth do I have to be afraid of anyway? They know me as Mary Delaney and won't give me another thought. I'll remain Mary Delaney for the rest of my time in Ireland and I'll have nothing to worry about."

I started back in the direction of Waterford and soon picked up a ride on a farm wagon that moved at a painfully slow pace. After the farmer had turned off at his farm, I continued on foot, considerably more quickly, I might add. By asking at a general store, I found that I could make for Tramore cross-country without going back into Waterford. I walked a little, then picked up another lift on a wagon, which deposited me on yet another quayside. It was a quaint and pretty little place with a whitewashed inn and several fishing boats bobbing in a peaceful ocean. I was directed to the blacksmith's shop and stood outside a ramshackle shed with the sign R. KELLY. BLACKSMITH tacked over the entrance to a dark interior. Inside I could see the silhouette of a large man, outlined against the glow of a fire, an enormous hammer rising and falling to the sound of rhythmic chinks.

I went inside.

"Mr. Kelly?" I asked.

"Yes. What do you want?"

He turned to face me, his large face running with sweat and streaked with dirt, his front covered in a filthy leather apron, the hammer still raised in his hand. I took an involuntary step back. "Are you Rory?" I asked. "Used to work for the Conroy family?"

"What if I am?" he demanded.

"I'm looking for the former Mary Ann Burke," I said, "and I was given to understand that she might be married to you."

He glared at me. "Mary Ann's been gone these many years," he growled. "Long gone. Dead and buried. Dead, buried, and forgotten."

He turned his back on me and sent sparks flying with a great crash of his hammer onto molten metal. I needed no urging to retreat into the open air. So that was that. I almost wept with frustration. To have tracked her this far, only to find that she had died—probably like so many women in childbirth. I realized I should have asked about children. It was possible that Tommy Burke might want to settle money on Mary Ann's offspring. I looked back into that glowing hellhole and at the mighty figure pounding away amid the sparks. Did I really have the nerve to face him again?

"You're being paid to do a job," I told myself sternly. "Not all jobs are pleasant or easy." With that I took a deep breath and stepped back inside.

"I'm sorry to disturb you again, sir," I said. I was about to tell him about Mary Ann's brother, but it occurred to me that this man might well be interested in news of a new and rich relative. The way he had spoken of her made me feel that he had little true affection for her, or her memory.

He looked up, the hammer poised in midair. "I meant to ask whether you and Mary Ann had any children. Her relatives in America would want to know."

"No children," he said. "She wasn't even able to produce me an heir, useless bit of rubbish that she was. And she didn't have any relatives either. She was an orphan, from the orphanage, so you've got the wrong person. Now get out of here and don't come back." He slammed down the hammer again.

I retreated for a second time and stood staring as the blows rained down on the metal. I didn't envy Mary Ann her lot, married to such a one. I wondered what had made her leave the comparative ease and refinement of a stately home for such an existence. Rory must have been a handsome brute in his youth to have made her throw all caution to the winds. I asked and found that there was a train station nearby. With any luck I could be back in Cork tonight and maybe Inspector Harris would release me to sail home to America.

Before I reached the train station, I realized I should have asked where her grave was. Tommy would want to know. I saw the spire of a simple gray stone church among the trees and found that there was a churchyard behind it, so I went in to look around.

I must have searched for a good hour and examined every stone without finding one with Mary Ann's name on it. I had just reluctantly abandoned my search and reached the lytch gate when I heard the scrunch of feet on gravel and an elderly priest came out of the church. He noticed me and came over.

"Good day," he said. "Visiting our lovely churchyard, are you? Isn't it a fine spot? I've often thought I'd like to be buried here myself some day. Was there a particular grave stone you were looking for?"

"There was, actually," I said, "but I couldn't find it. The blacksmith—Rory Kelly. It was his wife, Mary Ann, whose grave I was seeking. Do you happen to know if she's buried here?"

"Mary Ann Kelly?" He looked, if anything, amused.

"That's right."

"He told you she was dead, did he? Yes, that sounds like him. That Rory and his wretched, stubborn pride. She's not dead at all, you know. She left him years ago. Ran off with the local schoolteacher, Terrence Moynihan. He was a gifted man right enough—poet, playwright, orator, passionate about all things Irish was our Terry. Wasted in a backwater like this, of course. No wonder Mary Ann preferred him to that drunken lout. I can't say I blamed her for running off, even though as her priest I should have condemned it. But they upped and went to Dublin together, twenty years ago it would have been. I haven't heard word of either of them since."

"Dublin, you say?" I felt the surge of excitement as I said the words. In my youth I had dreamed of going to Dublin, of strolling down those wide streets like a fine lady. Now it seemed that at last this dream was going to come true. If Inspector Harris would let me go, I'd be off to Dublin in the morning.

❧ Seventeen ❧

Inspector Harris had no objection to my leaving for Dublin. The murder inquiry had stalled, and he was waiting for the *Majestic* to come back to Queenstown so that he could interview the stewards again. His current theory was that Rose might have had a flirtation going on with one of the ship's crew and invited him to Miss Sheehan's cabin when she knew it would be unoccupied. He then demanded more sexual favors from her than she was prepared to give and suffocated her by accident. That would explain the strange steward encountered by both Henry and myself. More believable than a passenger managing to obtain a steward's uniform and using it to gain access to a cabin. Also I got the feeling that this scenario suited him better than an unknown assailant sneaking in to kill Miss Sheehan. Servant girls are ten a penny, and a murder in the course of a rough sexual encounter would hardly be unknown among their class.

I didn't go along with this theory myself. What steward would risk his job by meeting a servant girl in a first-class cabin? I still felt in my gut that the intended victim had been Oona Sheehan herself. If I'd been conducting the investigation, I would have had the New York police find out who might have posed any kind of threat to her and why she got off that ship in such a hurry. That, to me, was the key to the whole thing. She had all those trunks with her. She had clearly planned to travel, but aborted the trip at the last moment. Maybe the police were pursuing this approach and just not keeping me informed. At any rate, I wasn't about to challenge Inspector Harris's latest theory because it meant that I was no longer a suspect and free to travel.

I packed up my things and departed on the express train for Dublin. Even the fact that it was a gray and drizzly day did not dampen my spirits as the train pulled into Kingsbridge Station. I could scarcely contain my excitement as I came out of the station and found myself on the banks of the river Liffy. A strong wind was blowing in from the North Sea and I had a bag to carry, but I set off anyway on foot, keeping to the south bank of the river. I wasn't about to be denied this first walk through the city of my dreams. I had decided that my first port of call should be the Shelbourne Hotel, to make sure that the trunks sent there in my name had been picked up. I didn't want to find that I was liable for storage costs for such a massive amount of baggage, and, in truth, I wanted to have a peek at the place for myself. I knew it was one of Dublin's grand hotels where the rich and famous stayed. Naturally I didn't think that such an establishment would be within my budget, but it would be exciting just to experience sweeping in through those doors and mingling with the fashionable set.

I started to walk along Victoria Quay. In fact I almost skipped, brimming over with excitement like a small child who can't wait to get to a party. I was here, alone, in the city I had dreamed of visiting, with money in my pocket and the chance to track down my quarry and return home a heroine. The first building I passed was a disappointment, I must say. Behind a high wall loomed a monstrosity with chimneys belching out smoke. Not the elegant Dublin I had imagined, to be sure. An ironwork sign over the main gate announced it to be the Guinness Brewery. But it turned out to be the one eyesore, and after it the city that unfolded before me was the Dublin of my fantasies. Across the river a magnificent building with a great green dome of copper and columns like a Roman temple sat on the quayside. I had seen pictures of it and recognized it as the Four Courts, where English justice was handed out to Irish miscreants.

The distance proved longer than I had expected and that suitcase became heavier by the minute. I had no wish to appear sweating and disheveled at the Shelbourne Hotel, so I hailed a passing cab and admired the view as we went along at a gentle pace. On our side of the river we passed a great church.

"Christchurch Cathedral," the cabby answered my question. "Church of Ireland, of course. They took over all the best churches for themselves, didn't they?"

I had to agree, but I also agreed that it was a grand-looking building. Behind it I caught a glimpse of what had to be Dublin Castle. I knew about that place right enough—seat of the British government representative in Ireland, seat of English power and dominance, and also the place to incarcerate those who might oppose her rule. I shuddered as we drove past.

When at last we came to O'Connell Bridge and I saw the famous thoroughfare of Sackville Street running away to the north with Nelson's Column and the O'Connell Memorial in the middle of it, I made the cabby stop and I jumped down. I had to go out onto the bridge, just to pause and savor it all. To my right were the glowing yellow stone buildings of Trinity College. Farther along the quay were more bridges and more grand Georgian buildings. Dark waters swirled below me, but around me the city was full of merrier life. Horse-drawn trams clip-clopped slowly across the bridge. Students in their black gowns swept toward the college like flocks of blackbirds, shouting to one another. Elegant folk passed in their carriages. And I was here, among them.

With a reluctant look up Sackville Street, I climbed back into the cab, which proceeded down Grafton Street with its busy shops and restaurants, coming out eventually to a lovely leafy park ringed by elegant Georgian buildings.

"Here we are, miss. Shelbourne Hotel," the cabby said, eyeing me with interest. Clearly he wasn't sure that I belonged at such a grand establishment as the Shelbourne and was waiting to see what I did next. As I was paying him, a carriage arrived and disgorged a lively group of passengers, the women dressed in the height of fashion with ostrich plumes dancing in jaunty little hats.

"That's the trouble with servants, isn't it?" one woman was saying loudly in strident upper-class English tones. "Simply unreliable, darling. Now I've no idea what I'm supposed to do."

"Come and have lunch with us and forget all about it," a second woman suggested. She turned to a distinguished white-haired man beside her and laid a dainty hand on his shoulder, "Shall you be lunching with us, Reggie? I shall be devastated if you refuse me."

"How could I refuse you anything, Grania? You know I'm completely bewitched by you," he said.

With that they passed into the building. I stood watching them go. I couldn't possibly follow them in, could I? I was painfully reminded that they belonged in a place like the Shelbourne, whereas I was an interloper. I was as far removed from them as from the man in the moon. Then I decided that such humility was quite unlike me. I'd not been known to hang back in deference to my betters; in fact, most of my life I had been scolded for having ideas above my station. I wanted that cabby to see me making my own grand entrance; and, what's more, I didn't want to find myself paying for luggage that wasn't mine. Miss Sheehan had promised me an extra fee for taking care of her trunks, but Miss Sheehan had not proved herself to be completely reliable so far, had she? So I plucked up my courage, instructed the cabby to hand my bag to the bellhop, and went in through the front door.

"May I help you, miss?" the young man at the reception desk asked in a not-too-friendly tone. I could see him sizing up whether I was respectable enough, of the correct class to be crossing his vestibule. I mentioned the trunks that had been shipped there in my name and asked if they had been collected yet. At this his face became friendly.

"Miss Murphy? We've been expecting you. Your room has been held for you all week."

"My room?"

"We were instructed to hold a room for you. Your luggage is inside, awaiting your arrival. Have you more bags to be collected?" He glanced down at the small valise at my feet.

"There must be some mistake," I said. "I was not proposing to stay here myself. I was merely carrying out the wishes of a friend to have luggage shipped here in my name."

He looked perplexed now. "You're not planning to stay in Dublin after all? Will you not be needing the room then?"

"I may be staying in Dublin, but I'm afraid the Shelbourne may well be a little too expensive for my pocket book," I said.

"But the room is already paid for," he said. "Two weeks in advance."

"Paid for? Who paid for it?"

"I have no way of knowing that, miss," he said. The look he was giving me hinted that it was none of his business to inquire into such things, and I suddenly realized that he thought I was here for some sort of illicit tryst. The thought was so absurd that I had to smile.

"It would probably be my employer in America who set the whole thing up for me," I said firmly.

"Probably," he agreed. "Would you like to sign the book, and then I'll have one of the boys show you up to your room."

As I signed the book beside my name I realized that I was registered here as Molly Murphy. If anyone was tracing me, it was as good as waving a flag from my window and shouting, "Here I am."

"Let me get your key, Miss Murphy," the clerk said. He was about to hand it to me when a man came up to the counter, literally brushing me aside.

"Still no messages for me?" he demanded.

"I'm afraid not, Mr. Fortwrangler," the clerk replied.

I dared not look at him.

"And still no word where Miss Oona Sheehan might be staying?"

"No word at all, Mr. Fortwrangler."

"I just can't understand it. She can't have vanished into thin air, can she?"

"I'm sure she has plenty of friends and family in the country," the clerk said patiently. "She may not want her whereabouts to be known."

"Look here," Artie Fortwrangler said. "There's a twenty-dollar bill for the guy who finds her for me. Spread the word around, won't you, Freddie?"

"I will, Mr. Fortwrangler, now if you'll excuse me, I have to get this young lady up to her room."

Artie Fortwrangler left me without even a second glance. I let out a sigh of relief. He didn't recognize me without the wig and makeup. But he was clearly staying at the same hotel. It might be wise to stay well away from him in future. The clerk snapped his fingers and my bag was whisked before me up a broad staircase to a grand room on the first floor overlooking the green. It would have been more delightful if the floor had not again been littered with those large trunks.

"You don't exactly travel light, do you, miss?" the bell boy said.

"I'm holding them for a friend," I said. "I had hoped she would have arranged to pick them up by now. Is there somewhere we could store them, do you think?"

"I'll ask for you," he said, accepted my tip and disappeared.

I was left with the obstacle course again. At the very least I should have asked the boy to drag the trunks into a corner. I attempted to do so myself. As I yanked it down the edge of the carpet onto the parquet I heard a distinct clunk. Clothing would make no such noise, so what on earth was in there? I tried to open the trunk, but it was one of the ones that was locked. By now I was well and truly curious. I tried every key I could lay my hands on—the wardrobe, my train case, and at last, in desperation, my hairpins. Suddenly I heard the lock click, and I lifted the lid. A lovely coffee-colored silk ball gown lay neatly folded. I lifted it out. Below it the next layer was tucked neatly into a blanket. I opened that up and found myself staring down at a layer of rifles.

⚙ Eighteen ⚙

I was finding it hard to breathe as I rummaged beneath those first rifles and found more of the same, each layer wrapped in a blanket. The whole trunk was full of guns. When I removed the dresses from the unlocked trunks I found that both had false bottoms and they too contained rifles and ammunition.

For a moment I wondered whether Miss Sheehan was a crook, and then, of course, I began to suspect where they were destined. I had come across Irishmen in America supporting the cause of the freedom fighters back in the old country by sending over money and guns. It had never crossed my mind that Miss Sheehan could be such a patriot. A cowardly one, however, I decided. It was I who would find myself in hot water if the guns were discovered, since they had been sent across the country in my name. And she was safely on the other side of the Atlantic. It did cross my mind to wonder if she knew about the guns or whether we were both being used by outside forces. Then I decided that she knew very well. Why else would she have jumped ship right before it sailed. Why else would she have had the trunks shipped in my name?

I'll call in the authorities, I thought, bristling with indignation. I'll let them know the truth. That whole business of trading cabins had nothing to do with unwanted admirers, it was all a hoax to make me do her dirty work for her. I paced up and down in a height of agitation. I didn't want those things in my room a minute longer. If the police raided now, I'd be hauled off to Dublin Castle and likely as not be facing the hangman's noose.

But then when I calmed down a little, I sat on the edge of my bed to think. There was a possibility that I'd still find myself under suspicion if I turned to the police. I was possibly still a suspect in the murder of Rose McCreedy. In their minds the rifles and the murder might be linked—maybe they were linked somehow. I paused to consider this new twist. I had always thought that Rose had been killed by someone who mistook her for Miss Sheehan, and I had thought that that someone would be a jilted lover or spurned admirer. But what if Rose knew more than was good for her? That meant that these were people not to be trifled with, one of whom had paid for my hotel room, someone who would not take it kindly if I betrayed him or her. I had no wish to end up like Rose.

And it would only be my word that the trunks were destined for Oona Sheehan and she, safely across the pond, didn't have to answer any of their questions. I would be seen as a junior lackey who had lost my nerve.

There was also the matter of patriotism. I was all in favor of home rule, wasn't I? And every home rule bill had been defeated in the English parliament, which seemed to indicate that our freedom wasn't to be won by peaceful means. But did I really want to encourage violence? The killing of innocent people? Soldiers, policemen, even bystanders?

I got up and paced again. This was a decision for which there was no right answer. I found that cold sweat was trickling down my forehead. A good Irishwoman would want the English out of her country, wouldn't she? Hadn't I grown up with no cousins or aunties or grandparents because my whole family had been wiped out in the potato famine while the English landowners did nothing but hasten evictions and burn cottages? And if I alerted the police to these guns, then maybe I would be responsible for bringing down a whole network of freedom fighters and thus delaying the Irish cause for years.

I decided to do nothing for now. Someone might come to pick up the trunks. I'd ask no questions, tell no lies and, get on with my own life. The rifles were none of my business. I was here to find out what had happened to Mary Ann Burke. I closed the trunk again, hearing the lock click back into place, then carefully replaced the layers of dresses over the false bottoms in the other trunks, spruced myself up, and went downstairs. My hotel room had been paid for, I had money to spend, and I was going to have a darned good meal in the dining room. The maître d' could tell, with that uncanny sense they seemed to possess, that I was not really the right class of person to be dining at the Shelbourne. He didn't exactly sniff, but he led me to a table behind a potted palm tree, with his nose in the air. This suited me just fine. I could observe and not be observed.

The merry party that had arrived just before me were seated at a big table at the center of the room, still talking and laughing with the ease of those born to the upper class. The elegant lady in the fashionable costume was holding court, telling an amusing story that held her tablemates enthralled.

"You are quite wicked, Grania," one of them said, when they had finished laughing.

"Not I. I am merely relaying the words of one with more wit and talent than I," she said. "You'll be coming to the opening tomorrow night, I've no doubt. Then I'll introduce you, and you'll meet him for yourself. He's going to be the talk of the town, I'll wager."

"And anything you take a wager on has a remarkable way of being a winner, as I sorely remember from last year's Grand National," one of the men remarked.

"Ah, well, I do know my horses," the lady replied.

"You certainly ride divinely."

"You are such a flatterer, Dermott."

The young man leaned closer. "So tell me, Grania. What do you think of Mr. Yeats as a dramatist? A poet, I agree, but will his play be a torment of dreary Celtic poetry?"

"It stars the delectable Maud, my love. Can you not endure dreary Celtic poetry for her sake?"

The young man sighed. "If one must, for the sake of art, then one must. But to tell you the truth, I'd rather be at the Music Hall, watching the cancan."

"You always were a philistine, Dermott."

"I resent that deeply. I thought that fellow Quinlan's work was splendid. Sent quite a shiver up a fellow's spine."

"There will never be another Cullen Quinlan," Grania said. "A great loss."

The mention of this Cullen subdued them, and they ate in silence while I studied the menu and ordered brown Windsor soup, roast beef, and Yorkshire pudding, and finished it off with bread-and-butter pudding. New York cuisine had a lot that was good about it, but you'd have to go a long way to beat good Irish beef and bread-and-butter pud!

After I had eaten I went to Reception and inquired about theaters in the city. I told the clerk I'd a mind to take in a good play tonight. If Terrence Moynihan had been a poet and playwright, then his name might be known among the theater crowd.

"Theaters? You're spoiled for choice," the clerk said. "There is a delightful musical at the Gaiety and a very good rendition of Mr. Dickens's *A Christmas Carol* at the Olympic. On the other hand, if your taste runs to the more highbrow, you'd better wait until tomorrow night when a new play opens at the Ambassador, written by none other than Mr. Yeats, the poet. His new Irish Literary Theatre, you know. And you won't be at all surprised to hear that Miss Maud Gonne is in the leading role."

"What do you mean?" I asked.

He leaned closer. "The whole of Dublin knows that he's sweet on her, but she won't have him. He proposes and she turns him down, over and over. That's what the crowd will be going to see tomorrow, not the beauty of his words, but the sparks flying between them."

"At the Ambassador, you say," I said.

He nodded. "And in the meantime tonight, go and enjoy yourself at the Gaiety. I hear the play was a smash success on Broadway in New York. Oona Sheehan was the star over there. She stays here sometimes, you know. What a vision of loveliness she is."

"She stays here, does she?" I asked. "Has anyone been here asking for her recently?"

"Why would they do that? The whole country knows when she comes to visit. They wouldn't need to ask for her. We have a line of young men waiting hopefully for her all around the green." He smiled.

I wasn't going to get any further on that tack.

"Tell me," I said, "have you heard of a playwright called Terrence Moynihan?"

He grinned. "I'm not the person to ask about playwrights. I wouldn't know Shakespeare from Oscar Wilde, except that one of them died in jail." He laughed at his own joke.

I bade him good day and went out into the street, wondering who might know about Terrence Moynihan. The priest in Tramore had called him poet, playwright, orator, and patriot, if I remembered correctly. Someone in intellectual circles in Dublin must have encountered him. And the most intellectual circle that I could think of would be Trinity College, just a stone's throw away up Grafton Street. As I approached it, I was again struck by the sheer beauty of those buildings. Carefree young men drifted between them, not even noticing how lovely they were. I walked around the railings and was about to enter through the main gate when a porter in black uniform stepped out of the gatehouse and stopped me.

"Where do you think you're going, miss?" he asked.

"To ask the college professors questions about a playwright," I said haughtily.

He laughed. "That's a good one. You know as well as I do that no females are allowed on college property. Nor will there ever be, no matter how hard they try. Go on then. Off with you."

Seething with righteous indignation, I had to retreat. I knew little about universities, but I had assumed that this was the twentieth century and women were no longer barred from places of higher learning. It seemed I was wrong. I stomped off, muttering and at a loss what to do next, and almost collided with a young woman.

"I see you've encountered the ever-civil watcher at the gate and been rudely repelled," she said, with a twinkle in her eye. She was petite but by no means delicate looking, and she spoke with no trace of an Irish brogue.

"I only wanted to speak to one of the professors," I said. "I had no idea that women would be barred from entering in that manner."

She laughed. "They'll fight the admission of women to Trinity with their dying breaths," she said. "Fortunately, we have crusaders on our side, campaigning with equal ferocity to have women admitted. Miss Alice Oldham is our greatest champion. Have you met her yet?"

"I've only just arrived in Dublin," I said. "I live in America these days."

"Where women have greater freedoms?" she asked.

"We are still denied the vote," I said. "Still not allowed to enter a saloon."

"Then you're equally oppressed," she said. "And presumably you haven't had a chance to attend a meeting of the Inghinidhe na hEireann."

"The what? I'm afraid I don't speak the Irish language."

"The daughters of Erin. It's a society for the promotion of women and all things Irish, founded by Maud Gonne."

"The actress?" How strange that the same names kept cropping up.

"Acting is the least of her talents," the young woman said. "She has great visions for the future of Ireland with an educated and liberated womanhood standing side by side with the men."

"Then I should most like to attend a meeting," I said.

"I'll be happy to introduce you next time we meet, if you are still in Dublin," she said.

"I'm only on a short visit," I said, "but I'd certainly like to come to a meeting with you if I'm still here."

"My name is Alice. Alice Wester." She held out her hand.

"And I am M—Mary Delaney." I only remembered the alias at the last moment. "I'm pleased to meet you, Miss Wester."

"Call me Alice, please. Within the Daughters of Erin we are all sisters alike. Queen Mab will be delighted to welcome you."

"Queen Mab?" I asked. "Wasn't she the queen of the fairies?"

"Indeed she was, but this one is living and breathing and mortal, and one of the leaders of our organization—although who she really is, I couldn't say."

She saw me looking perplexed and added. "Many of the ladies find it expedient to go by nicknames within the organization, just in case the English become too curious about our business. Not that we're doing anything wrong or illegal, you understand, but the promotion of Irish culture is seen by some as subversive. You've heard of the Gaelic

League, no doubt. Some of their members have disappeared before now, and what could be more harmless than reciting Gaelic poems?"

Gaelic poems—now that was a phrase that caught my interest. "I'm looking for a man who is a poet and a playwright," I said, "a Mr. Terrence Moynihan. You wouldn't have heard of him, would you?"

She wrinkled her pretty little button nose. "The name is somehow familiar, but no, I can't place him. You should attend the opening night of Mr. Yeat's new play tomorrow and ask your question there. All of those connected with the new Irish Literary Theatre will be in attendance, as well as all of the Dublin smart set, I've no doubt."

"I had certainly planned to be there," I said. "Do you know if there are any tickets left?"

"Let us walk to the theater together," Alice said. "I'm heading that way myself."

Together we crossed the O'Connell Bridge.

"Let me give you a word of warning," Alice said. "Avoid the little iron bridge you see over there."

"Is it dangerous in some way?" It looked perfectly harmless to me.

"Dangerous to the pocket book." She laughed. "It's a toll bridge. They'll extort a halfpenny a time from you for crossing."

"Then I'll remember to walk the extra distance and cross here," I said.

We walked up Sackville Street, past Nelson's Column.

"What's that very grand building on the left?" I asked. With its Roman portico, its columns and statues, it looked like a temple in the midst of this street of commerce.

"That? Oh, that's just the post office."

I sighed. "I had always expected Dublin to be a lovely place, and it's exceeded my expectations. Even the post office looks like a temple."

"It will be even lovelier when we govern ourselves rather than being ruled from London," Alice said. I noticed that she glanced over her shoulder, having made this utterance.

We reached the Ambassador Theatre and I managed to buy one of the last remaining seats.

"It's in the gods, unfortunately," the man at the box office said, "but better than nothing if you want to be there to see history made."

"I do," I said, and paid a very small sum. "What are the gods?" I whispered to Alice as we came out of the theater.

She looked at me strangely. "The very top seats in the upper balcony. Don't they use that term in America then?"

I wasn't about to admit that going to the theater wasn't something I did often.

"Not that I have heard," I said.

"I'll take my leave of you here and hope to see you tomorrow night," Alice said. "I'll also be attending, sitting up in the gods. That's where most of us students sit."

"You're a student?"

"Indeed I am. I'm attending University College, where they are more broad-minded about admitting women and less protestant in their outlook than Trinity. Until tomorrow then, Mary."

We parted, with me feeling uneasy about giving her a false name when she was being so friendly. But as she said herself, the Daughters of Erin often adopted nicknames. As I walked back down Sackville Street, I saw a familiar figure coming in my direction.

"Inspector Harris," I said. "What are you doing here?"

He tipped his hat to me. "Afternoon, Miss Murphy. Glad to see you're in good form. I'm here because I'm based in Dublin with the rest of the CID."

"So you've given up on the Rose McCreedy murder, have you?"

"Not at all," he said. "We have certain suspects who are being observed, and I have my men on the *Majestic* for the return crossing, finding out everything they can about those stewards."

"You still think it was a steward who killed her?"

"You don't?" he asked.

"I don't know what to think any more," I said. "I had always thought that Rose was mistaken for Oona Sheehan and killed by mistake. Now I'm not sure of that."

"Anything happened to make you change your mind?" He was looking at me keenly.

"Just that you seem to think that a steward killed her, and you're the professional," I said, in what I hoped was breezy manner.

"Where are you staying, Miss Murphy?"

"At the Shelbourne," I said.

"You're certainly living the life of Riley, are you not?"

"Not my idea. The room was booked for me."

"I see." He touched his hat again. "Your 'employer' again?" He put a satirical emphasis on the word. Then he touched his hat. "Well, I must be toddling along. Keep in touch, won't you. Anything that you feel might be useful in our investigation. You can always leave a message for me at the police station." And on he went, leaving me feeling quite shaken. Was it only by accident that we had bumped into one another, or was I being followed? The thought of those trunks, sitting right now in my room, made me go hot and cold all over. They had to go, and right away. I didn't care how, I didn't care where, just out of my room. I wanted nothing more to do with Oona Sheehan and her little schemes.

I crossed the street to the general post office and composed a telegraph to send to Miss Sheehan in New York.

YOUR TRUNKS STILL UNCOLLECTED. PLEASE ARRANGE PICKUP SOONEST. M. MURPHY.

I was horrified at the enormous fee they wanted to send these few words. It was pointed out to me that the words had to be sent through a cable all the way under the Atlantic Ocean. Put that way, I had to agree that the fee was not excessive, so I paid up and the cable was sent. I came out with a stamped receipt. At least this showed that the trunks weren't mine, and that I was trying to contact their true owner. And hopefully they would be whisked away from my room in the near future. It couldn't be soon enough for me.

❧ Nineteen ❧

As I walked back to the Shelbourne, down Grafton Street, I passed a bookshop. Amid the notices pasted in its window was one that caught my attention:

POETRY READING, SATURDAY EVENING.
*Mr. Desmond O'Connor reads from his Aran Island cycle and
recounts his journeys in the Far West.*

The address was Davy Byrne's on Duke Street, and the sponsoring society was the Gaelic League. If I learned nothing of Terrence Moynihan at the play tomorrow night, then the Gaelic League might turn up trumps.

I dined at the hotel and went to bed amid my mountains of luggage, but I didn't find it easy to sleep knowing what those trunks contained. Conflicting emotions raged through my head—anger at Oona Sheehan for using me so shamelessly to do her dirty work and anger at myself for being duped and flattered so easily. I could just see her smirking as she told me how closely I resembled her and how I fell for it. Lying there with the noises of a strange city outside my window, I suddenly felt very alone and far from home. The trouble was that I didn't know where I belonged any more. It wasn't my home in county Mayo I was missing, to be sure. My memories of that were of drudgery and boredom and dreaming of something better. But I missed my friends in New York, and I had to admit that I missed Daniel. He was probably missing me equally at this moment, living in limbo as he was and not knowing what his future might hold. In my current position of uncertainty, I understood his moods more charitably and chided myself for not being more loving and sympathetic to him. My desire to be an independent woman and to punish him for what he had put me through had made me act coolly to him when he most needed me. I got up and wrote him an encouraging note. I even signed it "Your Molly" this time.

That done, I fell asleep and only woke when the sun streamed in through my windows. I spent the day pleasantly enough, exploring the city. Each time I returned to my room, the trunks sat there untouched. I wondered how long it would take Oona Sheehan to act on my telegraph, and it occurred to me that maybe the person designated to retrieve her trunks might have been caught and was in jail. I had no idea what I'd do with them if they were still in my room when the time came for me to leave Ireland. Contact Inspector Harris, who seemed a reasonable sort of man, and tell him the truth, probably.

In the evening I contemplated wearing one of Oona's ball gowns, then decided that I'd be up in the gods with the students and should look inconspicuous. So it was the striped two-piece again, which was by now somewhat the worse for wear. But I did put my hair up and tucked a small feather into it. Then off I went into the night. It was a bitterly cold evening and the lacy shawl around my shoulders was no match for the wind sweeping in from the North Sea. I think windswept was also the word to describe my appearance when I finally landed up outside the theater.

There was quite a crowd around the Ambassador. I pushed my way through and made it up many flights of stairs to the gods. As soon as I found my seat and looked around, I spotted Alice waving at me from the other side of the balcony. I had hoped that I might be able to draw my seatmates into conversation and find out more from them about the Dublin literary life and Terrence Moynihan, but on one side of me were two large ladies who engaged in nonstop gossip about the people they were observing in the stalls through their opera glasses and on the other a young couple so clearly in love and oblivious to the rest of the world that I hadn't the heart to interrupt them.

During the interval I sought out Alice.

"What do you think of it so far?" she asked.

"Maud Gonne is lovely," I said. "I can understand why Mr. Yeats is besotted with her. Those eyes—they seem to take up half her face."

"But the language," Alice said patiently. "Don't you find the language stirring? An Irish play about Irish people, not other people's lives, but our own. Don't you find that wonderful and new and exciting?"

"Oh indeed," I said, realizing that I was probably neither a true scholar nor patriot. In truth, I was finding parts of it long-winded.

"Will you be coming to the party afterward?" Alice asked.

"Party?"

"There's going to be a celebration at a restaurant across the street," Alice said.

"But I'm not invited."

She laughed. "It will be a proper shindig, a free-for-all with the wine flowing like water if some of their other parties are anything to go by. Half of Dublin will be there."

"Then I'll join in the fun by all means," I said. If Terrence Moynihan had made any name for himself as a playwright then I should know by the end of tonight.

The play ended to riotous applause. Mr. Yeats was called on stage to take a bow. He appeared, looking every inch the poet, a lock of dark hair falling across his forehead, and solemnly kissed Maud Gonne's hand. The crowd applauded wildly.

"Give her a great big smacker," someone shouted from the gods. He didn't oblige but escorted her gallantly off the stage. We were swept down the stairs by the crowd and out into the chill night. We didn't need to ask where the party was to take place. We were born across the street like leaves floating in a current and into a brightly lit saloon, already crowded with people. Alice saw people she knew immediately, and I was left to stand there, examining the scene. A familiar voice attracted my attention, and there was the lovely Grania from the hotel, holding court, surrounded by a circle of admirers.

"So what did you think of the play?" a voice asked beside me and a serious-looking young man stood at my elbow. He was rather shabbily dressed, and I took him for another student.

"Interesting," I said cautiously. "I need more time to digest it. What did you think?"

"As a playwright, I think Mr. Yeats is a very fine poet," the young man replied with a twinkle in his eye. He held out his hand. "The name is Joyce," he said.

"Joyce? You have a woman's name?"

He laughed. "That's my family appellation. First name is James, but it's not polite to be on first-name terms with young ladies with whom one is not familiar."

I laughed too. "Well spoken, Mr. Joyce. My name is"—again I hesitated and opted for caution—"Mary Delaney, visiting Dublin from New York. Are you a student?"

"I am. Finishing up at University College here in the city. But also a writer, Miss Delaney," he said, "at least a hopeful writer."

"Ah, James, there you are, you fine fellow." A big hand was clapped on his shoulder, and he was borne into the crowd before I could find out whether he was another aspiring playwright and might have met Terrence Moynihan.

Trays of wine came around and I took a glass. At least sipping it gave me something to do. The rest of the people in the crowd seemed to know each other and were all engaged in animated discussions. I moved closer to Grania and her set, shamelessly listening in on her conversation.

"So is he going to be our new shining star of the theater?" someone was asking.

"The words are lovely to be sure," another chimed in, "but he doesn't possess the wit of an Oscar Wilde or a Bernard Shaw, and certainly not of a Ryan O'Hare."

I pricked up my ears now. I'd forgotten that Ryan also came from Ireland. I knew he'd come to fame in England, where he had been blacklisted for writing a wickedly satirical play about Victoria and Albert.

"And what about Cullen?" the first woman continued. "He would have topped them all by now, if he'd had a chance to go on writing. I certainly miss Cullen."

"We all miss Cullen," Grania said.

I had moved to the fringe of this group by now. "Who is Cullen?" I asked the young man standing beside me.

He looked surprised. "Cullen Quinlan? You've not heard of him? He was a fine young writer ten years ago, but he got himself too involved in the Brotherhood."

"The Brotherhood?"

"The Irish Republican Brotherhood. The secret society dedicated to getting rid of the English. You've not heard of them either? Where have you been, under a rock?"

I laughed uneasily. "No, in New York, I'm afraid."

"Ah, New York," he said, implying that was almost as bad as under a rock.

"Where I do happen to know Ryan O'Hare well," I said, playing my one trump card.

His face lit up. "You know Ryan? How is he doing these days?"

"Fair to middling, I should say. He's had his successes and his failures. In truth I think he's too wickedly witty for the New York crowd, who like their spectacles and big musical productions."

"Well, he would be, wouldn't he?" the young man agreed. "He was too wickedly witty for London, was he not?" He noticed the others in the group had turned their attention to us. "This young lady knows Ryan in New York," he said.

I was suddenly part of the circle. "Dear Ryan. And how is he doing in New York?" Grania asked, in her cool, elegant voice.

"He's had his successes," I said, "but he's had some bad luck too. One of his plays was due to open when President McKinley was shot. Another of his ideas was stolen from him. I'm afraid Ryan does talk rather expansively."

They all laughed at this.

"When you see him, tell him we miss him," Grania said. "Tell him Grania wants him to come home, Grania Hyde-Borne."

"I'll do that," I said.

"All the beautiful young men have left us." One of the men sighed. "Oscar and Ryan and Cullen. All so talented and such a treat for the eye as well."

"Don't let anyone hear you saying that, Tristan, or they'll get the wrong impression and you'll be following Oscar to jail."

"Such a terrible shame," an older woman said, "and such a sad end for a brilliant young man."

"It seems that all the true stars in the firmament are destined to flame briefly and then die," the man called Tristan said. "Oscar and Cullen. Who can say what they might have contributed to the world of literature in their mature years had they been allowed to keep on writing."

I turned to the young chap beside me who had been my supplier of information. "So what happened to Cullen?" I whispered.

"As I said, he became involved with the IRB, the Brotherhood. They attempted to blow up a barracks when there was that last push for home rule, and Cullen's name was implicated although I don't think he had any part in the planting of the explosives, mind you. But he was a known name, and it was decided to make an example of him. He was hauled off to jail and nothing has been heard of him since. We don't even know if he's alive or dead. Word has it that he died of typhoid. You know what the conditions are like in those places."

I nodded. I did know. I had visited Daniel in a similar place. If his case ever came to trial, it was just possible that a spiteful judge could send him back there. I shivered, then reminded myself that this was no time for personal worries. I had enough concerns on my plate right here in Dublin.

"So tell me," I said to the young man, "Do you happen to know a playwright called Terrence Moynihan?"

He frowned, then shook his head. "Can't say the name means anything to me. Ask Grania. She knows everyone. Grania!" he attracted her attention, "have you ever heard of Terrence Moynihan?"

"The name is familiar," she said. "Terrence Moynihan. Let me see. It was some time ago that I heard his name mentioned. A poet, wasn't he? But I haven't come across him personally, nor heard his name for quite a while."

So Mr. Moynihan had become a poet, rather than a playwright. I'd have to visit the Gaelic League on Saturday night to find out more. I had a feeling that if Grania Hyde-Borne didn't know him, he was no longer part of Dublin literary life.

More people crowded in upon Grania, and I found myself outside her little group. I looked around for Alice but couldn't see her. There probably wasn't any point in lingering any longer, and it was becoming impossibly loud for conversation anyway. As I fought my way to the door, a tall young man in a black frock coat grabbed my arm.

"Pardon me, but we've met before, I believe."

I recognized him right away, of course. It was Mr. Fitzpatrick, whom I had encountered when playing the part of Oona Sheehan on the ship. He was staring hard at me, but he obviously couldn't place me without my makeup and wig.

"Have we?" I asked innocently. "I don't believe so."

"I could have sworn your face looked familiar. Do you live in Dublin?"

"No, I'm just visiting from New York."

"Really? Then that is where I might have seen you. I also live in the States and often attend the theater in New York."

"There you are, then," I said. "Amazing as such a coincidence would be, we must have bumped into each other at a New York theater."

"Do you believe in coincidence?" he asked. "I rather think I'm in favor of predestination myself. You and I were destined to run into each other on both sides of the Atlantic, which must mean something important."

"I think it's more likely that you're mistaking me for someone else," I said. "I'm told I look typically Irish. I'm sure there are replicas of me in every major city of the world."

"Oh no, I wouldn't agree to that," he said. "Ripping play tonight, wasn't it? Of course a little highbrow for my taste. I go for musical comedies myself. Did you see Oona Sheehan in that last thing of hers? What was it called? She was a corker, an absolute corker."

I didn't like this turn the conversation was taking. It occurred to me that he had very possibly been in the courtroom at the inquest and had seen me unmasked there. Was that why he had introduced Oona Sheehan into the conversation—to observe my reaction? In which case why not just come out and say it? I decided that this was the moment to retreat.

"If you'll excuse me, Mr.—"

"Fitzpatrick," he said, with a little bow.

"Mr. Fitzpatrick," I finished, "I have a cab waiting and really have to go home. My family will be expecting me."

I didn't want him to know that I was all alone at a hotel.

"Wait," he called. "You didn't tell me your name."

"It's Delaney," I said. "Mary Delaney."

"Is it really?" he asked, his head cocked on one side. "Fancy that."

"I don't see what's so extraordinary about it," I said. "A very ordinary name, I'm sure. Now, if you'll excuse me."

I turned away. I thought he was going to try and follow me, but at that exact moment there were wild cheers from the doorway and Maud Gonne made her entrance on the arm of Mr. Yeats and followed by other members of the cast. I took the opportunity of all that confusion to slip out into the night, where I hailed a cab and got safely away.

❧ Twenty ❧

In the middle of the night a storm blew up. Rain peppered my windows and the wind howled down my chimney and found cracks through which to stir my curtains. I suppose the tension of being alone in a strange city, added to that of having found a murdered girl and knowing that I was surrounded by trunks full of illegal guns, was enough to make anyone sleep poorly. On this night I found sleep absolutely impossible. Thoughts raced through my head and when I half-slipped into dreams they were disturbing and confused.

I must have drifted into some kind of sleep in the wee hours because I woke to a leaden sky and a sodden dawn. The wind was still driving the rain almost horizontally. The milkman had hunched his shoulders to keep out the rain, and his horse stood head down and miserable. It was the kind of day that makes one long for roaring fires and tea and crumpets. Since I had no pressing need to go out, after breakfast I found a cozy chair in the lounge and sat down to think. If the Gaelic League had also never heard of Terrence Moynihan, where did I go from there? Somehow I had to discover whether he was still in Dublin, and if Mary Ann was still with him. It was all too possible that they had gone abroad to escape the vengeance of the horrible Mr. Kelly. He and Mary Ann could be living in London, Boston, or even Sydney by now.

The man in the wing-backed chair beside me kept rustling his newspaper annoyingly as he turned the pages. As I glanced up, an idea came to me. I could put an advertisement in a Dublin newspaper. I'm sure this was painfully obvious to anyone raised with a certain standard of culture, but newspapers were beyond our reach at home in Ballykillin. My father might have looked at one during his frequent visits to the pub, but he never brought one home for us. Had he done so, I might have known about things that were common knowledge to the rest of Ireland, like Cullen Quinlan and the Irish Republican Brotherhood.

I opened my little pad and composed a message. Seeking information on Terrence Moynihan, poet, and the former Mary Ann Burke. Anyone with information on contacting these people please refer to Box Number—.

I wasn't about to brave the storm and hoped that it might subside before the end of the day. In true Irish fashion of the weather never being the same for more than an hour, the rain did ease in the afternoon, at least enough for me to brave the long walk up Sackville Street to the offices of the *Irish Times*, where I placed my ad. I hesitated over whether to add the word "reward" but decided against it. Such an enticement might produce too many false leads.

As I walked back I had an odd feeling that I was being followed. I glanced around. The street was almost deserted and I saw nobody I recognized, but I quickened my pace. I was halfway down Sackville Street when the rains began again in earnest so that I was drenched through by the time St. Stephen's Green loomed through the fading afternoon light. I had forgotten how early it gets dark in Ireland the moment autumn closes in. The Shelbourne loomed like a safe harbor through the storm, and I ran up the steps and stood in the warm and comfortable foyer while lackeys rushed to relieve me of my sodden overcoat and hat.

"Fancy going out without an umbrella, miss," one of them said. "You'd better have some tea before you catch pneumonia."

Tea sounded like a good idea, so I let one of them carry my outer clothes up to my room while the other led me to a little table and had tea produced as if by magic. I had just finished my first cup and was pouring a second when I looked up to see a shadow standing over me. It was Mr. Fitzpatrick again, and he was beaming at me.

"Miss Delaney? I can't tell you how happy I am to find you here. I've been searching all over Dublin for where you might be staying and nobody had heard of a Mary Delaney. I was quite dejected. I believe you mentioned your family, and I thought I might have no hope of contacting you. And now here you are, at the Shelbourne and having tea. How delightful."

I don't know why I had taken such an instant dislike to him. Maybe it was because he made me feel uneasy. I couldn't help thinking that he knew exactly who I was and was enjoying this toying with me, like a cat playing with a mouse. To what end, I couldn't imagine.

Without being asked, he pulled over a chair and snapped his fingers for a second pot to be brought. "So tell me how you like Dublin so far. Is this your first visit? But surely not, for you say your family is here."

"It is my first visit," I said. "I am from—" I was about to say county Mayo when I realized I didn't wish to establish a connection to that county and to anyone who might have met Justin Hartley—"Galway myself, but I have an aunt and cousins who live here. And I am finding Dublin quite delightful."

He nodded. "I always enjoy coming here. Of course I live in the States, but my interest is in race horses, and everyone knows that the best horses are bred in Ireland. Hence I am enticed back here again and again."

"Do you have family here, Mr. Fitzpatrick?" I asked.

"Not anymore. My family immigrated to America, like so many of our countrymen. But I have come to know this city well, and I should be honored to show you around when the weather improves. There is to be a race meeting next week, point to point. Would you care to accompany me? It will be a jolly day and if one of my fillies wins, an even jollier return to the city. What do you say, Miss Delaney?"

"It's very kind of you, Mr. Fitzpatrick, but I can't think why you are showing me all this attention and consideration."

He blushed. "Isn't a chap allowed to show attention to the prettiest girl in town? I mean, dash it all, Miss Delaney, I'm a visitor here like you and it can be quite lonely so far from home, and it would be no fun watching horses win all alone, so you'd be doing me a great favor by saying yes."

A battle waged within me. I had no reason to see him as anything other than a keen young man. Perhaps I was overreacting, and he truly didn't realize that I was also Molly Murphy and had once been masquerading as Oona Sheehan. I managed a gracious smile. "You are too kind, Mr. Fitzpatrick. I accept your offer. I'd love to go the races with you."

"Next Tuesday? Where may I call for you?"

"I'll meet you here since it is so central and accessible for both of us."

"Shall we say ten o'clock then? And let's pray for good weather."

"You're very kind." I looked up to see the bellboy making a beeline for me. Since I knew he'd address me as Miss Murphy, I got to my feet hastily and went to intercept him.

"I just wanted to tell you, Miss Murphy, that the men have come for those trunks you're having shipped," he said. "They're up in your room now. I gather they have received full instructions so there's no need for you to go up, but I just thought I'd warn you so that you weren't alarmed if you barged in on them."

"Thank you," I said, "but I think I will go up and take a look for myself to make sure that they're not shipping anything I'll need during my stay."

I turned back to Mr. Fitzpatrick. "Please excuse me. There's something I must take care of right away."

He also got to his feet. "Is there anything I can do to help?"

"Nothing. But I must leave you. Until Tuesday then."

I didn't wait for a reply but hurried away and up the stairs. All but two of the trunks had already disappeared and two men were attempting to hoist one of the heaviest ones as I came in. They looked up, let go of the trunk and stood to attention.

"Sorry to disturb you, miss, but we were sent to collect the luggage," a big, ugly brute of a man said. "We're almost done."

He had a face like a boxer's and great paws for hands, and I was glad I was meeting him in the safety of the hotel. The other one simply looked like a half-wit.

I composed my features to look calm and disinterested. "That's quite all right. I'm glad it's finally going. I've had to clamber over it, and it's been most inconvenient." I waited until they had hoisted the trunk between them and then asked carelessly, "So who do you work for? Who sent you?"

"We work for the carter, miss. We got our instructions to come and pick up these trunks. We are in the right place, I hope."

"Quite right," I said. "And where are you taking them?"

"Just back to the warehouse, miss."

They had reached my doorway and were easing the trunk through it.

"And after that?"

He looked genuinely surprised. "I've no idea, miss. My job was to come and collect this luggage, and I just do what I'm told. Now if you'll excuse us, this blessed thing weighs a ton."

They staggered out. I went across to the window and peered down to the street. No sign of any vehicle. On impulse I decided to follow them. I ran out into the hall, but they were nowhere to be seen. Obviously they had been required to carry luggage down by some sort of back staircase and then, presumably, out of a tradesman's entrance. I snatched up my shawl from where it was lying on my dresser and raced down the stairs. I stood on the steps, scanning the street. Still no sign of any conveyance. And it was raining again. I put my shawl over my head and walked out onto the pavement.

"Are you requiring a cab, miss?" A hotel lackey stood ready at attention.

"No, thank you." I walked to the corner and looked into the alley at the side of the hotel. There was a horse and cart standing under a streetlamp and as I came around the corner, the two men appeared from a doorway, grunting as they tried to hoist the trunk into the back of the cart. I shrank back into the shadows. If they were indeed taking the trunks only back to their depot, then there was no point in following them. Besides, I didn't really want to know more than what was good for me, did I? The trunks were gone, and with them any danger to myself. I should be glad and leave them to it.

I was about to turn away when another man jumped down from the back of the cart.

"Is this the last of them then?" he asked, in a voice that made me stop and turn back to look at him.

"Jonnie and Donald are bringing down the last one now."

"Good, then let's get out of here," the man said, glancing up and down the alleyway.

He went to climb up to the driver's seat and the lamplight shone on his red hair. I must have gasped out loud because he looked up. For one brief moment our eyes met. I thought I must be seeing things; it was my brother.

☙ Twenty-one ☙

Liam!" I shouted and started to move toward him.

He shot me a frightened glance, then turned and fled, running away as fast as he could. I took off after him, down the alleyway, the clatter of our feet on the cobbles echoing from the sides of the buildings. The nails in Liam's boots struck sparks on the cobbles, so fast was he running. Back at home I had been a fast runner too, able to keep up with the boys in any footrace. But in those days I'd been barefoot, with light cotton skirts I could easily hoist up. Now I was dressed like a lady, hampered by my dainty shoes, my tight skirts and petticoats, and that neat little waistline that made it impossible to breathe.

"Jesus, Liam, slow down. Talk to your sister," I managed to gasp, but he kept on going, dodging from alleyway to alleyway. I had no idea in which direction we were heading, only that my side felt as if it was on fire and I couldn't go on much longer. When we had to cross a major road and a horse and carriage came hurtling toward us, he took the chance and sprinted in front of the horse. I had to stop for a moment while it passed by. In the time it took for me to cross the road, Liam had vanished. I was standing at the entrance to a maze of backstreets. From a nearby saloon came the sound of raucous laughter. I recoiled at the smell from an open drain at my feet. I started down a narrow, twisting street, then stopped when it branched again, vanishing into pitch darkness. There was no way I could pursue him into that warren at this time of night. I stood there, rain and sweat streaming down my face, almost weeping with frustration.

Then I realized how stupid I had been. All I had to do was follow the cart with the trunks on it and see where they were delivered. Even though it hurt to move and breathe, I ran all the way back and retraced my steps successfully to St. Stephen's Green. There was no sign of the cart anywhere. I tried all the streets that led from the green. I stopped passersby and asked if they had seen a cart go past, piled high with trunks, but none of them remembered seeing it. Who does pay attention to passing vehicles unless there is something strange about them?

Reluctantly I made my way upstairs to my room, now spacious and remarkably free of luggage. I ran a bath and lay back in the hot water, trying to calm my racing thoughts. What on earth was my little brother doing here in Dublin? Last time I had seen him he'd been an undersized and skinny fifteen year old, helping my father cut the peat on the croft, or with whatever laboring jobs the Hartley family needed on the estate. So what in heaven's name could have brought him here? He wouldn't have come all this way by himself to find work, when there were big cities like Galway and Limerick closer by. Surely he couldn't be mixed up in this republican business, could he? But if he were only working for a carter, doing an honest job, why run away from his sister? It did cross my mind that maybe he had been sent to Dublin by my father, or, worse still, by the Hartleys, looking for me. In which case, why run away when he had found me?

I asked myself if I could have made a mistake. It was almost two years since I'd set eyes on him last and in that time he'd have grown from fifteen to seventeen—from boy into a man. Would I still recognize him that easily? It was just possible that I had chased a complete stranger. But I didn't think so. I had looked into his eyes and seen recognition there.

Tomorrow I would find him, I told myself. I would keep looking for him until I did.

In the morning I inquired at the hotel about the carters who had come to pick up the luggage. I drew a blank there. They had come with a requisition slip, and I had already let the hotel staff know that I was expecting the trunks to be removed. I then asked for the name of firms of carters within the area. They gave me one or two. I went to visit them and from them acquired the names and addresses of their competitors. After a long morning of walking, I had not found the company that came to pick up those trunks last night.

I fortified myself with a good lunch of grilled herring with mustard sauce, followed by baked jam roll and custard, and then went out again, this time retracing my steps from the night before. I recognized the main road where I had been held up by the horse and carriage. On the other side was a large church, this one tall and gothic in contrast to the squat square Christchurch. The sign outside showed that it was St. Patrick's Cathedral—just how many cathedrals did one city need? Beyond it was the maze of small back streets. It didn't take me long to realize that my instincts the night before had been right. This was indeed a terrible slum. I wandered down filthy alleyways and narrow backstreets. Some of the houses must have been elegant once, but now they had become tenements, crammed with people just like in New York City. I walked from street to street, some with open drains, while ragged children observed me from doorways, mothers hung out washing, men stood together talking, and cats slunk between railings. It reminded me of the streets of the Lower East Side in New York, but without the vibrancy of life there. This was the Lower East Side with the life and color drained from it. These were people who seemed to have given up the fight and decided to exist rather than live.

I did stop to ask people I passed whether they knew a redheaded young man who looked a little like me and told them I was tracking down my young brother who had run away from home, but I got little help. For one thing there were redheads and skinny lads aplenty in the area, for another I might well be a wife seeking a runaway husband or even someone in league with the police. I offered some street urchins a reward if they found out where Liam Murphy was living and led me to him. They were certainly interested in the word "reward," but, as one of them said, "Dublin's an awful big place, miss."

I learned that the area I was in was called the Liberties. It had once been a self-governing center for weaving and trade and had been prosperous in the days before taxes on Irish goods made exporting impossible. For the last hundred years it had been the city's worst slum. I walked past dank tenements and desolate warehouses until I spotted the Guinness Brewery chimneys over the tenements and made my way toward the river Liffy. At least I now had my bearings, but no proof that Liam actually lived in this area. He might have used this confusing network of alleyways as a means of losing me and then come out the other side, free to go to his lodgings, wherever they might be.

I had to be content with telling myself that Liam knew where to find me if he wanted to make contact. If he didn't, there wasn't much more I could do but keep my eyes open as I went around the town. I came back to the hotel just in time for a change of clothes and a quick meal before I had to head out again, this time to my poetry reading, sponsored by the Gaelic League at Davy Byrne's on Duke Street. I asked directions to Duke Street from the hotel porter and was relieved to find it wasn't far away as the weather had worsened again, the wind was bitter, and my legs were already rebelling after a day's walking. I had changed into the warmest clothing I had brought, and wrapped a shawl around my shoulders before stepping out into the night. I didn't know at what number Davy Byrne lived, but I hoped that I'd arrive early enough on Duke Street to watch other people going into his house.

Duke Street was just behind Trinity College, and the whole area presented a lively scene on Saturday evening. Droves of young men, some of them already intoxicated, some arm in arm with young women of questionable repute, swept up the middle of the street, singing, laughing, shouting as they went. Some of them tried to persuade me to join them. Instead I asked them if they knew where Davy Byrne lived and was met with howls of laughter.

"That's Davy Byrne's over there," one of them pointed. "See the sign?"

Davy Byrne's was a public house, so it seemed. I hesitated outside in the darkness. In New York women were not allowed in most saloons and would only go into respectable drinking places accompanied by a man. Our pub at home had a ladies lounge around the side but decent ladies didn't frequent it. I'd been a few times with local lads, but there was nothing I hated more than watching grown men get drunk so I usually stayed well away. A group of men passed me and went in. Were ladies even allowed at meetings of the Gaelic League, I wondered? I stood there in the shadows until a middle-aged couple entered, then I stepped up hastily and followed them inside.

Inside was warm, with gas lamps casting a friendly glow on dark oak-paneled walls. There were simple oak benches around the walls, already full with an interesting assortment of young men, elderly professors, a couple of priests, shabby-looking individuals, and here and there a distinguished-looking matron. There were a couple of other young women, dressed rather in the bluestocking manner, one of them wearing glasses and both occupied with a book they were studying. I looked to see if there was any room beside them, but they were squashed into a corner, sharing a seat meant for one. So I stood awkwardly near the door until a young man called out, "Come over here to us, my dear. You can always sit on my lap."

"Nonsense. We can make room for the young lady over here," one of the matrons said firmly. "You two. Move over, please." Her look implied there was to be no hanky-panky in the establishment this evening. The men beside her moved to make room for me. I smiled gratefully and sat down. She was a large woman, with a mannish face, dressed head to toe in black, her hair scragged back into a severe-looking bun. But she had a serene, innocent look to her, and her face was remarkably devoid of wrinkles. In fact, she reminded me of the nuns who taught me in school, and I sat down cautiously beside her.

"Thank you. I wasn't even sure that women were allowed to attend," I said.

"What better way to resurrect our Irish culture than through the women, who will then teach it to the children," she said. "Are you a newcomer to town?"

I nodded. "I'm a visitor from New York," I said. "I heard about this meeting and wanted to see for myself what the Gaelic League had accomplished."

"Quite a lot," she said. "There are great stirrings all over Ireland. Our aim is to awaken interest in our past and our culture in the smallest villages of the land. We know that we're a nation of poets and musicians. Let's be proud of our own poetry and music and language too. You don't speak Irish, I take it?"

"I'm afraid not. We were never taught, although there were some people near my home who did."

"And where was that?"

"Up in—" I paused, conscious that people were listening, "In Galway," I said, latching onto a big enough city.

"Galway. How lovely," she said. "I'm Mrs. Boone, by the way. And your name is?"

"Mary Delaney," I said.

She nodded. "Welcome to the meeting, Mary. I hope it inspires you."

A barman came around with pints for those who had ordered them. I wondered if I was required to order something, and glanced at my female protector to see what she was doing. Before I could come to any conclusion the man next to me said, "and a half pint for the young lady here," and a glass was shoved into my hand. I turned to thank him and realized that I had met him before.

"It's Mr. Joyce, is it not?" I asked.

He smiled. "It is indeed. And you are—don't tell me—Miss Delaney."

"Quite right."

"I'm glad you've an interest in our native Irish poetry, Miss Delaney," he said.

"Oh, I have indeed," I said. "One poet in particular I had hoped to meet here. Terrence Moynihan. He used to write fine poetry, and I heard he'd left for Dublin some time ago."

Mr. Joyce frowned. "Terrence Moynihan? Now that's not a name I've heard. Maybe Kevin here would know better than I—he's been hanging around the city, imbibing equal measures of liquor and culture for as long as he can remember. Isn't that so, Kevin, my boy?"

"What? What's that you're saying, Joyce, old man?" One of the shabby fellows looked over in our direction, waving a half empty glass. It was hard to say how old he was—at least thirty but possibly a good bit older. He looked as if he was in need of a good meal, and his clothes were definitely in need of a brush and press.

"The young lady here is asking about a Dublin poet, and I've never

162

come across him. The name's Moynihan. Terrence Moynihan. Mean anything to you?"

The shabby man got to his feet, a little unsteadily, and came over to us.

"I remember Terry Moynihan," he said. "He wrote some fine stuff."

"Is he still in Dublin?" I asked excitedly. "I'd dearly love to hear him read his poems."

"Wouldn't we all," Kevin said. "But alas, poor Terry is no more. He had a little mix up with the Royal Irish Constabulary, and he was thrown in jail and never came out again."

"How long ago was this?" I asked.

He thought for a while. "Ten years, at least, I'd say."

"And what about his wife? Do you know what happened to her?"

He shook his head. "Terrence had no wife that I knew of."

"Well, they probably wouldn't have been legally married," I said. "I heard that he ran away with another man's wife. Her name was Mary Ann. Mary Ann Kelly when she was married, but before that it was Mary Ann Burke."

Kevin shook his head again. "Never met her. If Terry had her in Dublin with him, then he kept her hidden away." He was still frowning as he examined me. "But how would you know about Terrence Moynihan? Surely you'd have been nothing more than a little girl when Terrence was alive—certainly too young to appreciate the kind of political poetry that he wrote."

"To tell the truth," I said, as I weighed what truth I should be telling at this moment, "I was asked to look him up by a friend in New York who had been old enough to remember him in Dublin. You know what it's like when people hear that you're paying a visit to the old country—they all have someone they want you to look up for them."

"Is that a fact?" Kevin said. "I've never been out of Dublin myself."

"A stick-in-the-mud, that's what you are, Kevin my boy," Mr. Joyce said. "Travel broadens the mind, my friend. I aim to travel all over the world when I get through with my studies. I'll expect you to show me around New York, Miss Delaney."

"I'd be delighted to," I said. "It's a grand city."

"No city can beat old Dublin," Kevin said morosely. "Those Irishmen who desert their motherland are no true Irishmen. That's what I say. Rats leaving the sinking ship, every one of you."

He had just about reached that level of drunkenness that usually turns into fisticuffs with many Irishmen. Luckily I still had the matron beside me.

"Go back to your seat. Can't you see they're ready to begin," she said, in such a commanding voice that Kevin meekly obeyed her.

The program started. There was a report on the local branch of the Gaelic League and the great strides being made in fostering our native art and culture. There were language classes being offered, Irish music sessions, people collecting folk tales and dances. For the first time since coming to Ireland I felt that charge of enthusiasm that was so often present in New York. These people really believed they were about to reawaken the spirit of the country.

If they planned to do so, it surely wasn't with the poems of Desmond O'Connor. I think the best word to describe them is "longwinded." In the first poem—"Sea voyage," he took two pages just to describe the color of the sea, and then two more to describe the sound the sea made against the hull of the boat. Then he turned to the Gaelic and read the next pages in that language. I had to admit that the musical play at the Gaiety sounded like a much better way to spend an evening. But nobody else left so I was compelled to stick it out to the bitter end. I also wanted to make sure that nobody else present had any more information on Mary Ann and Terrence.

At last the poet finished to polite applause and we stood up stiffly. Some of the men made straight for the bar and another round of drinks. Demands for Jamesons echoed through the room as the menfolk moved on to stronger drink. Mr. Joyce had joined the crush at the bar. The matron was brushing herself down as if she might have picked up something unwanted on her clothing during the evening.

"A fine program, wasn't it?" she said to me. "How long are you staying? You should join our language classes."

"Not very long, I'm afraid," I said, "Although I'd dearly love to learn."

"My, but it's a difficult tongue." She shook her head. "Quite a challenge at my age. But I shall conquer it eventually."

With that she nodded to me. "Do you have someone to escort you home? Dublin is full of drunken rowdiness on a Saturday night."

"My hotel is only a stone's throw away, thank you," I said.

"I could arrange for someone to escort you without a problem," she insisted.

"Thank you, but I'm sure I'll be fine. I'll be back at my hotel in five minutes."

"Stay away from Grafton Street. It's full of drunken louts," she warned, putting on her bonnet.

"Are you coming, Mrs. Boone?" An elderly priest stood waiting for her at the doorway.

"Coming, Father," She glanced back at me with a concerned look as she went to join him.

I stayed around trying to find out from Kevin where Terrence Moynihan might have lived and who else might have known about him, but Kevin had sunk into the morose stage and kept muttering about the rats deserting their mother and going abroad. The men around the bar were becoming louder by the second, and it became clear that the respectable folk were going and I should probably join them.

I wrapped my shawl around my shoulders and left the warmth and brightness of Davy Byrne's. The matron had been right about Grafton Street. I could hear drunken revelry going on from where I stood, so I decided to turn the other way on Duke Street and make my way back to St. Stephen's Green by back roads. Luckily the green was such a large landmark that it wouldn't be hard to find it again, whichever route I took.

I reached the end of Duke Street and turned right, onto a quiet side road. After the noise and bustle, this street was poorly lit and deserted. One solitary lamp shone a circle of light onto the wet cobbles. They were uneven and slippery and I had to walk with care, so I was concentrating on not twisting my ankle rather than what was going on around me. I sensed, rather than heard, someone following me.

As I looked around something was thrown over my head—some

kind of heavy cloth. I tried to cry out but a hand clamped firmly over my face, making it almost impossible to breathe. I tried to squirm but the large blanket, or whatever it was, hampered my movements. I was picked up, half dragged, and suddenly dumped onto a hard surface. I heard a door slam. Before I could try to move, I was held down. It felt as if someone heavy was kneeling on my back. Then I was jerked around and dimly heard the clatter of hooves. I was being taken away in some kind of cart or carriage.

❧ Twenty-two ❧

Once the vehicle was in motion, the pressure on my back eased a little, which was good as I felt as if I had been having the life crushed out of me. But the thick wool cloth over my face still made it hard to breathe. Moreover it smelled disgusting, like some kind of animal blanket and when I half coughed, half choked, I got a mouthful of hair. I tried to move my hands so that I could free some space around my nose and mouth, but my hands were still pinned to my sides and I was still being held firmly down. I tried to wriggle, to squirm, to cry out, but the moment I did, the pressure on me increased again so I lay still.

I tried to think who might have kidnapped me and for what reason. This must surely be more than a simple robbery, for a blow to the back of my head would have been enough to knock me out and steal my purse. The words "white slave trade" did come into my mind, but this was Dublin, a peaceful backwater, not London or New York. I was becoming light-headed from lack of air. I could hear singing in my ears and sparks dancing in front of my eyes. The singing turned to roaring, and I was close to losing consciousness when I was jolted violently, grabbed again, and carried like a sack of potatoes. From the feel of it, I was being taken up steps. My biggest fear was that I was being carried onto a boat that would then sail off to Shanghai or wherever unfortunate girls were taken. When I look back on this it was a ridiculous fear, as being murdered right there and then in Dublin was a more likely fate—and I've never believed in fates worse than death, myself.

I could hear men's voices but the cloth over my head was too thick to make out exactly what they were saying, until I heard one voice say clearly, "Right. Let's have a look at her then."

I was set on my own two feet, and the blanket was taken from my head. I stood for a moment, blinking in the strong electric light and taking big gasping breaths before I had a chance to notice my surroundings. When I was finally able to breathe properly, I stared around me in amazement: I wasn't in the sort of seedy den, damp basement, or even ship's cabin that I had expected. I was in an elegant sitting room with Chippendale gilt furniture, a grand piano in one corner, Persian rugs on the polished wood floor, good art on the walls, and heavy red velvet curtains drawn over the windows.

A man was sitting on one of the Chippendale chairs. I had met plenty of men in my life I would call attractive, but this one was different from all the others. Daniel was definitely handsome; Ryan could almost be described as beautiful. This man was undoubtedly their equal in beauty—with a strong jaw, straight nose, dark hair worn rather long, and alarmingly blue eyes, but it wasn't his rugged good looks that instantly held my attention, it was something in the power of his personality. You could tell instantly that this was the sort of man whom others followed willingly, who was quite confident in himself and his leadership, who knew what he wanted and got it. Don't ask me how I could tell all this so quickly. I just knew as he fixed me with that steady gaze.

"All right, young woman," he said, in a voice that bore the trace of an Irish accent but was deep and cultured, "out with it."

My shock and fear had now subsided, and my relief at finding myself in a civilized-looking room allowed my normally feisty nature to resurface. I wasn't going to let this man see how afraid I was. I took a step toward him. "Look here. I have absolutely no idea who you are, or why you had the nerve to send your men to kidnap me. They've obviously made a mistake and brought in the wrong person. I demand that you release me instantly, or it will be the worse for you."

At this I saw those eyes light up and he actually laughed. "The worse for me? Did you hear that, boys? I like your spirit, whoever you are. Now supposing you start off by telling us who you really are, and who you are working for."

"Supposing you tell me why you had me brought here in such an undignified fashion," I said. "If you had merely wanted to talk to me, a civilized invitation would have worked just as well."

"Ah, but I couldn't risk that, my dear," he said. "When the enemy doesn't play by the rules, we can't either. And I may look like a civilized man, indeed I am, but lives are at stake here and I can't afford to take risks. You're going to tell us everything you know tonight, one way or the other."

I continued to stare at him as if he was speaking a foreign language. "I'm afraid I still have no idea what you are talking about. I can't think that I know anything that might be of interest to you or anyone else. You've obviously mixed me up with someone else."

"You're calling yourself Mary Delaney, are you not? And supposedly you've come over from America. But there's no Mary Delaney registered at any hotel in Dublin. So why are you using an assumed name if you're all above board?"

"Did it never occur to you that I might be staying with my family?"

"Possible," he said, "but you've been observed going in and out of the Shelbourne Hotel, where you must be staying under another name."

He leaned back, tipping the gilt-edged chair and stretching out his long legs. "So, to start with, you could tell me your real name and why you've been asking so many questions about Terrence Moynihan and Mary Ann Burke. And what you're doing here and who is paying you."

"As for what I am doing here and why I've been asking questions, that's easily answered and I've nothing to hide," I said. "If this is a civilized conversation, as you say it is, may I not sit down? I am at a disadvantage standing up while you seem quite at ease, and I'm actually still quite dizzy after being deprived of air under that rug or whatever it was. Horse blanket probably. It certainly smelled of animals."

He smiled again. On any other occasion I would have thought he had a bewitching smile, but at this moment his complete ease was unnerving me. I was all too aware that this man knew he had the power of life and death over me and wouldn't hesitate to use it.

"My apologies for the condition of the horse blanket," he said.

"Pray do take a seat. Brendan, could you find the young lady something to drink? Will water do, or do you need something stronger to steady your nerves?"

"Water would do just fine, thank you," I said. "I have no need of spirits."

He nodded as if he approved of this. I sat on the nearest chair.

"Proceed," he said. "You're going to tell us why we shouldn't be concerned about all the questions you've been asking."

"All right." I leaned toward him. "My name is Molly Murphy, and I am a private investigator in New York City. I was hired by an Irishman who has lived in America for most of his life to come to Ireland to try and find his sister, Mary Ann, who was left behind when the family fled during the famine. I have traced her as far as Dublin, where I understood she was living with a man called Terrence Moynihan. Hence my visit to the Gaelic League poetry reading. I was sure that other poets might know of Mr. Moynihan's whereabouts."

"And did they?"

"One of them told me that he'd died in jail at least ten years ago."

"That is correct. Terrence Moynihan was arrested because of an inflammatory pamphlet he wrote on civil disobedience. He was thrown into a jail cell, awaiting trial, and caught consumption while he was there. He never had the strongest of constitutions, and he didn't last out the year."

"If you know this, then what became of Mary Ann?"

He shook his head. "I have no knowledge of a wife. Within the Brotherhood we keep personal details to ourselves. You can't reveal under torture what you don't know. That's why most of the boys choose nicknames these days. It's better not to know."

"You're with the Irish republicans then? The secret society called the Brotherhood?"

He nodded. "That's correct."

"If it's so secret, why risk identifying yourself to me?"

He smiled again. "Because, my dear, if we discover that you are some kind of informer, and you're working for the hated English, you'll not be leaving this house alive."

"You wouldn't really kill me," I said, with more bravado than I felt.

"I wouldn't want to, but if it was your life versus fifty or a hundred others, then I'd have to sacrifice you for the common good, just as I've been prepared to sacrifice myself for the common good. It's our cause that counts, not individual lives." He looked up as the door opened. "Ah good. A glass of water for Miss Murphy."

I took it and drank, gratefully.

"I don't know what I have to say to convince you that I am not a spy of the English," I said, as I put the empty glass down on the table. "I'm exactly who I say I am."

"I assure you it won't be hard to check out your story. But if you are merely an investigator, looking for one Mary Ann Burke, what were you doing chasing one of our young men the other night? I am told you chased one of our lads and asked about him all over the Liberties?"

"That's also an easy question to answer. I chased him because he's my brother."

For the first time I saw I had surprised him. "Your brother?"

"His name is Liam Murphy, is it not? And I am Molly Murphy, his older sister. Of course I wanted to speak to him. I couldn't imagine what he was doing in Dublin when I had left him as a fifteen-year-old boy in county Mayo."

The man in the chair snapped his fingers. "Brendan, do you know this Liam Murphy that she is talking about?"

"I do, sir. He's just joined us. A new recruit."

"Then go and have the boy fetched right away."

"He's likely to be out making merry on a Saturday night," the young man who had brought me the water answered.

"I don't care if he's in bed with his fancy girl, you tell him I want to see him right now. This is the army, boy, the republican army, and you'd better get used to it."

"Sorry, sir. I'll bring him right away," the lad mumbled and disappeared.

❧ Twenty-three ❧

I was left alone in the room with the charismatic man. He seemed relaxed and pleasant and yet the tension in the air was so strong you could cut it with a knife. I had the feeling that he could just as easily snap his fingers and command one of those boys to end my life, if he so chose. I wanted to ask him his name, but I didn't dare. I found that my knees were shaking and was glad that they were hidden by my skirts. But I wasn't about to play the helpless female. I had the feeling that all the strange things that had happened to me so far on this journey must be somehow linked, and that the man in the gilt chair knew the answers.

Then there were voices in the hallway outside. I looked around, expecting Liam to enter through the double doors. Instead the last person in the world I expected to see came in. It was Grania Hyde-Borne, the society lady.

"What is going on, Cullen, my sweetest," she said, crossing the room to the man and putting her delicate gloved hand on his shoulder. "I go to the theater, and when I return I hear the boys mumbling about kidnapping a spy."

"You tipped us off to her yourself, Grania," he said.

"I did?" Grania turned those lovely eyes on me and registered surprise. "You? You were at the reception after the play the other night. You're the one who knows Ryan O'Hare."

"And she was also at the Gaelic League tonight, asking questions about Terrence Moynihan."

"I see." Grania perched on the edge of the sofa, close to the man. "And have we found out why she's so interested in knowing what happened to Terry?"

"I've explained to this gentleman," I said. "I'm an investigator from New York City, and I was sent over here to try and locate a Mary Ann Burke, who was left behind by her family when they came to America during the famine. That's the whole story. I'm no spy, I'm not interested in your republican struggles, and I'm no danger to anyone, so please just let me go about my business."

"Not as easy as that, sweetheart," the man said.

"Oh, come now, Cullen," Grania leaned over and patted his knee. "Aren't you overreacting? I'm sure she's as harmless as she looks."

"Just a minute," I said as the wheels in my brain started working. "Your name is Cullen? Not Cullen Quinlan, the playwright everyone was talking about the other night? But you can't be. He's dead."

"Have you not heard of the resurrection of the flesh?" Cullen asked, turning to Grania with a grin. "Cullen Quinlan in the flesh, my darlin', alive and well, but a playwright no longer."

"But how?" I began.

"For your information I was being held in a damned English jail. One of our boys was due to be hanged. They allowed a bevy of priests to come in and hear our confessions. Twelve priests came in and twelve went out again—only I was one of those twelve, looking very humble with my Franciscan hood over my head. The real Franciscan stayed behind, and only gave the alarm that he'd been overpowered, tied up, and gagged when he knew I was already on a ship bound for France. I've been in hiding in France ever since."

"So what on earth are you doing back in Ireland?" I blurted out. "Surely there is a price on your head?"

"Bound to be," he said easily. "But what the Brotherhood needs now is leadership. We were in tatters. And there's such apathy among the masses, even though home rule has suffered defeat after defeat. Most of them don't care if we're ruled by England or by the Queen of Sheba as long as they get their daily crust of bread and their pint of stout. Someone has to breathe the fire into them, and right now I'm the only one who can do it."

"If anyone can do it, you can, Cullen," Grania said adoringly.

"As long as the enemy doesn't find out my whereabouts," Cullen said.

"Who would ever suspect that the fun-loving society hostess, Grania Hyde-Borne, was harboring a dangerous criminal at her house," Grania said, looking delighted with herself. "Keeping you here was a stroke of genius, though I say so myself."

"But what about your husband," I said, "what about your servants?"

"My husband is currently at our house in London, and most of the servants with him," Grania said. "Unfortunately I could not travel with him because of my health. Those servants who have stayed on here with me, I'd trust with my life. So we're completely safe, unless the English are using subtler means these days—innocent-looking young girls, for example."

They were both staring at me, but I'd had enough of being accused.

"I'm Irish born and bred," I said. "Do you think I'd work for the English? And I don't know why you are questioning me when it's I who should be questioning you. I came over here on a simple, innocent errand, minding my own business. You and your cronies are the ones who have used me to your own advantage and put my life in danger."

"Used you? How so?" Cullen asked.

"Those trunks. I presume they were destined for you and your men. Did you think I wouldn't look inside? And what if the customs men or the police had looked inside? I would have been the one who would be in jail right now, probably awaiting execution."

"What trunks are these?" Cullen asked.

"Don't pretend you know nothing about the trunks full of rifles, shipped in my name," I said. "I take it that Oona Sheehan is in league with you, or were you using her against her knowledge too?"

"Oona Sheehan?" Cullen asked sharply, sitting forward in his chair. "God Almighty, what's she got to do with anything?"

"She was the one the trunks belonged to. She was the one who tricked me into changing cabins with her on the ship and . . ." I broke off as my thoughts went one step further. "Was it you who had Rose

McCreedy killed? Did she know what was in the trunks and start to talk when she should have kept silent?"

"I'm afraid you've lost me," Cullen said. "I know of no trunks, nor any Rose McCreedy."

"Rose McCreedy was Miss Sheehan's maid. She was murdered in Miss Sheehan's cabin, which I was occupying at the time."

"I know nothing of any of this," Cullen said, "and I can assure you that the Brotherhood doesn't go around killing maids."

"Let me intervene here. I'm the one who knows about the trunks," Grania said.

"A shipment of arms arrived, and I wasn't told?" Cullen said shortly. "Exactly what I've been saying about no chain of command here and the right hand not knowing what the left—"

Grania held up her own small hand. "Keep your hair on, Cullen. You couldn't have known, since we only received word of them yesterday in a telegraph cable from New York and I haven't had a chance to speak to you since then. I gather they've been picked up and taken to a safe place, awaiting our instructions. So they were sent as part of Oona's luggage, were they? God bless her."

"God bless her?" I said angrily. "She tricked me into taking her place and impersonating her on the ship, into having the trunks shipped as part of my luggage. I was the one who fell under suspicion when her maid was murdered. For all I know, I may still be under suspicion."

Cullen was frowning now. "And who did you tell about the contents of these trunks?"

"Why nobody, of course," I said. "I guessed right away where the rifles were destined. I may not be an ardent patriot myself, but I wasn't about to do anything to hinder the fight for freedom either."

"You hear that, Cullen," Grania said. "She's one of us. I knew we could trust her."

"We're not trusting her out of our sight, Grania," Cullen said. "In fact, we're now in a most difficult position as to what to do with her. We could put her on a boat back to America, but we'll never be able to rest easy."

"You don't have to do anything with me," I said.

Who knows how the conversation might have developed, but at

that moment there came the loud sound of footsteps, there was a knock on the door and several lads entered. In the midst of them was Liam, looking white-faced and afraid.

I stood up, unprepared for the rush of emotion I felt on seeing my little brother, now a good head taller than me, his boyish faced replaced by the square jaw of a man.

"Liam," I said. I started toward him to give him a hug, then saw him back away.

"Molly, it *is* you." I saw his Adam's apple move up and down. "Holy Mother of God."

"Why did you run off last night? You didn't want to acknowledge your own sister?"

"At first I thought I was seeing a ghost," he said. "And I'm not supposed to be here." He glanced nervously around the room. "Nobody's supposed to know I'm here. It could ruin everything."

"I don't know you, boy," Cullen said sharply. "Why don't I know you?"

"I just got here, sir," Liam said. "I'm with William O'Brien and his United Irish League, working up in the Northwest."

"Then what are you doing here?" Cullen asked. "Has Mr. O'Brien given up his fight for land reform and decided to join our struggles?"

"No, sir. Mr. O'Brien isn't here with me. I came by myself when I heard the news."

"News? What news is this?"

"About Kilmainham Gaol, sir. I thought I might be of help."

Cullen was frowning now. "You might be of help?"

"Yes, sir. You see, my brother is one of the lads in Kilmainham. If there's a plan to rescue him, I want to be in on it."

"Who said anything about a plan?" Cullen demanded.

"Mr. O'Brien got word of it and told me. He sent me down here with letters to the Brotherhood. I've signed on. I've been staying with these lads and helping out with whatever needs to be done."

"Our brother is in jail?" I asked, not thinking that it probably wasn't wise to interrupt Cullen Quinlan. "You're saying that Joseph is in jail?"

Liam nodded, his face now looking ridiculously young and scared. "They're going to hang him, Molly."

"Holy Mother of God, what did he do?" I asked.

"Killed a man, by mistake, mark you. He was only trying to protect Malachy."

"Malachy?" I felt a cold hand clutching at my heart at the mention of my youngest brother, the one who had always been my favorite. "What's been going on, Liam?"

Liam shuffled his feet uncomfortably. "Plenty's been going on since you left, Molly. Da went to pieces after you disappeared. He started drinking too much. You know he's always been a one for his drink, but it got really bad and the house became no better than a pigsty. The Hartleys sacked him right away because he couldn't do the work, and he just sort of gave up. Then Joseph and he got into a fight—a real fight, mind you, with fisticuffs, and Joseph took off and left. I couldn't stand it there either, but I wouldn't leave because of young Malachy. Then Da fell into the river on his way home from the pub one night and drowned."

"Drowned? You're saying our father is dead?"

He nodded, pressing his lips together.

"God rest his soul," I muttered, wondering if I actually felt grief at this news. "And Malachy? What's happened to him?"

"I tried to carry on and look after Malachy," he said, "but the next thing I know, I'm told that the Hartleys needed our cottage back, and I find that they've put Malachy up for sale."

"For sale?" I couldn't believe what I was hearing. "Like a slave, you mean? I don't believe it. This is the twentieth century. Such things can't be allowed."

"Oh, but they are. They have hiring fairs all over where the farmers come to buy young boys as indentured servants. No better than slaves, really. Just like buying a new farm horse. Well, I went and found Joseph. It turned out that he had already joined the United Irish League and was working with Mr. O'Brien trying to pressure the big landowners to hand over land to their tenants like the law says they should. Well, Joseph was always the one with a temper. He was fighting mad, I can tell you. 'We're not letting those bastards sell Malachy into slavery,' he said. So off he went with a group of lads to rescue him. There was a bit of a fight and men came at them with clubs and guns. Our lads fought back, and a land agent got beaten up and killed. The Irish League managed to spirit away young Malachy and myself, but Joseph was on the run and he got caught. And he put up a fight then too, and damaged a few members of the constabulary, so I hear. So naturally they threw the book at him. He's sentenced to be hanged."

Unwittingly my hand went up to make the sign of the cross. My father dead, two brothers on the run and in hiding, and one sentenced to be hanged. It was almost more than I could take in. Grania must have sensed this. She came over to me.

"Sit down, my dear. Cullen, get her a brandy. She looks about ready to pass out."

"I'm all right," I said, but for once I welcomed the brandy. The burning liquid did seem to spread warmth into my frozen limbs. "But what's become of Malachy?"

"Don't worry about him. He's been taken in by one of Mr. O'Brien's supporters who has boys of his own. He'll be just fine there."

Cullen shifted in his seat. "So, young man, how do you think your being here is going to be of any help to your brother?"

Liam glanced around again, "I'm not sure if I should be talking in front of these people."

"They've all sworn an oath, except for your sister, and I don't imagine she'd betray her own family. Go on, let's hear what you've got to say."

"I was told, sir, that there was a plan to break certain men out of Kilmainham Gaol. I wanted to make sure that Joseph was among them."

"If the plan is such common knowledge that it reaches the far corners of Ireland, then there's no way it will be carried out," Cullen said. "I'm not risking the very fabric of our organization at this critical stage."

"But sir, it has to take place," Liam said. "You can't let Joseph hang. And it's not the whole of Ireland that knows, just Mr. O'Brien, and he only sent me down here because it was my brother and he thought I might be of help."

"So you think you're better at infiltrating a jail that has been called the Irish Bastille than any of the men we have trained, are you?" Cullen demanded.

"No sir. It's just that Joseph and me look alike, almost like twins, wouldn't you say, Molly? I thought that somehow I might act as a decoy—add to the confusion, you might say—have the guards chase me by mistake." He stood there with his hands on his hips, staring at Cullen. "I don't know what kind of plan you've got in mind, sir, but I'm ready to do whatever you want to help."

A weary smile crossed Cullen's face. "You're a brave lad, Liam. I like that. But I have to warn you that this is going to be no bun-fight. We're hoping to spring some of our men from jail; but more than anything, we want to send a message to the English that we're here, and we're alive and arming ourselves, and we're making preparations for the big fight that will come one day soon. We want to scare the pants off them, Liam. Maybe we'll get nobody out and maybe most of us will die trying, but by God it will be a rallying call to our countrymen, won't it?"

I could see now why I sensed immediately that he was a leader, one that men would follow into battle. I heard myself saying, "If there's anything that I can do to help you, then count me in."

❧ Twenty-four ❧

"At least we appear to have a new supply of weapons, although I can't think why I wasn't notified about them sooner." Cullen still looked perturbed. It was later that evening and the boys, including Liam, had been sent on their way. I would dearly have liked the chance to talk to him, and to hug him too, but he had gone without much of a backward glance at me when ordered to do so. I got the feeling he was worried about getting emotional in front of the other lads. I was left alone with Grania and Cullen, and not at all sure about what might happen next.

"I told you, Cullen," Grania said, "we only received word about them yesterday."

"We?"

"The message was sent to Maude Donne at the theater. It concerned stage properties for an upcoming play, donated by Oona and sounding quite innocent. Maude naturally passed the message along to Queen Mab."

"Queen Mab," Cullen said scornfully. "So she's in charge now, is she?"

"Not of the Daughters of Erin, per se, but of the organization's more militant branch, yes."

"And you women will be running the battles from now on?"

"The Daughters of Erin have done their part so far and will continue to do whatever is required of us," Grania said stiffly, "and as to that, it made more sense to send the message in this way, when your organization is sure to be more closely watched than ours. At least now we have the weapons safely hidden and waiting for when they will be needed."

Cullen continued to scowl. "And it seems that my own lads were used to transport them."

"Obviously our women don't possess the strength to haul around trunks full of weapons, so Queen Mab enlisted them," Grania said.

"Queen Mab enlisted them," Cullen repeated scornfully.

"You're being unreasonable, Cullen. If all our little groups can't work together, what hope do we have of uniting when the big push comes some day. And it's sheer arrogance to think that you men will be the only ones with a say in how our country is to be ruled."

Cullen looked at her and then he laughed. "I can see you taking over from Queen Victoria, Grania. You'd love every minute of it."

She smiled too. "Contrary to popular belief, I'd be happier carrying on with my life of leisure. I enjoy my theater and art shows and trips to Paris for the fashions. I'd hate to give them up to have to rule a country. I'm sure you'll do it much better than I."

"I don't expect to be alive that long," Cullen said.

"Don't say that." Grania shivered.

"We have to face facts, Grania. It's only a matter of time before they find out I'm back in Ireland, and then you know very well that my life isn't worth a damn. Most likely it will be a sniper's bullet so that they don't have to bother incarcerating me again."

I had been looking from one to the other, following this conversation with awe. It was like watching a play. I decided she was every bit as brave as he. He had nothing to lose at this stage, but she had a grand life with all the money and freedom she could want, and she was prepared to risk it all. And my own little brother was all ready to follow them. And in the heat of emotion, I had volunteered to help them. I wondered how brave I'd be when it came to it.

"I think we need refreshments, don't you?" Grania said. She went across to a bellpull and almost immediately a young maid appeared. "Francoise," she said, and proceeded to address her in French. The girl curtseyed, "Oui, Madame," she said, and hurried out.

I saw why Grania didn't have to worry about our meetings being overheard by her staff.

Cullen looked more relaxed. He took out a pipe and lit it. "I'm still amazed that Oona is working for us over in America," he said. "I thought she'd renounced the cause long ago in favor of fame and fortune."

"Isn't it obvious why she's doing it?" Grania said. "She's doing it for you. She heard you were back in circulation and still carries a torch for you, Cullen."

"Don't be ridiculous," Cullen said. "That was all years ago."

"You forget that we women can carry a torch for life."

The way she looked at him made me realize something. These two were lovers, or had been. I'd led a sheltered life and didn't know much about such things, but I had seen Daniel look at me in that way.

I went to stand up. "If you'll forgive me, I'm tired and I need to go back to my hotel room."

"Don't be silly, Molly," Grania said. "We can't let you go out alone at this time of night. You're staying here. We've plenty of room. And in the morning I'll send one of the staff round for your things. Much more comfortable than a stuffy old hotel."

I saw that I wasn't going to be allowed to escape. They might be acting like civilized people, but I was still to be held a prisoner.

"You really don't have to worry about me," I said. "You said yourself that I'm not likely to betray my own brother."

"I'm sure you're not," Cullen said, "but the enemy has many spies and some of them are highly skilled at wheedling information out of unsuspecting young ladies. To tell you the truth, I haven't quite made up my mind as to whether you and your brother are among the enemy's latest choice of spies."

"Don't be ridiculous," I said. "You heard why Liam is here."

"What better way to learn our plans than to pretend to be working with us? When I've done a little checking of my own, I'll decide how much you are to be trusted, and what I'm to do with you."

"I've already offered to work with you, but I've also my own job to do," I said. "I'm being paid by a man in America to locate his lost sister.

I have to do my very best to find her. And since I know she came to Dublin with Terrence Moynihan, then I must begin with his old address and work from there. She may still be close by."

"I doubt very much that you'll find her," Cullen said.

"Why do you say that?"

"I never heard any mention of Terrence Moynihan having a wife. She certainly was never seen in public with him."

"She wouldn't have been married to him. She was married to a man called Kelly, down near Waterford."

"Waterford, Grania. Your part of the world, is it not?"

"Long ago, yes," Grania said. "So she fled from her husband, did she?"

"A great brute of a man," I said. "I can understand why she ran away."

"Then it seems all too possible that Mr. Kelly found his errant wife and killed her, don't you think?" Grania looked at Cullen.

"All too possible," Cullen said. "I never saw Terrence with a woman. I never heard him mention her. So I'm afraid Grania's suggestion does seem the most likely."

"Unless she decided that she'd made a mistake and didn't want to stay with Terrence Moynihan," I said. "She might have decided to leave him and go somewhere else. But I've no idea where that would be. She was raised in an orphanage. She had no home."

"You're looking for a needle in a haystack," Cullen said. "She could be anywhere in Ireland, if she's still alive. She could have gone to try her luck in England. And if she was left behind in the days of the famine, then she'd be quite an old woman by now. Not everyone lives to beyond fifty."

"But I must keep on trying," I said. "Please let me do what I have to."

"Don't you want to help your brother escape from Kilmainham?" Cullen asked.

"Of course I do."

"Then you'll stay on here, until we've made our plans," Cullen said. "You won't find it a bad life, I'll tell you that. Grania spoils us hopelessly."

"And in a couple of days you'll have the chance to meet the Daughters of Erin," Grania said. "We've a meeting at this house."

"Saints preserve us," Cullen said with a sigh.

Food was brought, but I found it hard to swallow. At last Grania noted that my eyes were shutting of their own accord and had me led up the stairs to bed. A hot water bottle greeted me among crisply starched sheets. I lay hugging it to me, trying to get warm, trying to come to terms with this latest twist in my adventure. My father was dead, one brother under sentence of death, and the other working with a revolutionary group, while the youngest was hidden away. I had thought, when I escaped to New York, that I had freed myself from my family, whom I saw as annoying and demanding. Now I realized that family ties cannot so easily be cut. My brothers might have been ungrateful, tracked in mud, and demanded food at all hours; but I still cared about them.

I had made a brave promise to Cullen Quinlan that I would help them in any way they needed me. Now, as I lay awake, I had time to consider that promise. Of course I wanted to help free Joseph from prison, but I hadn't really thought what that might entail. Fighting? Killing people? Did I really want to help bring down the government and perhaps set anarchy in its place? Was the English rule really so bad for us? And what was I really prepared to do anyway—learn how to shoot a gun? To kill innocent people, if so ordered?

I hugged that hot water bottle to me, feeling its firm and comforting warmth through its flannel cover. It seemed I had little choice but to go along with them until I knew more. I was either for them or against them. And if I was against them, Cullen had already told me I'd be disposed of. I was now committed to being part of their plot, whatever happened.

❧ Twenty-five ❧

I was woken by the French maid bearing a tray of tea and biscuits, and found myself in a delightful room with lace curtains letting in leafy sunlight. Before I had had a chance to drink the tea the maid returned bearing a jug of hot water. A fire was already burning in my fireplace. There were clean clothes laid out for me. I didn't think that staying here for a while would prove too much of a hardship. Of course a voice in my head nagged that I was actually being held here against my will. For the second time in a matter of weeks, I was in a beautiful prison.

In the light of day my brave offer to help rescue Joseph seemed overdramatic and ridiculous. How could I possibly help break into a jail? Exploits like that should be left to trained men. In truth I wanted no part of it, much as I hoped Joseph could be rescued. I didn't feel that patriotic fire burning in my belly. I wandered around the room and considered how I might escape.

It occurred to me that Inspector Harris might have been keeping an eye on me at the Shelbourne and would notice I was missing. But what good would that do me, unless he'd actually had a man following me to witness my kidnapping. And he wasn't likely to have had me followed, was he? Not when it appeared I was no longer a suspect. Then, for some reason, I thought of Mr. Fitzpatrick, appearing out of the blue and seeming so interested in striking up a friendship. I was hardly a Dublin beauty, when compared to Grania, and I certainly wasn't an heiress . . .

so was it possible that he was working with the police and keeping an eye on me for them?

In which case I was probably now in worse trouble than before. Inspector Harris might construe this to mean that I was trying to give him the slip. And what about Mary Ann? How could I look for her when I was cooped up here? She was the only reason I was in Ireland, after all. But then I figured that Tom Burke had given me no time frame. As long as I was not living off his money, then my time was my own. If I had to spend a few days at the pleasure of Grania Hyde-Borne, then it wasn't really the worst fate in the world, was it? The most sensible thing was to stop worrying and see what happened next. Having talked myself into not feeling guilty, I washed, dressed, and went down to a good breakfast of smoked haddock, scrambled eggs, and kidneys.

I was on the toast and marmalade when Grania came to join me. "Your things have been collected from the Shelbourne and they have been told that you will not be returning," she said. "You have received unexpected news from America and are traveling home on the next boat."

"I see," I said. "So I am to be kept here as a prisoner?"

"Not a prisoner. Heavens, no. A welcome houseguest," she said. "I trust you found the room to your liking?"

"It's a lovely room," I said, "and I have been made most comfortable. But I do have a job to do in Ireland. I'm being paid to find Mary Ann Burke."

"I tell you what," she said, moving her chair confidentially closer to me. "I'll send out my spies, if you like. I know Cullen won't approve of our drawing attention to ourselves around the city by asking questions at this point, but I'll use the most discreet of the Daughters of Erin. They may be able to find out if your Mary Ann is still in the city and what happened to her after Terrence died."

"Would you do that?" I beamed at her. "I can't thank you enough."

"I'm only too happy to help." She patted my shoulder as if I was a cherished pet.

"Grania, why are you doing all this?" I asked.

"Helping you? Because you need help."

"No, I meant working with the Brotherhood, taking terrible risks?"

She laughed merrily. "As for the terrible risks, I'm afraid you overestimate my part. I am merely a facilitator. I bring people together, I pass along messages. I know everybody, you see. I present a wonderfully visible, respectable face to the world. And I have a big house where secret meetings can be held when my husband is away."

"Your husband is away a lot?"

"He finds Ireland deadly dull," she said, "so he prefers to spend his winters at our London home and springtime in Paris. Usually I join him, only this year, knowing Cullen was to return, I pleaded ill health. When the prison break actually occurs, I shall be on the boat bound for Liverpool, on my way to join my husband."

"But you still haven't answered my question," I said. "Are you doing it for Cullen?"

"For Cullen?" she asked, looking amused if anything. "Why would I be doing it for Cullen? I'm not under his command."

"But under his spell?" I said cautiously. "You yourself suggested that Oona Sheehan only agreed to the little scheme with the trunks because she still carried a torch for Cullen."

She laughed merrily. "And you think I still carry a torch for him? How sweet you are. Darling, I'm a married woman."

"That hasn't exactly prevented other people from falling in love."

"I'll be quite honest with you," she said. "I'm certainly not in love with my husband. I married him because of what he could offer—money, power, a chance to travel, to live well. And I did have a brief and heady romance with Cullen when we were considerably younger. But Cullen is only in love with one thing—Ireland. I need someone who will adore me for myself, not for what I can offer. So Cullen and I remain devoted friends, no more."

"Then I return to my question," I said. "Why risk all this—your home, your position, your money? Surely you are one of the Anglo-Irish, aren't you? You must be in favor of keeping English rule?"

"On the contrary," she said. "I am fervently opposed to it. I rather think that your personality is like mine—we don't like to be ruled by anybody. But if anybody's going to rule us, it should be our own people, with our own interests at heart. As for being Anglo-Irish—my family has lived in Ireland for four hundred years. I think that makes us Irish, don't you? And my thinking is this: Ireland could have been a prosperous country—should be a prosperous country. But we have been brought to our knees by unfair taxes and restrictions, by the English siphoning off all the best in Irish produce for themselves, and by the restrictions placed on Catholics. We have been turned into second-class subjects in our own land. Most of our people are too cowed to speak for themselves. They need people like me and Cullen to stir them into action."

"So you are prepared to risk everything."

"If need be."

"I wish I had your kind of zeal burning inside me," I said. "I have a strong sense of justice, but I don't think I'd risk my life to change the government in my country."

"We all have our own paths to follow," Grania said. "I wouldn't force anyone into following mine." She got up. "Come. Let us go up to your room and make sure that you have everything that you need. I'm afraid it's no use trying to communicate with Francoise unless you speak French."

We had reached the dining room door when an elderly man appeared. "Are you done with your breakfast, my lady?" he asked.

"Quite finished, thank you, Bertie."

She whisked me past him. My heart was beating rather fast.

"My lady?" I stammered. "I didn't realize. I apologize for my rudeness."

"What rudeness?"

"Calling you by your first name."

She laughed merrily. "My dear, within the Sisterhood and the Brotherhood we are all first names, and you are now a sister. Hence you are Molly and I am Grania."

"I thought everyone had to have a nickname."

"My sweet, it's impossible for me to disguise who I am. Everyone in Dublin knows Grania. They think I am a social butterfly, light, flippant, and therefore harmless. It is working wonderfully so far."

With that she took my hand and swept me up to my room. My clothes had been put away and the window was open, letting in good, fresh air with just a tang of salt in it. It was the sort of place where I could have been blissfully happy in other circumstances. At this moment there seemed no way to unclench the tight knot in my stomach.

"Go down to the library and choose reading materials for yourself," she said, "because I do get a lot of visitors and I rather think that you should stay out of sight, just in case."

As we came down the stairs again, the elderly retainer was returning from the front door, bearing a salver. "The post has arrived, m'lady," he said. "Should I take it through to the morning room? There's a letter from Lord Ashburton."

"Oh dear, is there?" A frown crossed her lovely face. "Well, I suppose I had better read it immediately." She took the letters from the salver. I hesitated in the hallway, not sure what was required of me, but she turned as she reached a door and said, "Come, Molly."

I followed her into a bright, uncluttered room with chinz-covered chairs. She went over to a ladies secretary, took out a letter opener, and slit open the envelope. I remained standing near the doorway, not because she had not instructed me to sit down, but because I was trying to recall why the name had been so familiar to me. Someone had used that name recently.

"Who is Lord Ashburton?" I couldn't resist asking.

She looked up, amused. "My husband, of course."

Almost as she said the words, I heard the echo in my head. Sir Toby Conroy at Ormond Hall saying, "She's quite the society lady these days—Lady Ashburton."

I stared at her, trying to piece things together. "You're Toby Conroy's sister," I blurted out.

She looked surprised. "Yes I am. Do you know Toby?"

"I went to your family seat, looking for Mary Ann Burke," I said. "Why didn't you tell me that you knew her?"

There was a long pause and then she said, "That is the Mary Ann you are looking for?"

I nodded. "She was your nursemaid, I believe. She ran off with a groom."

"My Mary Ann? How extraordinary," she said. "You know, it never crossed my mind that we were talking about the same person. I don't think I ever knew her surname—well, servants don't have surnames, do they? And I think I always called her nursie, although I did know her name was Mary Ann. And as to running off with a groom—I had no idea what happened to her. One day she was there and the next day she wasn't, and nanny said I was never to mention her again. I pined for her for quite a while. Are you absolutely sure she was the one who came to Dublin with Terrence Moynihan? I really can't picture my Mary Ann running off with a revolutionary poet."

"Yes, I'm sure," I said.

"Well, now I have a double incentive for sending out my spies to look for her," Grania said. "Rest assured I'll leave no stone unturned. If she's still in Dublin, I'll find her for you. I'd certainly love to see her again myself. I was very fond of her. Now, if you'll excuse me, I have to read my husband's letter."

I wandered over to the window and found that it overlooked an elegant square of tall, Georgian townhouses. Nannies were pushing prams, tradesmen were making deliveries and ladies were out for a morning stroll. It all looked very jolly and very normal. I wondered what would happen if I just went to the front door of the house and then walked away. Would they come after me? Would I be allowed to leave the country?

Then, of course, I reminded myself that I wasn't about to leave Liam and Joseph in the lurch. I perched on an upright cane chair and picked up a magazine. I had scarcely opened it before I heard a gasp from Grania.

"Oh, dear God," she said.

"What's wrong?"

"Just about everything," she said. "Gerald is coming home this weekend. He's bought a filly and he wants to see her race. He's sending the servants ahead, and he'll be arriving on Friday, damnation."

I looked at her with interest. She was the only woman I had heard swear, apart from those in the gutter who knew no better.

She looked up at me, frowning. "That's certainly put a spoke in our wheel, hasn't it? I won't be able to hold any more meetings at the house, and you and Cullen certainly won't be able to stay here any longer. I suppose I could spirit you away to our place in the country, but you'd be no use to the cause stuck miles from the nearest railway. I'll have to work fast to find a new place to hide you—and I have a luncheon engagement today too. And the Daughters of Erin are supposed to be meeting here tomorrow evening. Let us just pray that Gerald's servants don't make it back here too quickly, or we'll be in a real soup." She got up. "I'd better go and wake Cullen. He's a notoriously late sleeper. He'll have to help me decide what to do next."

A few minutes later Cullen came stomping downstairs, unshaven and rather disheveled. I must say his current appearance truly made him look the part of the revolutionary and all the more glamorous in my eyes.

"I thought you said he was in London for the winter season," he complained. "You were sure of it."

"He usually is. How was I to know he'd take it into his head to buy a racehorse and then want to see it perform in Ireland before he had it shipped across to England?"

"Well, there's nothing we can do about it, I suppose," Cullen said, "but it's the most infernal nuisance. I must be gone right away. I can't risk anyone seeing me here."

"We have a couple of days before the first of the servants arrive, I'm sure," Grania said. "I have a luncheon appointment, but after it I'll put my thinking cap on and decide where you could hole up."

"Can't you cancel the luncheon?" Cullen growled. "It is rather important, Grania. Not only my life, but the fate of the Brotherhood does hang in the balance."

Grania laughed. "My darling, always so dramatic," she said. "You did write the most lovely plays. I wish you hadn't stopped." She went over to him and stroked his cheek. "I can't do anything that would set people talking, you know that. If Grania doesn't go to lunch with her friends, they'll be dropping by at the house to find out why. I promise you'll be hidden away by the time Gerald gets here. Now do go and shave—you look like a South American bandit."

❧ Twenty-six ❧

I wasn't privy to the undercover maneuverings that were going on, but I had my bags packed and ready to leave should I be required to do so at a moment's notice. I reported this to Cullen when I encountered him in the drawing room.

"It's not quite as desperate for you, Molly," Cullen said. "If necessary you could stay on for a few days. Grania is always showing hospitality to friends of friends, and I'm sure she'll come up with a perfect story for you."

"But it would be wiser if I weren't seen," I said, "since I closely resemble my brothers."

He looked at me long and hard. "As you say, it would be wiser, although the resemblance is only superficial, mainly in the hair. Your face is ten times more handsome."

I didn't quite know how to handle that and felt myself blushing. I hadn't been aware that he had noticed me as anything more than a nuisance and potential spy. He came across the room and stood close to me. Then he put a hand on my shoulder and bent his head toward me. For a moment I thought he was going to kiss me, but then he said in a low voice, "Oh, and one more thing, Molly, while we're alone. Grania will be holding a meeting of her Daughters of Erin here tomorrow night. Obviously she'll want you to attend. Not all those women can be trusted, so don't say anything you might regret later. Not a word about your brothers. You're a friend of the family, visiting from New York. That should suffice. Got it?"

"Yes," I said, "but I thought—"

"Grania is sometimes too trusting," he muttered. "It may be our downfall."

He glanced up as Grania came into the room.

"I hope you're not trying to seduce our little Molly, Cullen," she said.

"I was merely giving her some fatherly advice, if you must know, Grania," he said.

"I know you too well, my sweet." She flashed him a challenging smile.

"One must have some pleasures in life," Cullen said. "God knows I've given up just about everything else."

"You keep an eye on him, Molly," she said to me. "He's not to be trusted."

"On the contrary," Cullen replied. "I am to be trusted in all things that matter, and Molly is quite safe with me."

He withdrew his hand from my shoulder, gave me a friendly pat, and left the room. I watched him go with just a pang of regret.

Cullen disappeared later that day. When I asked about him, Grania merely shrugged. "He decided he should be gone before our Daughters of Erin meet tomorrow. I don't think he quite trusts us. And he certainly underestimates us. He thinks us to be a gaggle of well-intentioned women whose only function should be charitable acts, but with no place in Irish politics or republican struggles."

"But obviously your group is involved in such struggles," I said. "It was your Queen Mab who received word of the shipment of rifles."

"The Brotherhood is closely watched," Grania said. "Of course, the English aren't quite sure that the Brotherhood, per se, has resurrected itself, but they watch all those with ties to the republican movement. Hence it makes sense to give a greater role to us women."

"But aren't the Daughters of Erin watched too? They are not in any way a secret organization, are they? I met a young woman the other day who talked openly about your group and invited me to a meeting."

"Ah, but that's the beauty of it." Grania smiled. "Our lovely foundress, Maude Gonne, whom you saw in the play the other night, had visions of an organization of women who could better social conditions in Ireland and further the spread of Irish culture. An exemplary ideal. We all support it. But within the group there are those of us who work more militantly for the republican cause. Only *we* know who we are. Our very existence depends upon utter secrecy. We use our noms de guerre—"

I nodded. "Your leader, Queen Mab."

"Most of our members have no idea who Queen Mab is. It is essential that she remain in the background and secret or she would be no use at all."

The way she smiled made a sudden thought cross my mind. Grania herself was Queen Mab! I remembered Cullen teasing her about wanting to take the place of Queen Victoria. Supplanting one queen with another. I decided to be a keen observer at the upcoming meeting. At that moment it seemed all like a rather exciting game. Then, of course, I remembered that it wasn't a game at all: my brother was under a death sentence and so was Cullen if he was caught. Maybe so were we all.

The following evening the drawing room was filled with chairs and women started to arrive. Among the early arrivals was Maud Gonne, looking even more beautiful without her stage makeup. She embraced Grania and went around the room, shaking hands. I was introduced as a visitor from America and passed over without a flicker of interest. The room began to fill. I recognized the two bluestockings from the Gaelic League. Then Alice Wester came in. Alice's face lit up when she saw me.

"Miss Delaney—Mary. How delighted I am to see you here. We lost each other in the crowd at the theater the other night, and I was afraid you would have no way of hearing about our meeting. And now here you are. Let me introduce you to some of our sisters." She slipped her arm through mine and led me around the room. It was all on a first-name basis and I had no way of knowing whether those were true first names or nicknames—noms de guerre, as Grania had put it. The two bluestockings were Maeve and Tara, both important names in Irish history. Then I was presented to a bevy of older ladies and recognized my protector from the Gaelic League—the severe-looking matron in black who had made room for me beside her and worried about my going home alone. Wouldn't she be interested to hear that her fears had been justified, and I had been kidnapped?

"So you made it to our meeting," she said. "Splendid. What was your name again?"

"This is Mary," Alice Wester said. "She's visiting us from America. Maybe she can go home and start a chapter of our organization over there."

"I believe we already have women working for the cause in America," one of the other matrons said. "Don't we, Mrs. Boone?"

"I believe we do," my matron agreed. "I'm sure we could put Mary in touch with similarly minded women when she goes home, if she finds that she is attracted to the promotion of Irish culture and the improvement of women."

"I'd certainly be interested," I said, not at all sure that I was telling the truth, but wanting to be accepted at this point.

Grania clapped her hands for attention and introduced Maud Gonne. Maud gave a long, impassioned speech about heroines of Irish history and how we were all called upon to be heroines and to keep our history alive. One of the bluestockings followed with a speech on the shocking infant mortality rate in the slums and how we could help improve sanitary conditions there. Tea and biscuits were handed around. It was a very civilized evening, probably similar to evenings repeated in women's institutes all over the country. I half expected to be instructed on how to make pickles next. I looked from one earnest, innocent face to the next and found it hard to believe that some of these women hid guns, ran messages, and were on the front lines of the fight for freedom.

We were still in the middle of tea, biscuits, and gossip when Grania's elderly retainer came in. "I'm sorry to disturb you, m'lady," he said, "but you have visitors."

"Visitors? Not my husband already?"

"No, m'lady. Your brother and his fiancée and Captain Hartley. I've put them in the library."

I thought my heart might leap right out of my mouth. So my fears were justified. Sir Toby Conroy's fiancée was indeed one of the Hartleys and her brother was really my archenemy. I looked around the room, trying to see if there was anywhere for me to hide. There were heavy drapes at the windows. There was a piano in the corner, but I had thirty or so women who would notice one of their members crawling under a piano. My one hope was that I'd be overlooked amid a sea of female faces.

"Didn't you tell my brother that I was otherwise occupied at the moment?" Grania said.

"I did tell him that you already had visitors, your ladyship, but Sir Toby asked me to tell you that they had just arrived in town and Miss Henrietta had set her heart on greeting you immediately and introducing you to her brother."

"I see." Grania looked around at us and raised her eyes in frustration. "This is so inconvenient. Please excuse me, ladies. My brother can be most tiresome. I sincerely hope they are not expecting to stay here."

She swept out of the room. My heart was still pounding violently. If Sir Toby and the Hartleys were really going to stay in the house, then I was doomed. Grania would have no reason not to introduce me as a friend from America. My one chance would be to leave with the rest of the women. Maybe Alice Wester could put me up for the night, if I could give her a reasonable explanation for my desire to escape. I tried to think of one but my brain wouldn't work.

"We should probably leave, ladies," Maud Gonne said. "The meeting was almost over, wasn't it, and I don't want to deprive Grania of the chance of seeing her brother."

She started to put on her cape. Others followed suit. I stood there, not knowing what to do. If I followed them out into the night, wearing no outer clothing, someone was sure to notice. But I couldn't stay where I was either. My knees were weak at the thought that Grania, being of a social nature, might well bring in her brother and the Hartleys and introduce them to the group.

If they were in the library, I might be able to slip up the stairs without being noticed. But that would just be a temporary respite. I'd then have to make it down the stairs again, with my bags. I could hear Grania's voice floating across the marble entrance hall.

"But of course, darlings. On any other occasion . . ."

"I'll go and tell Grania we are leaving," Maud said. "Until next time then, ladies. Keep up the good work. On with the fight."

"Miss Delaney," Mrs. Boone tapped my arm, "could I ask you to take my arm and help me down the front steps? I'm afraid my eyesight is not what it was and I am in perpetual fear of falling."

"Of course," I said.

She slipped her arm through mine. "I'm most grateful to you, Miss Delaney," she said in a louder voice and patted my hand.

Then we were crossing the front hall with the rest of the women. Down the front steps. Out onto the pavement of the square. Maud Gonne was climbing into a waiting carriage. Hansom cabs were cruising past, hoping for fares. Mrs. Boone waved a brolly, and one came to a halt beside us.

"Would you be a dear and assist me aboard?" she said. "Can I drop you off somewhere?"

"I was staying here with Lady Ashburton," I said, "but I rather fear there won't be room for me if her brother has now arrived."

"And her husband is due home any minute, is he not?" she said. "Definitely an overcrowded household. I tell you what—you're welcome to come and stay with me, if you don't mind considerably less grand conditions. I could share with you my collection of Irish poetry. I'm rather proud of it. And you'd bring some youth and gaiety into a lonely old woman's life. What do you say?"

"I would like that very much," I said. "Do you think I could I come with you right away?"

"I was going to suggest the very same thing. Hop in." She patted the seat beside her.

I needed no second urging. "I'm afraid my belongings are up in my bedroom at the house." I glanced at the door.

"Here, take my shawl," she said. "It's not more than a ten-minute ride. You'll not freeze to death traveling half a mile."

The cabby cracked his whip and we were off. I had escaped.

❧ Twenty-seven ❧

I must say I compliment you. You're quick on the uptake, I'll say that for you," Mrs. Boone said as the cab left the square. "Either that or you're a thoroughly nice, simple country girl who was brought up to help old women."

I turned to look at her. Her face in the darkness looked as if it was made of white marble, surrounded by all that black. Her expression was still serene. How much should I tell her, I wondered.

"I should have let Lady Ashburton know I was leaving," I said. "She'll worry about what has happened to me."

"I shouldn't think so for a second," she said. "It was all arranged."

"That I was to go with you?"

"Exactly. You had to be out of the house before the husband came home, and you certainly didn't want to be caught there by Grania's half-wit of a brother, who can't be trusted to hold his tongue about anything."

"I don't know how much you've been told," I said, "but my name's not really Mary Delaney and . . ."

She patted my knee. "Never reveal anything about yourself unless you have to. That is rule number one for survival. I'll call you Mary and you call me Mrs. Boone."

"Very well, Mrs. Boone," I said. I leaned back against the leather upholstery as a sigh of relief escaped from my lips. I was in good hands, so it seemed. All would be well.

We came out onto the quay and were trotting along the bank of the Liffy, retracing the route I had walked on my arrival from the station.

"Adam and Eve, you said?" The cabby called down to us.

"That is correct," Mrs. Boone replied.

"Here you are then, my dear."

"Thank you, but I am not your dear," Mrs. Boone said. "Nor is it likely that I will ever be your dear."

I heard the cabby laughing. The horse was brought to a halt outside a tall building. The cabby came around to help us down. I looked up at the building with surprise. "It's a church," I said.

"That's right. St. Francis. One moment while I pay the cabby, then we'll get you inside. The wind is quite raw tonight."

"What is Adam and Eve then?" I asked.

"The old nickname for the church, dating back to the days before emancipation, when Catholic worshippers would have to enter the chapel through the Adam and Eve pub. Follow me, please, and watch your step."

I noticed that she set off at a good pace, and didn't need any help on the uneven surface of the path to the church.

"I'm to be housed in a church?" I called after her. It looked dark, devoid of life, and a little frightening. Thoughts did go through my mind that I'd become a liability and was to be dispatched.

"In the rectory," she said. "I am the housekeeper."

"But what about the priests?"

"There is only one priest. He is a very spiritual man, lost in his devotions and notices very little," she said. "Besides, he now suffers badly from rheumatics and can't make the stairs. You'll be in the attic and quite safe. Watch your step here."

She led me around the side of the church and into a tall brick building beyond.

"He goes to bed early, so that he's up to say six o'clock mass," Mrs. Boone whispered to me. "But try to go quietly up the stairs."

The hallway was dimly lit, but warm and smelled of baking. Up a long flight of steps we went, then across a landing and up a second flight. These steps were uncarpeted and creaked alarmingly.

"Here we are." She pushed open a door. "Wait while I light the lamp. There's no gas up here." I heard a match strike and then the hiss of a lamp and the room was bathed in warm light. It was Spartan, to be sure, with an iron-framed bed, a chest of drawers and a marble-topped table on which stood a basin and water jug. The ceiling sloped and there was one small window

"It's not the Ritz, but you'll be comfortable enough," she said. "Chamber pot under the bed. I'll bring you up hot water in the morning and your breakfast while Father is saying mass. Fortunately there are masses at six, seven, and eight on weekdays. You'll have to make do with one of my nightgowns tonight. It will be large for you, but it will keep you warm."

"Thank you," I said. "You're very kind."

"Just doing my Christian duty," she said. "I'm one of the members of our group with no family and sufficient space, so of course I volunteered to house a sister in distress. Good night, now. And please stay put and don't come downstairs until I tell you to."

She closed the door behind her. I undressed in the light of the lamp, then turned it out and climbed into bed. The darkness was absolute. I lay there, listening to the wind in the chimney, the tooting of tug boats farther down the river, feeling cold and abandoned and fervently wishing myself back in Patchin Place, in my own little house with Sid and Gus across the alleyway. I even wished that Daniel was here. I wanted to feel his strong arms around me, my head resting on his shoulder. I had thought that having a husband would be a nuisance but now it seemed like a good idea to have a man to take care of me. It even seemed like a good idea to give up this crazy notion of being a lady detective and settle down to bake scones and do embroidery—which will tell you what an emotional mood I was in that night.

I had almost drifted off to sleep when I heard a noise. It was the slightest of creaks on a floorboard, but it was enough to jerk me instantly awake and alert. Mrs. Boone had said that nobody ever came up here. I couldn't believe that she'd be coming up again herself just to check on me. I lay there, every muscle tense, holding my breath, and heard nothing more. I told myself that it was probably a house cat, prowling for mice and had just settled down again when another floorboard creaked, this time closer to my door. I was up and out of bed in a second. The darkness was almost complete. I could just make out the shape of the window, the whiteness of the counterpane on the bed, but nothing more. I stood beside the bed, heart pounding and listening.

Again there was silence. Then slowly my door began to open. I was too frightened even to scream. I kept telling myself that it was only Mrs Boone, come to see if I was sleeping. I sensed a large presence rather than saw it, and then I heard the sound of the door shutting, trapping me in the room with the person, whoever it was. Not Mrs. Boone then. Definitely not. I tried to remember where the table with the water jug was positioned. A good dousing with cold water would surprise any intruder enough for me to make it to the door and escape down the stairs. I wondered where Mrs. Boone slept and if I dared to call for help.

I heard a muttered curse as the intruder blundered into the bedside table. Definitely a male curse. But he was still standing between me and the door. Then a hissing noise and a match was struck. He looked up and saw me. I let out a scream. He gasped. The match went flying and was extinguished.

In a flash he had grabbed me, twisting my arm behind my back and clamping a big hand over my mouth.

"Don't try to move or scream or I'll break your neck," he said calmly. "All right. Out with it. Who are you?"

I recognized the voice. "Cullen?" I tried to say through his fingers. "It's Molly Murphy. Let go of me."

He released me, struck another match and lit the lamp.

"Jesus, Mary, and Joseph," he exclaimed, looking at me standing there in a voluminous nightgown. "What the devil do you think you're doing?"

"More to the point, what do you think you are doing, barging into a lady's bedroom in the middle of the night."

"Lady's bedroom? This is my room. I'm staying here."

"Mrs. Boone put me in here. If you don't believe me, I suggest you go down and wake her."

"But she put me—wait a second," he said. He carried the lamp to the door, held it up on the landing, then looked back at me. "She put me in the room next door," he said sheepishly. "I've never had to find my way to my door in the darkness before. I must have lost my way. I apologize profusely."

"Apology accepted," I said.

He started to laugh. "I had no idea there was anyone else staying here. She told me I'd be quite private and quite safe up here. I've just got back from a meeting."

"You scared the living daylights out of me," I managed to say.

"I scared the daylights out of you? My dear girl, the feeling was mutual, I can assure you."

"You're lucky I couldn't locate something to bash you over the head with," I said. "Or you'd be lying there unconscious right now."

"Would I now? I think I might have underestimated you, Miss Murphy." He was still smiling. Then he became grim again. "I tell you what I thought—that the English had located me and sent someone to bump me off," he said. "When did you get here?"

"A couple of hours ago," I said. "Grania's brother arrived so Mrs. Boone spirited me home with her."

"She thinks on her feet, our Mrs. Boone." Cullen nodded with approval.

"And she didn't tell me anyone else was staying up here. In fact, she said I'd be quite safe and private."

"She was told not to reveal my whereabouts to anyone and was leaving it up to me as to whether I made my presence known or not. Normally I'd have been asleep by this time, but something came up at the last minute and I had to go out to meet some fellows." He looked at me and grinned. "So it seems that for the second time we're sharing a domicile, Miss Murphy."

I must have been hugging my arms to myself, suddenly shivery. He noticed. "I've a bottle of Jamesons in my room. I think we could both do with a drink after that little scare. Hold up the lamp; I'll go and find it."

He came back with the bottle, and a glass into which he poured a generous tot for me.

"I don't really drink spirits," I protested.

"Go on. Drink it up. It will do you good." He pressed the glass into my hands. I drank, coughed, and drank again. "This little encounter was good for us both," he said. "From now on we'll be on our toes, and we'll need to be. The enemy is not as stupid as they look. We must expect for plans to go wrong and not to panic."

"You're talking about the prison break," I said.

"That's exactly what I'm talking about," he said. "We've set a date. October Twenty-second. Just over a week away."

"Will you be wanting me to help out in any way?"

"We're counting on it," he said. "In fact, the whole plan depends upon it."

"Doing what, exactly?"

"I can't tell you yet." He put a hand on my shoulder. "You'd better get back to sleep, before Mrs. Boone hears us talking up here and jumps to the wrong kind of conclusions."

He started for the door, then turned back and gave me a wicked smile. For the second time in one night I found it hard to get to sleep.

❧ Twenty-eight ❧

The next morning Mrs. Boone brought me up a bowl of porridge and some rashers of bacon.

"I've sent a boy to fetch your things," she said. "They should be here any minute. Did you sleep well?"

"Apart from bumping into Cullen Quinlan in the middle of the night, and nearly dying of fright," I said dryly. "Why didn't you warn me he was staying in the next room?"

"I wasn't sure whether Mr. Quinlan wanted that fact known. And it must never be mentioned to anyone but me," she said. "Even Lady Ashburton doesn't know where Mr. Quinlan has gone. The authorities must have no whiff of the fact that he is in Dublin until the event. Many lives depend on it."

I glanced up at her. She was calmly laying out a knife, fork, and spoon onto the marble-topped table.

"Are you the one they call Queen Mab?" I asked.

"Queen Mab?" She looked amused. "The only Queen Mab I've heard of is the queen of the fairies, and I don't think I have the build, my dear. Think of the size wings you'd need to lift this body off the ground." She chuckled. "Now don't let your breakfast get cold."

I ate then went over to the window, admiring the glimpses of the river and the Four Courts between the church roof and the next buildings, but then I wondered how long I'd be expected to stay up here. At least Grania's house had a grand library and Grania herself was good company, as was Cullen. Would he be sharing my solitude, I wondered, and was rather surprised by the quickening of my pulse I felt at such a thought.

Rubbish, I said to myself. The last thing in the world I wanted at this moment was to develop an attraction for an older revolutionary. What I really wanted was to catch the next boat home, to be back in my old life having croissants and coffee with Sid and Gus, unexpected visits from Ryan, all the excitement of life in New York. Oh, and Daniel, of course.

I heard the clip-clop of hooves as a carriage went past and spotted a constable walking along the far bank of the river. Would he hear me if I opened the window and yelled to him? Which made my thoughts turn to Inspector Harris. What must he be thinking of me now? By vanishing without a trace, had I again become his number-one suspect in Rose McCreedy's murder? I wondered whether his investigation was still proceeding, whether any new details had come to light when the *Majestic* had docked again in Queenstown.

The constable disappeared between the buildings, and I turned away from the window. It was the waiting and uncertainty and worry that I found so hard to take—knowing that I was to be part of a dangerous plot, knowing that my brother was destined to be hanged if we didn't rescue him, knowing that I might still be a suspect in a murder and that Justin Hartley was in the same city as me. I felt as if I was walking down a dark tunnel and there was no escape, no turning back. Cullen, I could sense, was excited as well as apprehensive. He was ready to strike that next blow against the British. There was nothing I wanted to do less. All I was concerned about was saving my brother and then getting away from here as rapidly as possible. It was an agony being cooped up with too much time to think. I wished I had asked Mrs. Boone whether I was to stay hidden all the time or whether I could go out for an occasional walk.

That question was answered later that day. There came a tap on my door. I expected it was Mrs. Boone, come to collect my lunch tray—a good, hearty Irish stew, by the way, followed by stewed apples and custard. I opened the door and saw Cullen standing there.

"Get your coat. We're going for a walk," Cullen said.

"Has something happened?" I asked nervously.

"No, I just felt like going for a walk, and I hate walking alone." He helped me on with my coat.

"All right, if you think it's wise," I said.

"We can't be wise all the time," he answered. "Tie a scarf over your head so that your hair won't be so noticeable."

We crept down the stairs together and then out into bright sunshine.

"I was going mad, stuck up there in that poky little room," he said, as we came out of the churchyard and crossed to the Liffy. "I expect you were too."

"I was," I said. "I was brought up in the outdoors. I like my freedom."

"And yet you choose to live in New York, which is all buildings and no outdoors," he said.

"Oh no. There is plenty of good walking in New York. Central Park, for example. You can get lost in Central Park and feel you are in the middle of the country. And there is splendid walking along the waterfront, down at the Battery. I have Washington Square just a stone's throw from my house."

"You sound as if you have a good life there," he said.

"I do."

"Then I hope you get back to it safely," he said. "And is a young man part of this good life?"

"There is a man," I said slowly, "but I'm still not sure if he's destined to be my partner for life. There are—complications."

"But you miss him?"

"Yes," I said. "I definitely miss him."

He sighed. "I envy you that."

"I'm sure you have lady friends a plenty," I teased. "Oona Sheehan still pines for you, so I hear."

"Ah yes. Dear Oona," he said. "That relationship was doomed to failure."

"How so?"

He smiled. "She wanted a lap dog, a devoted admirer who wrote her love notes every day. I could never be anyone's lap dog."

"I can see that."

I looked at him and our eyes met.

"I rather suspect that you're not too great at the lap dog business either," he said.

I laughed. "Absolutely hopeless. I'm too strong willed, I'm afraid."

"I like that in a woman," he said.

"So where are we going?" I asked, because the subject was becoming uncomfortable. "Just for a stroll to stretch our legs?"

"That's right. A nice, middle-class couple out for a stroll. You may take my arm if you like." He didn't wait for an answer but slipped my hand through his arm, patting it into place. "It's been a long time since I've done this. It's rather nice."

We passed the Guinness Brewery. At Kingsbridge Station the road left the river bank and followed the railway line inland.

"Should we cross to the north bank of the river here?" I asked. "We seem to be going into a less pleasant area."

"We do indeed," Cullen said. "In fact that building to our right, beyond the railway, is one of my least favorite in Ireland. That's the Clancy Barracks, my girl—home of a regiment of Inniskilling Dragoons. The might of King Edward, just waiting to keep the peace."

"Then why go this way?" I tugged on his arm. "Let's turn around."

"Because there is something I want to show you," he said. We walked on until we came to a road junction and there on the other side loomed the grim façade of a brick building. It was tall, with hardly any windows, and an iron fence around it.

"Now there's an ugly building if ever I saw one," I said.

"That, my dear, is Kilmainham Gaol," Cullen said. "I wanted you to see it, to see what we were up against. And I also wanted to take a closer inspection for myself. A lone man—well, he could be noticed. But a happy young couple like ourselves—nobody is going to look at us twice."

"So you brought me out as your decoy," I said.

He laughed. "I suppose you could put it that way."

"Nice little stroll indeed," I said, and attempted to withdraw my arm.

"You need to study it too," he said. "Let us cross the road and look at it from the other side."

"It looks formidable," I said. "Only one entrance and no windows at ground level. I don't see how anybody could break in."

"You are going to get us in, my sweet," he said, and patted my hand again. "It's all up to you."

It was in solemn mood that we walked home again, neither of us speaking, but lost in our thoughts. That night we ate supper together in Cullen's room, shared the bottle of Jameson's, and laughed, the grim task ahead for the moment forgotten.

I saw nothing of Cullen the next day, or the day after that. Mrs. Boone brought me food and I thought it wise not to ask questions. I tried not to think about that jail and what possible part I might have to play. I tried not to think about my little brother, shut up in a cell without light or open air. I had to help rescue him, whatever the ultimate cost.

The next afternoon Mrs. Boone came up to my room. "I've a favor to ask," she said. "There's a message needs to be delivered right away, and Father is holding a meeting of the Parish Council, so they'll need me to serve their teas. Would you be kind enough to take it for me?"

"Yes, I'd be happy to," I said.

She handed me a slim envelope. "There's a bookshop on Grafton Street. If you drop it off with the proprietor there—he's an older man with white hair—and tell him it comes from Mrs. Boone, he'll know what to do with it."

"I can do that," I said.

"I've a cape with a hood," she said. "Maybe it's better if you're not seen or recognized."

I came downstairs and she handed me a heavy Irish tweed cape. I put it on and pulled the hood over my head.

"Come straight back, won't you," she said.

"Don't worry. I will."

She let me out of the front door. I heard her call, "Coming, Father. Just been giving those old clothes to a poor, destitute woman."

The wind hit me full in the face as I came out to the Liffy and I was glad of that warm cape and hood. I went along bent forward against the wind and almost ran into one of the benches along the riverside. As it was I banged my shin and let out an exclamation, making the man sitting on the bench look up. Recognition dawned, and his face lit up in a big smile.

"Miss Delaney! I am so glad to meet you again."

"Oh, Mr. Fitzpatrick," I stammered. I had forgotten all about him. "How do you do?"

"All the better for seeing you, Miss Delaney," he said, still beaming at me. "When you didn't appear for our little assignation on Tuesday, I feared you had left the city without telling me."

"Assignation?"

"You had promised to come to the races with me, remember? I had to go alone and had the most infernal bad luck all afternoon. You would have been my one bright spark in the day and cheered my gloomy mood, I am sure. As it was, I came home in deepest depression."

"I'm so sorry," I said. "I met friends of the family unexpectedly and got taken off to their place."

"You must come and have dinner with me," he said. "I sail home for New York shortly."

"I told you, I am currently staying with friends."

"But surely your friends won't object to your having dinner with a charming young man like myself," he said, "or is there a jealous male among the friends who is likely to challenge me to a duel?"

"There may be," I said, and laughed.

"I do believe you are turning me down flat," he said. "Ah well. I can handle rejection as well as the next guy, I suppose, but may I not walk with you at least?"

"I'm only going on an errand for an elderly friend," I said. "Nowhere exciting."

"Maybe I find your company exciting," he said. "Whither shall this errand lead us?"

"Nowhere you'd want to go," I said, thinking quickly. "Some hair pins, various medicinal preparations, and face cream, some crochet yarn, and a new novel to read. Such are the ways elderly ladies fill their days. She doesn't go out much any more."

"Perhaps she would welcome a visit from a young buck like myself," he said. "I've been told I have a way with elderly ladies."

"I really don't think so," I said. "She's not that kind of elderly lady."

"They all are in the end. A few words of flattery and flirtation from a handsome young man like myself, and I can have them positively eating out of my hand."

"This one would be biting your hand, I can promise you," I said. His smugness was beginning to annoy me. He was clearly brought up to privilege, never had to do a day's work in his life, and thought that he was God's gift to women. I decided that my initial reaction to him of distrust and dislike had been well-founded.

"Very well, Mr. Fitzpatrick," I said. "You can come with me to buy hair pins and face cream if you like, but then I must take my leave of you."

"You are being a spoil sport, Miss Delaney," he said grouchily. "You know I couldn't bear standing around in a chemist's shop while you ladies discuss the merits of various face creams. I shall accept my rejection like a man and do the various chores I've been putting off—like visits to my own relatives."

He touched his hat to me and I watched him go with relief. I had been trying to think how I could pass across a message with the annoying Mr. Fitzpatrick breathing down my back. "Pompous ass," I muttered myself. Our assignation, how dramatic, making it sound like a secret tryst.

I walked on. The word continued to annoy me. Assignation. Then I realized where I had last heard it: spoken by the executioner at the costume party on board the *Majestic*. "We have a confirmed assignation, you and I," he had said, and I had laughed it off. But some time that evening Rose had been murdered. I paused and looked back. Surely the oafish Mr. Fitzpatrick couldn't have been the executioner? Hadn't he denied even being at the ball? I took this one stage further: so was it also possible he had killed Rose, thinking he was killing Oona Sheehan? But why? I tried to remember my encounter with him, when I was disguised as Oona. He had been remarkably restrained and correct, if I remembered rightly, and hoped he would have a chance to run into me in Dublin. Not like the enthusiastic puppy love of an Artie Fortwrangler or some of those other men who had tried to make it to my door.

I continued without incident to the bookshop, waited until it was devoid of customers, and handed over the note. The old man took it gravely.

"More book requests from Mrs. Boone, I'll wager," he said. "Doesn't that woman have anything to do but read?"

I came out, put my hood over my head and made my way back to the rectory. As I was about to cross the road someone came running toward me. "Miss Delaney. Wait up!"

Oh no. Mr. Fitzpatrick again.

"We seem destined to bump into each other this afternoon," he said. "Here I was, minding my own business, and suddenly you show up again. You see, you can't escape from it. It is fate that we are to be together."

"What are you doing here, Mr. Fitzpatrick?" I asked. Now I was no longer feeling annoyed, but distinctly uneasy. I sensed that he might have been waiting here for me to return. I asked myself why he was pursuing me so relentlessly and couldn't come up with an explanation. Certainly not for my beauty or my prospects.

"Paying a courtesy call on my aged aunt," he said. "And what are you doing? Going into the church to say a quick prayer?"

"Your aunt? Mrs. Boone is your aunt?"

"Absolutely. Don't tell me you know her too? That's the most amazing coincidence. Dublin really is a small place after all."

Now I really was unsure of myself. Another idea was forming in my head. Was Mr. Fitzpatrick who he made himself out to be, or was he really one of us? Had he been sent to make sure the guns crossed the Atlantic safely? No matter, I decided. Mrs. Boone would dispatch him quickly enough if he was an imposter. I tapped on the front door, found it unlocked, and let myself in, with Mr. Fitzpatrick breathing down my neck.

"Mrs. Boone?" I called from the entrance hall.

"In here, my dear. In the kitchen, to your left. Come on in."

"I've someone with me," I called. "He says he's your nephew."

"My nephew? Really?"

She emerged from the kitchen, wiping floury hands on a large apron. "Now let me take a look at the young man who says he is my nephew."

"Aunty." Mr. Fitzpatrick opened his arms wide in a dramatic gesture. "All these years I've been looking forward to meeting you."

"I'm afraid you've got the wrong person," Mrs. Boone said. "I have no nephews. I was an orphan. So I suggest you run off and go to find your true aunt."

"But you are my true aunt," he said. "I wasn't sure until I saw you, but now I'm absolutely certain I've got it right. Your eyes, you see. The way they slant down at the sides and something about the way you carry your head. It reminds me of my dear departed mother and of my Uncle Tommy."

"Uncle Tommy?" She was still standing in the kitchen doorway, hands on hips and frowning.

"Tommy Burke," he said. "You are Mary Ann Burke, are you not?"

❧ Twenty-nine ❧

Mrs. Boone glared at me. "What have you been telling him, you foolish girl?"

"Me? I told him nothing, except I was staying with a crotchety old lady who was a friend of the family. I had no idea, not the least idea."

Even as I spoke I realized why I had seen something I deemed to be masculine in her features. It was the strong resemblance to Tommy Burke.

"What do you mean, you hadn't the least idea," Mr. Fitzpatrick said scornfully. "Why else are you here when you were sent by my uncle on a mission to find this woman, Miss Molly Murphy?"

I must have reacted at the mention of my real name because he laughed. "Did you think for a moment I bought that Delaney nonsense? I knew who you were the first time we met—on the deck of the *Majestic* when you were wearing that ridiculous Oona Sheehan wig. Oh yes, I heard all about the stupid idea to trade cabins as well. Oona was dining with my uncle and shared her little plan with him."

"So why didn't you let me know you knew the truth?" I demanded angrily. "Why let me go on making a fool of myself?"

"Isn't that simple to answer? So you would lead me to her—save me the trouble of seeking her out for myself. I've always been a lazy fellow at heart. And a selfish one too, so I'm told. Not willing to share my uncle's fortune with a previously unknown aunt anyway."

I had been observing him closely as he spoke, and I'm afraid that I was realizing many hard truths—things I should have known and recognized before and didn't. He had been the executioner at the fancy dress ball, and what's more, he had been warning me what he planned to do to me. "I am your executioner," he had said. Only he killed Rose by mistake. We had got it all wrong, Inspector Harris and I. The murderer hadn't been out to get Miss Sheehan: I had been his target all along. The easiest course of action for him would have been to prevent me from ever reaching Ireland. I looked at his affable face and knew I had to tread very carefully. I couldn't tell what Mrs. Boone was thinking. She certainly didn't appear to be worried.

"I gave up that name and that identity long ago," she said, "when Terrence died. When Terrence was murdered by the English, I made a vow that I'd devote the rest of my life to the republican cause. So you can go back to America, young man, and tell your family that Mary Ann Burke does not exist."

He actually laughed. "Quite right. Well spoken. That's exactly what I'll tell them. How easy you've made it for me."

He reached into an inside pocket of his overcoat and produced a pistol with one fluid movement. Before either of us could react, he had jammed the gun into my side.

"Into the kitchen, both of you. And you, Mary Ann, shut the door. Is there anyone else in the house?"

"Father Flannigan is in his study, and the Parish Council is expected in half an hour," Mrs. Boone said.

"Too late to be any use to either of you," he said. "By the time they get here, you'll both be dead."

"May I ask why you have developed such a hatred for an aunt you've never even known?" Mrs. Boone asked. She still seemed calm and in control of herself, but then she didn't have the barrel of a gun pressed into her ribs.

"Oh, I don't hate you, dear Auntie," he said. "It's just that my uncle has a large fortune and he was planning to settle the bulk of it on you, if he could find you."

"My family has certainly taken its time to come and reclaim me," she said dryly. "Where were they when I was in the orphanage? When I was in service?"

"Tommy Burke only found out about your existence when his mother was dying and spoke of you in her final rambling." I managed to make the words come out, even though I was finding it hard to breathe evenly. "Before that he had no idea that a baby sister had been left behind when they went to America. He wanted to make amends immediately. That's why he sent me to find you."

"Unfortunately your search came to naught," Fitzpatrick said, giving the gun an extra little jab into my side. "Two women found shot to death in a rectory. And I on the boat to England from where I shall return home. My uncle need never know that I have been in Ireland or ever met you."

"You would kill for money?" Mrs. Boone demanded. "You poor stupid boy. Money is not worth killing for."

"On the contrary, one can only truly lead a happy life with sufficient money and I'm not allowing two meddling women to get in the way of my future happiness."

"And how do you think you are going to carry out this deed?" Mrs. Boone said, still sounding remarkably calm—disinterested almost. "You can't shoot us here, you know. Father Flannigan's study is just across the hall, and he has ears like a hawk. He'd be in here in a second, and he used to a fine boxer in his younger days. And that back door is always kept locked—nasty rusty lock too, so I wouldn't count on making my escape that way. No, you'd have to force your way past Father Flannigan into the hall and risk running into the Parish Council who will be arriving at any moment."

"You—unlock the back door," Fitzpatrick said, no longer sounding the affable oaf. He prodded me forward with the gun.

"I can't," I whimpered, deciding that the helpless female impersonation might serve us best at this stage. "My hands are shaking so badly that I won't be able to do it. I think I might faint."

"Do it!" he shouted.

"I wouldn't yell, if I were you," Mrs. Boone said. "Father Flanningan will be in here, and I don't think that even you can fight off three of us, especially not Father when his temper is roused. But you are hopeless, girl. You go to pieces at the least little thing." And she rolled her eyes upward in a gesture of despair. For a moment I thought she was condemning me. Then I saw the rack hanging in the ceiling. It had a couple of big pots, some ladles and drying cloths on it. With my eyes I traced down the wall to where the cord to raise and lower it was secured. If one of us could only get over to it. If we could lure him to the right spot—

"Here," she said, still sounding annoyed. "Out of the way, I'll open the lock for you, if you must." She pushed us aside and started to wrestle with the lock on the back door. "It hasn't been opened in years," she said. "We keep it locked for safety reasons. Never know who might be prowling along the waterfront. Ah, wait a minute, I can feel it moving just a little."

I glanced at him. His eyes were on her, while she reached up and struggled with the lock. I was close to that cord on the wall, but not close enough to risk it. Somehow I had to get the gun out of my side first.

Suddenly Mrs. Boone spun around, looking surprised. "Father Flannigan!" she exclaimed.

Fitzpatrick turned instinctively to look at the closed door. I gave him an almighty shove and released the cord. A shot fired upward over my head as the rack crashed down onto him, knocking him to the floor in a jumble of cloths and pots. One of the large pots must have struck him with some force because he just lay there stunned for a second— long enough for Mrs. Boone to retrieve the gun.

"Stay where you are, boy," she commanded, when he groaned. "Don't try to move. I should warn you that I'm rather good with one of these things, and you wouldn't be the first man I've killed. Molly, there is twine in that drawer behind you. Tie his wrists together please, then his legs."

He started to struggle as I tied his wrists but I managed to bind them together securely before he could free himself from the rack. Then I started on his legs. By now he was wide awake again, and I had to sit on his legs to keep him from lashing out.

"You stupid old woman!" Fitzpatrick shouted. "What do you think you're going to do now, eh? Do you think I'm afraid of you?"

"Oh, and use one of those pudding cloths for his mouth, please," she continued.

I did a thorough job on this, and we raised the rack off him.

"Well done, Molly," she said. "You performed admirably. I can see now why Cullen thought you were a good choice. A cool head indeed."

"But what are we going to do with him now?" I asked.

"This is most inconvenient," she said. "It comes at a bad time. Go up and see if Cullen—"

As she said the words, the kitchen door opened and Cullen himself entered. "I thought I heard a shot," he said, looking around suspiciously. "Holy Mother, what's going on here?"

"A rather annoying complication," Mrs. Boone said. "This young man followed Molly from New York with the idea of dispatching the both of us. He's my nephew, you see, and he didn't want to share his uncle's fortune."

"We have to get rid of him right away," Cullen said. "I'll send for some of the lads and have him taken out of town."

I looked down at Mr. Fitzpatrick, now lying trussed like a chicken, his eyes staring at us in terror.

"You're not going to kill him?" I blurted out.

"I don't see what option we've got," Cullen said. "He was planning to kill the two of you, wasn't he?"

"Yes, but that's no excuse," I said.

"I can't risk keeping him alive," Cullen said. "What do you think, Mab? My inclination is to have him taken out to sea and then thrown overboard. We've got the boat standing by."

"Yes, but it's not without risk."

"Can't you just put him on a liner and send him home?" I said. "If he knows your men will kill him if he sets foot in Ireland again, that should be deterrent enough."

"Who knows what connections he has?" Cullen said. "He might be in Whitehall's pocket."

"His family fled in the famine," I said. "Mary Ann was the only one left behind. What connections could he possibly have?"

"We can't risk his contacting the authorities under any circumstances," Cullen said firmly. "I'm sorry, but he has to go."

Fitzpatrick whimpered.

Mrs. Boone looked down at him. "I don't like killing unnecessarily," she said, "but we can't just let him walk away. We can't even trust him to make his own way home."

Fitzpatrick made more pathetic noises through the cloth.

"So what's the answer?" Cullen demanded in surly fashion. "Invite him to stay to tea?"

"Tea?" Mrs. Boone put her hand to her mouth. "Lord have mercy, we'll have the Parish Council arriving any minute, wanting their teas. You, Cullen, put the kettle on and Molly, take those scones off the rack and put them on that plate over there. I'd best take the first tray into the dining room right away so they don't come looking for me. The gun's on the table if you need it."

She picked up a tray of cutlery, leaving me and Cullen looking at each other over Fitzpatrick's trussed body.

"It seems the two of you handled yourselves rather well," Cullen said. "I take it he was the one who started out with the gun?"

"Jabbed into my side," I said. "Mrs. Boone certainly knows a thing or two."

"Yes, well she would, wouldn't she, after what she's been through," he said, and I realized that I had got it right after all. He had slipped and called her Mab. Mary Ann Burke. Her own initials all the time: Queen Mab.

She came back in, wiping off her apron. "I'd better change out of this before I take the teapot in," she said. "I'm all covered in flour. That will never do."

Cullen prodded Fitzpatrick with his toe. "You'll be all right for a while if I go to get the lads and set up the transportation?" he asked.

"Oh, we'll manage just fine," Mary Ann said easily. "And I had a grand thought while I was putting out those teacups—Molly will send a cable to my brother in America. She'll tell him what this boy tried to do, and urge him to take appropriate action when the boy gets home."

"What? You're thinking of letting him go home?" Cullen demanded. "Are you out of your senses?"

More noises came from Fitzpatrick's gagged mouth.

"I thought if you were going to France anyway, you could drop him off there. Then it would be up to him where he took his useless hide."

Cullen prodded him with his foot. "You hear that, you pathetic specimen? Your life's being saved for now by these two kind women you tried to kill. But I swear this to you—put one toe out of line and it will give me great pleasure to finish you off."

He slipped out of the back door, which opened quite easily. He had only been gone a minute or two before there were voices in the front hall. Then a tap on the kitchen door. My heart leaped to my mouth, and I tried to stand in front of the trussed Mr. Fitzpatrick. An elderly priest poked his head around the door.

"They've arrived, Mrs. Boone. If you'd be good enough to serve tea in a few minutes?"

"Coming, Father," she said serenely.

As the door closed behind him she caught my eye and smiled. "Deaf as a post *and* blind as a bat," she said.

❧ Thirty ❧

It seemed only a few minutes before some lads arrived and hauled away Fitzpatrick under a tarpaulin on a cart. After he had gone, the tension didn't leave the house with him. It was as if this little detour had reminded us of what lay ahead and thrust all our plans into high gear. At least, not my plans. I knew a lot of planning was going on, both in the house and out of it, but I wasn't included in the details. I knew that Cullen was slipping in and out at odd hours. I heard creaks on the stairs at night, but I was left in the dark. I've never been the most patient person, and I felt that I was about to explode. Finally I waited until I heard the stairboards creaking, and I leaped out to accost Cullen.

"I need you to tell me what's happening," I said.

Cullen shrugged. "Oh, this and that, you know."

At that I did explode. "Look here," I said. "You want me to be part of your absurd scheme. You want me to put my life at risk and yet you tell me nothing? That's just not good enough for me. I'm not a pawn or a puppet, you know. If I'm to put my life at risk, then I need to know what I'm committing to."

Cullen put an arm around me, which, if it was intended to calm me down, had the reverse effect. "Come inside," he said, and led me into his room, closing the door behind us.

"Look, Molly, it's better if you don't know too much," he said gently. "Nobody knows more than he has to. That way, if any of us is captured, we can't be forced to give away information we don't have."

I shuddered. "You don't make it sound very encouraging. What exactly are our chances of success?"

Cullen sighed. "To tell you the truth, I couldn't say, Molly. I've been out of Ireland for ten years and the Brotherhood fell apart during that time. These new lads are untried and pretty much untrained. We have no real explosives expert. Whether they'll hold up under pressure, I couldn't tell you. But we have to go ahead, whatever the chances of success. The only way to achieve independence is to make the English behave badly enough that they stir our countrymen out of apathy and onto our side. And we have to start small."

"So we don't really know whether we can actually rescue my brother?"

"I'd be lying to you if I said I was confident we would succeed, Molly, but I tell you this: we'll give it a damned good try. And if you're having second thoughts about your part in it, then I don't blame you, and I'll think none the less of you if you decided to catch the next boat back to America."

"You'd let me go back to America?" I asked. "I thought I was your prisoner."

"I wouldn't keep you here against your will. I know you can be trusted now, and I know that you're that one element we need to get us into that jail, but I wouldn't force you to do it, Molly. You can go home now if you want to."

"I don't think I'd be allowed to do that, not until Rose McCreedy's murder is officially solved," I said. "But I can't tell Inspector Harris the truth, not while you're holding Mr. Fitzpatrick prisoner anyway."

"It might make things rather inconvenient for us." Cullen gave a wry smile.

That smile didn't make me feel any easier. "You have got Mr. Fitzpatrick safe and sound, haven't you?"

"Oh yes," he said. "As safe as houses."

I didn't know whether to believe him, but there was nothing I could do about it either way. I had done my best for someone who had wished only the worst for me and would have had no compunction about killing me. If he was now feeding the fishes, then it was better I didn't know about it.

"I tell you what," Cullen said. "You can write your inspector a letter telling him what really happened when you're safely home in New York."

"If I'm safely home in New York," I said. "From what you're saying, that fact isn't at all guaranteed."

"I've just told you that you don't have to have any part in this."

"Do you really think I'd be happy sailing home to New York, knowing that I could have helped rescue my brother and chose not to?" I demanded. "I swore I was ready to help you, and I won't go back on my word, however afraid I am."

He reached out and took my hands in his. "You're a grand girl, Molly. I knew that the moment I set eyes on you when you came out fighting from under that horse blanket."

I pulled my hands away because the close contact was making me uneasy.

"Can't you at least tell me what my part in this marvelous scheme of yours will be? I'll not be required to shoot anyone, will I, because I don't think I have it in me to kill another human being."

"Your part is simplicity itself," Cullen said. "You are required to be Joseph Murphy's sister, wanting to see her brother one last time before she sails back to America. They will let you in and that way we'll have someone inside the jail. You're our Trojan horse, Molly."

"How do we know they'll let me in?" I asked.

"Because you'll have a letter from the Home Secretary in London giving his permission."

"The Home Secretary—what makes you think he'll give his permission?"

He smiled. "Because the letter is already written and in our possession. We happen to have an excellent forger at our disposal."

I stared at him. I think until now I suppose I had looked upon this as some kind of lark. Oh, I knew sure enough it was a dangerous lark, but a lark nonetheless. Now there were forged letters from the Home Secretary, and I was the one who was to get them into the jail. I was only just beginning to realize the ramifications of what it might mean if I was caught. Suddenly I was so afraid that I felt physically sick.

"And after I'm in there, what then?" I made myself ask in a calm and level tone.

"We haven't quite agreed on that," Cullen said. "The idea is to over-power the guard and get hold of his keys."

"Jesus, Mary, and Joseph," I muttered. "What is it that you think I am? Queen Maeve and the Blessed Virgin all rolled into one? Now how do you expect me to overpower a guard?"

"You'll have your smelling salts with you, like all delicate young ladies."

"I've never touched smelling salts in my life."

"I'm sure of it," he said, chuckling. "However, this time you'll be carrying smelling salts. Only the bottle will contain chloroform. You'll sprinkle a few drops on your hankie, hold it over the guard's face, and there you are."

"There I am?"

He was still smiling. "You'll be ready to hand over his keys when our lads break in."

"I will, will I?"

"You will. This is what's going to happen. We assume that your brother will be brought to meet you in the interview room near the front entrance. You'll claim to feel faint, use your smelling salts, and overpower the guard. Take off the guard's jacket and put it on your brother. After you've been in there ten minutes, there will be an explosion at the main entrance," he said. "Lots of smoke, confusion. You'll run out shouting for your brother to stop, letting everyone know that he's getting away."

"Why would I do that?"

"Because at that very moment your other brother, Liam, will appear outside the front door, dressed in prison garb. He'll be spotted through the confusion. Everyone will set off to chase him. Some of us will slip in, overpower any other guards we find, and release what prisoners we can."

"And what about Joseph? How will he get out?"

"He'll be wearing a guard's jacket. What would be more natural than for him to run out and give chase with the other guards?"

"And me? How do I get out?" I tried not to let the fear show in my voice.

"You'll make your way to the front entrance and slip out any way you can during the confusion."

"It sounds too simple for words," I said. "Make my way to the front door? Isn't it likely the guards are going to stop me?"

"Then you will play your trump card, my dear. The helpless and terrified female, innocently visiting her brother when this terrible thing happened. You'll cling to their strong arms and beg them to save you."

"I see," I said.

"We'll have transport waiting and a ship ready at the mouth of the Liffy to take us to France."

"To France?"

"Where else do you think we'd go? To London, and book ourselves into the Tower?"

"So Liam and Joseph will be going to France?"

"Hopefully to train and come back home to run future missions for the Brotherhood."

"I see," I said again. I didn't know what else to say. In truth I was numb with shock about the whole thing. I wanted to do this less than anything else in my life so far, and that included fleeing to America after I thought I had killed Justin Hartley. But I didn't want my brother to be hanged either. There was no way out except through Kilmainham Goal.

In the meantime there were several days of waiting ahead of me. Several long days with nothing to do except replay that jail scene over and over in my mind. It was all too fantastic to be real. I felt like an overwound watch spring about to snap. Being cooped up in that attic bedroom was more than I could bear. It rained, washing out all color from the scene outside my window, and adding to the gloom that now hovered over me. My nights were full of disturbed dreams in which a noose figured prominently and that executioner from the ship kept appearing.

I had begun to understand what Daniel had been going through. Now, for the first time I truly appreciated what it was like to fear for one's life, to be cooped up with one's whole future in jeopardy. Of course he had been short tempered and tense. Of course he had tried to prevent me from doing anything dangerous. I should have been more understanding. I had worried about making a future commitment to Daniel, thinking that the fault was his, when in fact it had been my own. Spouses support each other in their hour of need. I pictured his smile, his dark unruly hair, the way he looked at me and wished fervently that he would somehow know I was in danger and come to take me away.

After a couple of days like this, I could stand it no longer. I came down the stairs and let myself into the kitchen. Mary Ann looked up from the table where she was rolling dough.

"Molly, what is it?"

"I can't stand it up there," I said. "I'm going mad. Put me to work. Give me something to do with my hands. If Father asks, I'm a new kitchen maid you're training."

She smiled. "Very well. There's an apron hanging on the hook over there. You can get started cutting out these tarts."

We worked side by side.

"Lady Ashburton inquired about you this morning," she said. "She hoped all was well with you and sent you her best wishes."

"Lady Ashburton? You saw her?"

"At a meeting of a ladies' charity group of which we are both members. Lord Ashburton is now in residence. So are her brother and retinue."

She looked at my face. I tried to keep my expression that of calm disinterest, but her eyes narrowed. "I meant to ask you about that," she said. "You were awfully anxious to leave that house. I could tell at the time. You were looking around the room, checking for escape routes. Why was that?"

"This is entirely between ourselves, and not to get back to Grania or anyone else," I began.

"Naturally. I am not one to gossip, as I'm sure you know by now."

"I didn't wish to encounter Grania's brother. I was educated with his fiancée, Henrietta Hartley, and her brother, Justin Hartley, is my archenemy."

"How so?"

I looked away from her. "He tried to force himself on me when I was a peasant on his estate. I fought him off. He slipped and hit his head on our stove. I thought I had killed him, which was why I fled to America. It turns out I had just gravely injured him—an injury from which he will never fully recover or ever forgive me." There was silence. "There. Now you know."

"Don't worry, my dear," she said. "There is no reason you should ever have to encounter him again. Cullen said you had courage. I—I hope it will all turn out well for you."

"This prison break they are planning," I said softly, "will you be part of it?"

"Oh, good Lord, no." She laughed. "Can you see this bulk climbing in and out of prison cells? I'd be more liability than asset. Besides, I'm more use to everyone alive than dead."

I must have gasped because she corrected herself quickly. "I didn't mean it like that. Cullen has everything well planned. You've a good chance of getting away. He's grown fond of you, you know."

"Yes, I know," I said.

"Then perhaps I should warn you not to become fond of him. I don't want a broken heart to be added to your list of problems."

"I'll try to resist his charm," I said, with a smile.

"Cullen has sacrificed any hope of a normal life for our cause," she said, not smiling in return.

"Just as you have, apparently."

"Oh no, my dear," she said. "My hopes for a normal life died with my Terrence. I found true happiness, you see. Not everyone is lucky enough to meet their soul mate. I made a horrible mistake when I married Kelly. I was bored, stuck out in the country, and he was handsome enough to turn any young girl's head. But he turned out to be a drunken, mindless brute. Then Terrence appeared, and he was everything I'd ever dreamed of in a man—bright, witty, kind, passionate. And I watched him waste away and die of consumption before my eyes after he'd been held in that English goal."

She went back to her work and I to mine. She had found true love, I thought. Would I feel that my life was over if Daniel died? Would he feel that way about me? And what about Cullen? I wondered whether Mary Ann had seen something I had missed, and that I was already just a little bit in love with him.

On October Twenty-first, the day before Kilmainham Goal, Cullen came to my room.

"I came to see how you were holding up," he said.

"Oh, never felt better in my life," I retorted. "Stuck up here, watching the rain, thinking about what it would feel like to be hanged."

"So you're scared?"

"Of course I'm scared," I snapped at him. "I'm terrified, if you want to know. I'm not like you. I haven't done this kind of thing before."

"We're all scared, Molly," he said.

"Even you?"

"Especially me. I've already faced the prospect of life in jail once before, and now I might be facing it again. That would be worse for me than the hangman's noose. Forty years of never seeing the sun, or the green fields, or cows and horses, or watching children play or women dancing. . . . It's a lot to give up."

"A terrible lot."

He put a hand on my shoulder and caressed it gently.

"It's not too late to back out, Molly," he said. "I wouldn't want that kind of future for you. You should marry and have children and live out your days happily."

I was sorely tempted. "And if I backed out," I said hesitantly, "how would you get yourselves into that jail?"

"I expect we'd manage," he said. "We'd send your brother in to visit Joseph instead of you."

That did it, of course. Liam's life for mine. As things stood now, it was Liam in this whole venture who had the best chance for escape. He was a fast runner, and I had seen how quickly he could lose himself in the maze of backstreets. I knew I'd never forgive myself if he was condemned to death or spent the rest of his life in jail because I had taken the easy way out.

"I'm not backing out now, Cullen," I said. "You can count on me."

"Molly," he said, and unexpectedly his arms came around me. He held me so fiercely I could hardly breathe.

We stood there, wrapped in each other's arms, my head on his shoulder. Then he bent to brush my cheek with the lightest of kisses and released me, still feeling breathless.

"So—is there anything you'd like to do today?" he asked.

"The condemned's last meal?" I asked.

"Any letters you'd like posted?"

This brought me rapidly to harsh reality. Did I want to write a farewell letter to Daniel? To Sid and Gus?

"I'll write them," I said, "but I'll give them to Mrs. Boone. I only want them posted if I"—I stopped. I couldn't say the words.

I went through to my room and sat staring at the writing paper on the table.

"My dearest Daniel," I wrote. "If you read this, I am no longer alive or I'm a captive. I had to do what I could to save my brother. It was probably foolish of me, but you know I've never been the most sensible of women. I love—" I picked up the sheet of paper, crumpled it and threw it into the waste bin. How could I put down feelings on paper when I wasn't even sure of them myself?

❧ Thirty-one ❧

October Twenty-second dawned bright and crystal clear. The sky was like spun blue glass and every bare tree branch, every building and lamppost etched in fine detail against that blue arc. Just when mist and cloud and rain would have been useful to hide what was about to happen, we would be spotlighted like players on a stage. It was as if the elements were mocking us.

Mary Ann, or Mrs. Boone as I still thought of her, brought up a breakfast tray as the sun streamed in through my casement window. "You'll be needing your strength, I've no doubt," she said, and placed it on the marble-topped table. It contained a dish of porridge, a smoked haddock with a fried egg on top and several slices of toast. I tried to eat, but somehow I didn't feel hungry.

"You should get all your belongings packed up right away," she said when she came to collect the tray and tut-tutted over the amount I had left. "Someone will be coming for them."

"My belongings?" It had a horrible finality to it. Did they now take for granted that I wouldn't be needing any of my worldly goods again?

"It wouldn't do for them to find any trace of you here, just in case the place is searched," she said.

"Where will they be taken?" I asked.

"To the ship," she said. "More than that I can't tell you."

When she returned to collect the tray I remembered something that had been bothering me. "Mrs. Boone, I mean Mary Ann—you will write to your brother, won't you? He sent me to find you and I'd hate him to think that I'd failed or hadn't bothered to do the job."

"I don't know that I have any wish to contact my brother," she said. "But I'll do what you wish, just to let him know I'm alive and well and you did your job just fine."

She picked up the tray. "And it may prove useful at some stage to have a powerful ally in America."

I packed up everything and again thought about writing letters home. But I couldn't bring myself to do so. Around noon Mrs. Boone offered lunch but neither Cullen nor I were in any mood to eat. The waiting seemed endless. At last Cullen tapped on my door.

"Time to go. Are you ready?"

I nodded. He led me down the stairs. There was no sign of Mrs. Boone, and I realized she probably didn't want to say good-bye. I walked beside Cullen into the back streets of the Liberties, and at last we were admitted to a ramshackle house over a stable. Inside the room was dark, with tattered curtains drawn across the window, and it didn't smell too wholesome either, with the odor of unwashed bodies competing with the horse manure rising from the stable below. As far as I could make out in the gloom, there were several boys present, a couple of whom I had seen before at Grania's, and one of whom was my brother. The tension in the atmosphere was palpable, although the boys attempted bravado, with insults and jokes as their instructions were given. I was handed the bottle of smelling salts, which now contained chloroform and shown how many drops to use and how to administer it. Then I was handed a basket of baked goods.

"Isn't this a little obvious?" I asked. "They are bound to search a basket like this."

"Of course they are," Cullen said. "They'll immediately think of files baked into the soda bread; knives in the plum cake. And of course they'll find nothing and feel rather stupid. Then we hope they'll let down their guard a trifle."

"I feel like Little Red Riding Hood, going to see her grandma," I said, and Cullen laughed.

"So you are," he agreed.

"But the grandma was a wolf in disguise with big teeth and he ate her up," I reminded him.

I came back into the main room to find the boys pouring over a street plan of the city. We were shown a plan of the best escape routes to cut across the Liberties and emerge on the riverbank close to where the boat would be waiting for us. It would be tied up by the Grand Canal docks, seaward of the last bridge at the mouth of the Liffy and the open sea. The craft was to be a fishing smack, complete with nets and busy fishermen making ready on deck, but we'd know it from other fishing boats by the small green flag of Ireland that would be flying somewhere visible.

After that we waited some more. The boys passed around a flask of something, helping to bolster their courage, but they didn't offer it to me, for which I was glad. I couldn't have swallowed if I'd tried. At last Cullen consulted his watch.

"Right, boys. Four o'clock. I think this is it," Cullen said. "Ready to go?"

They nodded, eyes unnaturally bright.

"Let's show the English bastards a thing or two, shall we then?" Cullen roared. "Let's strike a blow for freedom, for independence, for Ireland."

A loud cheer went up and the boys scrambled for the door as if they couldn't wait for the battle to be enjoined.

Liam slipped into place beside me. "Good luck then, Molly. Look, if something happens to Joseph and me, and we aren't around any more— you'll get in touch with young Malachy, won't you? Mr. O'Brien in Westport knows where he's staying."

"You'll be fine, Liam," I said. "We'll all be fine."

He grinned at me. "This is a queer business and that's a fact, isn't it? Who'd have thought when we played follow the leader over the rocks on the beach and you fell into that tide pool that we'd someday be doing something like this?"

"Never in a million years," I agreed.

"We had some good times, didn't we, Molly?" he said. "I know life was hard, and it was especially hard work for you after Mam died, but we had some grand old times."

I nodded, for once my heart too full to speak. I reached out to take his hand, then thought better of it.

"Right, advance troops move out," Cullen said. "First wave is me, Molly, Billy, and Tinker with the cart. Next wave, Liam and Paddy, you're to count to two hundred and then follow. Once we're out of this house you don't speak to each other, you don't acknowledge each other in any way, got it?" The boys nodded. "And whatever happens, don't panic." He looked around the group. "God go with you, boys. See you at the boat, then."

He opened the door. As I went to pass him, he took my hand and held it fast. "Take care of yourself, Molly, won't you? No stupid heroics. If they catch you, play the helpless female card—that Cullen Quinlan, he seduced me, so I didn't really know what I was doing. Bat your eyelids, cry, faint. Whatever it takes. They'll never hang a woman."

I hardly found that encouraging, but I knew what he was trying to do.

"Don't worry about me. I'll be just fine," I said.

"I know you will. You're a grand girl." He brought my hand up to his lips and kissed it. Then he released me and we both stepped outside into the fierce sunlight. Cullen led me at a great pace through the maze of backstreets. We attracted interested stares from the occasional housewife gossiping on her doorstep, or a cluster of men lolling against a corner with nothing better to do, but no more than any stranger to the neighborhood would have done. At last we stepped out of the maze of backstreets and there, across the road was Kilmainham Goal.

It loomed over us, bigger and more formidable than I remembered—a towering mountain of solid brick, surrounded by an iron fence, its massive studded oak door firmly shut.

"This is it," Cullen whispered. "Off you go. You've got ten minutes to do your stuff." He pulled out a pocket watch, then sauntered on, as if he hadn't a care in the world.

I took a deep breath and then crossed the street to the jail. There was a bell to the right of the great studded front door. I tugged on it and heard a jangle echoing inside. After what seemed an eternity, a small door within the massive one was opened and a uniformed guard looked out. I gave him my most winning smile.

"Hello," I said. "Am I in the right place? This is the jail, isn't it?"

"Well, it's not Buckingham Palace, you can count on that," he said, scowling at me.

"I'm here on a sad mission, to see my little brother," I said. "I've come down from our home in Connemara to say good-bye to him."

"Your brother?"

"Joseph Murphy. He's—he's set to be executed, you know. I've come to say good-bye. I've a letter here, from His Majesty's home office in London, giving me permission for the visit." I fished in the basket I was carrying and produced the letter.

This caused the old man to pay attention. He scratched his head and looked entirely uncomfortable.

"Wait here," he said.

He disappeared in through the small door, closing it behind him and leaving me waiting outside. After what seemed like another long wait, the door was opened again and this time two more senior officers came out and examined my letter.

"We weren't informed of this, Miss Murphy," one of them said.

"I'm sorry you weren't informed," I said, "but it's the Home Secretary himself who signed the letter for me, and my own member of parliament who asked him to do so."

One of them started to mutter about calling Dublin Castle for confirmation, but I cut in, "Look, Officer, have you no heart? The Home Secretary was apparently most touched by my plight. My little brother—all I had left in the world, you know. I came all the way here on my own. I'm just asking for a few minutes with him, to say good-bye. What can be so hard about that?"

The two men exchanged glances. Finally one of them said, "Very well. Let her in. But that basket will need to be searched."

He attempted to take it from me.

I resisted. "You're not going to deny the boy a slice of his sister's soda bread, are you? Nor his favorite plum cake?"

"There's many a weapon been smuggled in a cake before now," one of the men said. "Let's take a look, shall we?"

With that he broke open the soda bread, then the cake, then a couple of the rock cakes. When all that was left were some biscuits too small to hide anything larger than a darning needle, he handed the basket back to me. "All in order, miss. Sorry I had to mess them about a bit, but we can't be too careful, can we?"

"Of course not, Officer," I said, smiling sweetly at him. "You can never be too careful."

"Now your purse," the other said and took it roughly from me. It was only a fabric dolly bag, not big enough to conceal a gun, for example. He opened it wide.

"There's just the things a lady always needs—my handkerchief, my smelling salts, a comb, and a few coins," I said. "See for yourself."

He nodded and handed it back to me.

"All right then. This way. Watch your step." He stood aside to let me through the little pass door. I stepped into the main foyer of the jail. The area was lit by a large central skylight and tier after tier of iron balconies rose up around that central well. It provided a gloomy sort of light, like being inside an aquarium. "Wait here, please," one of the officers said. "Johnson!" He barked at the original warder. "Go and fetch the officer from level two."

"Very good, sir."

Johnson set off, up the first flight of iron stairs, the loud clanking sounds of his feet reverberating through the building. Two more officers marched across the stone floor of the foyer. From above came an exchange of angry male voices and then something like an animal snarl. I found myself shivering in the damp cold. More from fear than from cold, probably. It would never work. The whole thing was impossible. The place was a steel-and-stone fortress. I was risking my life for nothing.

"This way then, Miss Murphy," the senior man said, and indicated I should follow him. I did so with leaden feet. He pushed open a door in the wall to my right, just behind the entrance. "Wait in here."

It was a small dark room, and reminded me painfully of the room in The Tombs where I had been brought to see Daniel. Same damp musty smell, same feel of hopelessness. There were two wooden chairs and I was offered one of these. I sat, hardly daring to breathe. Wasn't all this taking too long? What if the explosion at the front door happened even before Joseph had been let out of his cell?

More boots on the stone floor and another guard arrived. He was a beefy man with big lambchop whiskers, and instantly I tried to picture myself clamping a chloroformed handkerchief over his face.

"This is Miss Murphy. She's got a letter from the Home Secretary to let her visit her brother—isn't that nice?" the first officer said with clear sarcasm.

"Murphy? Right. So I should take her in then, should I?"

They were both looking at me with steel-hard eyes. At least they were making my task easier. If I had to knock somebody out, I'd rather it was an unsympathetic type.

"No, bring him down here."

"Do I need to manacle him?"

"Just the cuffs will do."

"Very good, sir."

Both officers went out, closing the door behind me. I was left alone to wait. I was so tempted to check the chloroform bottle, but I suspected I might be observed through a peephole, so I sat like a demure little miss, fighting back the urge to flee.

At last I heard more feet and a voice saying, "In you go, then. And only a few minutes, mind." He opened the door. "Visitor for you, Murphy." He shoved Joseph into the room, almost making him fall over me. As he fought to recover his balance, Joseph's startled face looked at me, then recognition dawned.

"Molly! What in heaven's name? I thought you were dead. I can't believe it."

I hugged him. He was all skin and bone. I could feel his backbone through the coarse shirt with arrows on it. His skin was as gray and pasty as uncooked dough, and there were great sunken circles around his eyes. It almost broke my heart to look at him.

"That's enough of that." The guard roughly pushed us apart. "Sit down, Murphy. You too, miss."

"What are you doing here?" Joseph was looking at me with excited anticipation. "Have you come to get me out? Did they hear my appeal?"

"I don't know anything about your appeal, Joseph," I said. "I only know that I had to visit you while I was in Ireland, to give you my love and Liam's love . . ."

His face lit up. "Liam? You've seen him?"

"Briefly," I said. "He's well and wishes you well."

"And Malachy?"

"I haven't seen him yet, but I gather he's being well looked after."

"He's a grand little chap." A big smile spread across his face as if he could see Malachy standing beside me. "Got a temper on him like me."

"And me," I said. "I've brought you some of your favorite foods, Joseph."

"Really?" He peered into the basket and a frown crossed his face. I thought for one awful moment that he was going to say he didn't like soda bread, but instead he said, "I never knew you could bake plum cake, Molly."

"When could we ever afford the ingredients?" I demanded. "It was soda bread or nothing, wasn't it? And lucky if there was a mutton bone to stew."

"What did you bring me, the leftovers?" Joseph asked. He attempted to grasp a jagged piece of soda bread with his handcuffed hands.

"Those guards at the gate went through everything," I said. "They thought I might be smuggling you a file or a knife."

Joseph laughed. "A lot of good they would do in this hellhole. What would I do, cut my way out through the brick walls?"

The warder shifted from one foot to the other, making the keys jangle. A thought struck me. "There's plenty for all," I said, holding up the basket to him. "If you'd like a bite for yourself, Officer. I'm known for my light hand at baking."

"I won't say no," the warder said, and took a big piece of plum cake, stuffing it into his mouth.

I wondered how much of the ten minutes had gone by now. Surely it must have taken all of ten minutes to examine my letter, then the basket, and then to have Joseph fetched. If I was going to act, it had to be now. I put my hand into my purse and drew out my handkerchief. "My, but it's clammy in here, isn't it?" I said. "Oppressive. I feel as if I might faint."

"Out of the way, Murphy. Let the young lady sit down," the guard said, his mouth still full of plum cake.

Joseph stood aside, and the officer assisted me to sit on the nearest chair.

"You'd better sit down too, Murphy."

Joseph sat.

"I don't know what came over me," I twittered in best feminine fashion. "It must be the shock of seeing my little brother like this. I never was of strong constitution. Always did have a weak heart, didn't I, Joe."

Again I glanced at him to make sure he didn't contradict me. But instead he nodded. "Yes, she was always the delicate one of the family," he agreed. "It's good of you to come and put yourself through this, Molly."

I had taken out the bottle. "I'll be right as rain in a minute," I said. "Just a whiff of my smelling salts." I opened it, shook out drops onto the handkerchief as I had been instructed, and then, without warning, jumped up and thrust it into Shaw's face. His mouth was still full of cake. He spluttered. I caught an elbow in the side that almost winded me. Joe was on his feet instantly, butting his head into the man's stomach to knock him back against the wall, while I tried valiantly to keep that handkerchief over his face. He fought for a moment or two then he collapsed onto the floor.

"Quick" I hissed to Joseph, who was standing like a statue, staring down at the warder in horror. "I don't know how long we've got. Quick."

I was down on my knees wrestling with the clip that held the guards keys to his belt. "We need his keys."

"What's the point?" Joe said. "I'll never get out. There's only the one door."

"Which will be blown out, if all goes according to plan," I said.

"Which of the keys opens those handcuffs?"

"I've no idea," he said, looking at the great bunch. "A small one, obviously."

"Obviously," I snapped, my nerves stretched to breaking point. I tried one, then another, then another.

"We'll never get you into his jacket in time. When you hear the blast, I'm going to yell, 'Run, Joe, run,' but you stay hidden. Then we'll try to sneak out in the confusion. As soon as you get out, run like hell. Go through the Liberties and make for the river. At the docks by the

Grand Canal, look for a fishing boat flying a green flag. It will take you to France."

"Jesus, Mary, and Joseph." He crossed himself. "I can't believe it's my own sister telling me this."

"I wish I could get these dratted handcuffs off you. You'll be so obvious running with handcuffs on," I said. "Maybe I should take the guard's jacket off and put it over your shoulders."

"I don't know, Molly," he said.

"Here, take the basket. You can hide your hands in it as you run."

"I'd look stupid with a woman's basket," he commented.

"Better stupid than dead," I snapped, remembering suddenly how very annoying my brothers used to be. "At least I've got the keys to hand over to our boys. Where are the political prisoners kept?"

"Second level, like me. There's a whole string of us."

"That's good. Then we've the right keys."

I glanced down nervously at the guard, who was still lying there. Shouldn't we tie him up or something? Then another chilling thought came to me—the attempt outside the door had failed, and Joe and I were sitting ducks. I had just chloroformed a guard. The penalty for that would be tremendous. I couldn't stand being shut in that little room a moment longer. Surely ten minutes must have passed long ago.

"I'm going to take a peek outside," I said. "If all's clear we can sneak toward the front door, and be ready when they blast it out."

I opened the door a few inches and peered out cautiously. I found myself staring into another face—a face I recognized but failed to put a name to right away.

"Well done, Miss Murphy. I have to congratulate you," a voice said, and I realized who he was. It was the detective inspector from the ship—the one in the tweed jacket who had followed me around. And behind him stood another familiar figure—Detective Inspector Harris.

❧ Thirty-two ❧

The door of the cell was flung open and a uniformed constable grabbed Joseph, while the first detective took me by the arm.

"How did you know I'd be here?" I demanded. "How did you find out?"

"It was elementary, my dear Watson, as the fictional Mr. Holmes would say," the detective said, holding me with my arm twisted behind my back. "We have been tailing you since the ship. We'd had Oona Sheehan in our sights for quite a while, you know. And when we found out that she was leaving the ship in a hurry at the last moment, and leaving all her luggage behind, we thought it expedient to examine that luggage. Very interesting personal belongings, wouldn't you say?"

"You knew about the guns in the trunks?" I stared, openmouthed.

"Oh, indeed we did."

"Then why did you do nothing?"

"Because, my dear, we were anxious to know for whom they were intended. So all we had to do was wait and watch. I must say we were concerned when you vanished for a while. But we received a telephone call at headquarters a few minutes ago to say that you'd shown up here, so here we all are. Now, I presume you are not a major player in this little farce, in fact likely as not you've been suckered into it, so we'll just wait for your little pals to show up, shall we?"

"You've got it all wrong," I said defiantly. "When I heard that my brother was in jail here, I just wanted to see him one last time. And it was only at the last second that I decided to have a go at that guard and see if there was any way I could help Joseph escape."

"Pull the other one; it's got bells on," Inspector Harris said with a chuckle. "So the maid got wind of what was being shipped in those trunks, did she? What was it, blackmail? You decided she was a danger to your little scheme, and you had to finish her off? Did you do it alone, or did you have an accomplice on board?"

"Look, Inspector." I could hear my voice rising. "Everything I told you before is true. I had no idea I was being tricked on that boat. I had no idea those trunks contained guns until I tried to move them in my hotel room and they clanked. I had no idea for whom those guns were destined. And what's more I'm fed up with being used and manipulated for other people's purposes. I know who killed Rose McCreedy although I'll never be able to prove it now, but I can assure you it wasn't me."

As if on cue at the end of this speech, there was a terrific explosion. I was hurled backward as dust and debris came flying at me. It felt as if all the air was being sucked from my lungs and the sound was so loud that my head was ringing. I think I struck the wall. Anyway, I found myself lying on my back with dust and debris all over me. I picked myself up and staggered to my feet. Smoke and dust and a horrible acrid smell made it hard to see and harder to breathe. There were shouts and groans and the sound of running feet on stone. The inspector from the ship was staggering to his feet, clutching a bleeding head. It looked as if a part of the wall had collapsed on us. I couldn't even see Inspector Harris. But I could see Joseph. He was just standing there, his mouth open in horror.

The inspector let go of his bleeding head and tried to make a grab for me. I darted away, looking around frantically for our lads, so that I could hand over the keys. But nobody appeared. I could feel cold air blowing in through what had been the door, sending the smoke and dust swirling.

"Run, Joe. Get away while you can," I shouted, then plunged myself in the direction of the doorway. Ahead of me was chaos. Police whistles blowing, shouts, screams, and then shots fired. Running feet caught up with me. I decided to take a terrible chance as a warder reached me.

"Oh, Officer, I'm so glad to see you," I gasped, grabbing at his arm.

"I was here on a visit and then there was this terrible explosion. What is it? A gas main?"

"No, miss. I think that some idiots are trying to blow up the building. Here, take my arm. I'll get you safely out, don't you worry."

He led me toward the door with infuriating slowness. The smoke and dust were so thick, it was impossible to see what lay ahead. We stepped over some chunks of rubble, and I saw something on the floor in front of me. For a moment I couldn't think what it was until I realized it was an arm. I swallowed back bile that rose in my throat. The stench of burning was overpowering. It stung my nostrils and made my eyes water. I tried to breathe and started coughing. All around there was coughing and retching and groaning too. Men staggered past us, not seeming to notice me. I recoiled in horror as I came to what used to be the doorway. Jagged shards of wood hung suspended in space. Rubble was piled high, and among that rubble were bodies. I could see that some of them were wearing uniforms but not all. I wanted to look at faces, but couldn't. If Liam was lying at the bottom of that pile, or Cullen, then I didn't want to know.

"Thank you, Officer," I managed to gasp. "I can get out now. Just let me get away from here. Most grateful to you."

He must have been as much in shock as I was. I slid my arm from his and grabbed the jagged edge of what used to be the door frame, stepped cautiously over bodies and rubble, and was outside. The sun was setting, glowing red through the dusty haze, and a mist had come up from the river, curling low along the street. A crowd was already gathering. I looked around. There was no sign of the cart and horses, no sign of Liam or Joseph or Cullen or anyone I could recognize. But there were plenty of blue uniforms milling around in confusion.

Then someone yelled and I saw a figure running across the street. A shot rang out. The figure went sprawling, staggered to his feet and kept on running. Men in blue uniforms gave chase. More shots were fired. There were screams of alarm from the crowd. I took the opportunity to merge with a group of women, pulling my hood up over my head. Gradually I eased my way to the edge of the crowd.

Then there was a barked command, the tramp of marching feet and a platoon of the Iniskilling Dragoons, stationed just across the road, came out of their barracks at a trot, bayonets at the ready. I darted across the street ahead of them. When they were between me and the jail, I turned and fled into the mist.

I was running down a wide street, tree lined, elegant, but it wasn't the street that led into the Liberties. In fact, I had no idea where it led. In contrast to the other streets, it was deserted. The shape of a big building loomed ahead of me. From what I could see in the growing darkness it had that same elegant Georgian design as the Four Courts, and I had a moment's panic that it might be some kind of government headquarters into which I was now blundering. I thought I heard running feet and shouts behind me, and I steeled myself for a shot in the back. I glanced to either side of me. On the riverside mist hovered over a stretch of open ground. Not a good place to seek cover. The other side of the street was bordered by a high wall. The running feet were definitely gaining on me, and I was finding it hard to breathe. When I found an opening in the wall I ran through it, not even stopping to think what I might find.

It was now almost dark and getting mistier by the moment. I ran past a line of yew trees, then gasped as a white figure, brandishing a sword, rose up in front of me. It took a moment for my heart to calm down enough to recognize that it was a marble statue of an angel, probably St. Michael by the look of him, and that I had stumbled into a cemetery. I dodged between grave stones, past Celtic crosses, around more angels. I could hear those running feet clearly approaching now. I came to a mausoleum, elaborately decorated with urns and cherubs, climbed the low iron fence, and cowered beside one of its corner pillars. I'd be fine here unless they had lanterns or dogs with them.

The sound of footsteps had stopped. I crouched low without moving, trying to regulate the great gasps of breath. I heard nothing more and was about to straighten up when there came the distinct crunch of a foot on gravel, on the other side of the mausoleum. Farther away, on the other side of the wall, there were shouts. It sounded as if they were coming this way.

I looked around, deciding whether I should stay where I was or attempt to run. I could see no safer hiding place, pulled the black cape around me, and decided to bluff it out. Then suddenly shouts erupted again, and I was almost knocked over as someone stumbled into me. I waited to feel hands grab me or a bayonet spear me, but instead the person dropped to the ground beside me and I heard ragged breathing. I pulled my hood aside to look and saw Cullen, pressing himself against the marble, clutching his side, panting in rasping breaths. His eyes suddenly spotted me, registering recognition and warning at the same time. I took the cape and flung it over the two of us.

Feet crunched on gravel. More shouts. Then someone called "This way!" and the footsteps receded. Cullen and I huddled together without moving. I straightened up, looked around, and whispered, "I think they've gone."

He didn't move and I was afraid for a moment that he was dead. Then he stood up, in obvious pain, still clutching at his side.

"Are you all right?" I asked.

"They shot at me," he said. "I seem to be bleeding pretty badly."

"We need something stop the bleeding." I tried to think clearly then lifted my skirt, untied my petticoat and stepped out of it.

"I must be pretty bad," Cullen muttered with a grimace. "The sight of a pretty woman undressing, and it doesn't rouse me."

"Show me where it is."

He lifted his jacket and I saw the right side of his white shirt was sodden with a big dark stain. I folded the petticoat into a pad. "Keep that pressed to it. There's nothing more I can do here and now. We should get you to a doctor."

"Are you mad? We can't wait around to see a doctor. The boat will leave without us. They won't wait forever."

"A lot of good the boat will be if you die on the way to France," I said.

"Someone on board will know what to do," he said. "I don't think the bullet struck any vital organ or I'd be dead by now. It's just a question of stopping the blood."

"All right." I took a deep breath and tried to sound calm and in control, even though I was trembling. "Can you walk, do you think?"

"I have to," he said.

"Lean on me," I whispered.

"I'll manage. You'll need all of your own strength. And Molly—if they come after us, don't stick around to wait for me. Run like hell."

"Such heroics," I said, and heard him chuckle.

We made our way through the cemetery and came out to the still-deserted street. After we'd gone a few hundred yards I could see the river ahead of us. Cullen was staggering rather than walking.

"How far is it to the docks where we're meeting the boat?"

"Maybe three miles," he said.

"You'll never make it. Look, we're close to the river. Why don't I drop you off at St. Francis. Mrs. Boone can look after you."

"We agreed we wouldn't go back there," Cullen said. "She's too important to put at risk."

"But you can't walk three miles."

"That's true."

"And we can't risk taking a cab. You'd bleed all over the seat."

"That's true as well."

"So what are we going to do?"

He was breathing heavily now. "You leave me and go on alone. The boat won't wait forever."

"I'm not leaving you." I tried to think.

"We could go down to the river and see if we can find ourselves a little boat," Cullen said at last. "Do you know how to row?"

"Of course, but that's stealing."

"Molly—we're about to be hanged for murder. I don't think stealing a boat will make much difference at this stage," he snapped.

I saw his point. "Come on, then. Let's take this alleyway."

We came out to the river, now shrouded in a blanket of sea mist. Perfect for our intentions, in fact. We crossed the road and kept walking until we found steps down to the water. I went down, but no boats were in sight. We continued and tried again. Still nothing. Cullen was coughing—a rasping rattle that shook his whole body. "He won't make it out of here alive," I thought. Another set of steps led down opposite a public house, from which came raucous singing. It occurred to me to go in there and ask for help, but then fortune finally smiled on us. I heard the creak of oars and a boat came into view. What's more it was heading for the steps. I watched as a wiry little man stepped out, tied it up, then headed up the steps and into the pub.

As soon as he had disappeared inside the pub I helped Cullen down into the boat, untied it, and cast off. Luck was with us. The tide was in full ebb, which made the rowing easy. We passed under one bridge and the next. I kept expecting to hear shouts or shots as we were detected, but none came. At last we passed the great shape of the Custom's House.

"The docks are just up ahead," Cullen said. "Pull in to the next landing place."

He seemed a little more lively and cheerful and handed me the rope as I climbed out. "I am certainly more agile without that blasted petticoat," I said, and he chuckled.

I helped him out and we came up to the quay.

"Fishing boat. Green flag," he said.

I searched up and down the quay. It was empty.

✖ Thirty-three ✖

Cullen and I looked at each other.

"Are you sure this is the right place?" I heard the tremble in my voice.

He nodded. "Right where the Grand Canal Docks meet the Liffy, they said. And see—that's where the docks begin."

"Maybe there was a hitch and they had to tie up somewhere else." I tried to stay positive. "You stay there and I'll look."

"You can't look the whole length of the Liffy," he snapped. "We have to just face it. The boat has gone without us. It wasn't safe to wait any longer."

"Then what do we do now?" Until this moment there had been hope. Now hope was rapidly fading. "We have to go back to Mrs. Boone. There's nothing else we can do."

"I've told you, we're not going there," he said firmly. He closed his eyes. Then he attempted a deep breath, gasped in pain, and put his hand to his side. "There is an emergency plan," he said, almost in a whisper. "Another place where a boat could pick us up if they are warned in time."

"Right. Let's get there."

"But it's several miles out of Dublin."

"Oh wonderful," I said, my patience and optimism now worn remarkably thin. "We'll just run several miles out of Dublin then, shall we?"

"Grania," he said. "We'll have to risk going to Grania."

253

"Are you mad? If you're worried about putting Mrs. Boone in danger, then what about Grania?"

"I think we'd be fairly safe there. They probably won't think of checking on her. Especially as her husband is now in residence."

"Oh sure. Her husband. That makes it all the more inviting."

"We need help from somewhere, Molly. And we have to get out of Dublin. Come on. We're but a stone's throw from Grania's here. I can make it just fine."

I took his arm to support him, and he didn't refuse me. We cut inland and soon came to the elegant outline of Merrion Square and Grania's house.

"We can't just walk up and ring the front doorbell," I said.

"No, I grant you we can't do that," he agreed. "What time is it? Not yet eight o'clock. That means the servants will be fully occupied. We'd better go round to the mews and wait."

We did so, standing shivering in the alleyway beside the stable door.

"The groom must be still at supper," Cullen said. He leaned back against the woodwork and closed his eyes.

"Are you all right?"

"I don't know," he said. "I don't know how badly I was hit."

"What happened at the prison?"

"Utter disaster. They must have been tipped off to us. Just as we were setting the explosives, a whole band of RIC showed up. I yelled for the others to run, then I pressed the plunger. At least that gave the boys in blue a shock. And did quite a bit of damage too, from what I could see. But they started shooting at us. I didn't even have a chance to get inside. I had to run away with the rest. What a shambles."

"My brothers," I began, not wanting to know the answer. "What about Liam? Did he get away?"

"I've no idea. I saw some of our boys go down."

"I think they shot Joseph," I said. "I told him to run but there were police everywhere, and it was all I could do to escape."

"You did just grand," he said.

I shook my head, fighting back tears. "I was the one who caused the disaster," I said. "Oh, not intentionally, I promise you. But it seems the police had been tailing me from the ship. They had found out about the shipment of rifles, but let me go ahead, waiting to see where I went and what I did."

Cullen nodded. "As I said, the enemy is not stupid." He grimaced and his hand went to his side. "I'm afraid your petticoat is quite soaked through," he said.

At that moment a light shone from a side door and the groom returned, whistling merrily as he sauntered across the mews. The whistling ceased abruptly as he noticed figures lurking in the shadows, and he gave a yell of alarm when Cullen lurched out on him.

"Oh, it's you, sir," the boy stammered.

"We're in trouble, Johnnie," Cullen whispered. "You'll not have heard the news yet, but we had a little run in with the police and we have to get away from here. I need you to take a message to your mistress."

Fear registered in the groom's eyes. "They have guests for dinner, sir. It's more than my job's worth to disturb her."

"Then do you have access to pen and paper, man? I'll write her a note."

"I have pen and paper up in my room. You'd better come up."

We went up the rickety outside staircase and into a low-ceilinged room. Johnnie found Cullen a notepad and pen and ink, and Cullen sat composing a note.

"Take this to the butler and tell him he has to get it to your mistress somehow or other. It's a matter of life and death. Do you understand me, boy?"

The frightened groom nodded, his eyes as wide as saucers.

"And we'll need to borrow a couple of horses."

"Borrow our horses, sir? Without asking the mistress?"

"We've no time to waste, Johnnie. We must get out of the city while we still can."

I'd been taking no part in this, but now I was listening with growing alarm.

"Hold on there," I interjected. "It's no use asking for a horse for me. I can't ride. I've never ridden a horse in my life, apart from sitting on an old cart horse and being led around a field once."

"Damn," Cullen swore under his breath. "Then you'll have to ride pillion behind me."

"I'm not sure about this. Not until her ladyship . . . ," Johnnie began.

"I'll take good care of the damned horse and make sure it's returned. I can't say better than that. Now are you with me, or will I have to take out my pistol and shoot you?"

The boy looked terrified. "I'm with you, sir. Just as long as I don't get in trouble."

"I've explained all in my note, Johnnie boy. You just deliver it as soon as we've gone. I promise you won't get in trouble on our account."

"Very well, sir. What horse should I give you?"

"One that won't be required in the morning or missed too quickly."

"Then it had better be Old Traveler. The master don't ride him no more, not since he bought that devil Satan."

"Old Traveler—he's got the wind to make the journey, has he?"

"Oh yes, he's a grand horse. Steady as a rock."

"Then be a good lad and saddle him up for us."

"And while you're doing that, do you have bandages and antiseptics?" I asked. "Mr. Quinlan has been wounded."

"Only for the horses, miss," the boy replied.

"Better than nothing," I said. "Bring me what you've got."

He returned. "Let me take a look at that wound, Cullen," I said.

"We've no time now."

"At least let me put a clean pad on you and bandage you up so you don't start bleeding again while the boy saddles up the horse."

"Very well."

I eased away his shirt and heard the boy gasp when he saw the dark bloody mess that was Cullen's side. I didn't feel too well myself, but I dabbed it with antiseptic, put on a pad, and bandaged him as tightly as I dared.

"That will have to do, Molly," Cullen said. "We can't wait another minute. For all we know, the roads will already be watched."

We went down to the stable below. The groom was hefting a saddle onto the back of what seemed to be an enormous horse. I couldn't believe this was happening. The past weeks had turned into an ever-expanding nightmare, the kind of dream in which one runs from one monster to the next. Was it ever going to end, I wondered, or would it finish in that greatest nightmare of all—a walk up the steps to a gallows?

The horse was saddled and bridled. Johnnie was about to lead it out when we heard the sound of boots on cobbles.

"You, in there," a voice barked. "I need a mount, immediately."

I had been right about the nightmare ever growing in intensity. It was Justin Hartley, and he came into the stable. I shrank back into a corner, but Justin only cast a cursory glance around until he spotted Johnnie. "Oh, you've a horse saddled up for me already have you? My man must have informed you I was going out." He stepped toward Traveler and then flicked his whip at Johnnie in anger. "Not that horse, you fool. Lord Ashburton has told me I may ride Satan, and I'll ride none other. Now get him saddled up for me right away before I give you a dashed good thrashing."

"Right away, Mr. Hartley, sir," the boy said, and led out a handsome black horse. Cullen and I stayed motionless in our corner until Justin Hartley swung himself up into the saddle and galloped off into the night.

"A most unpleasant fellow," Cullen muttered to me. "But that was a close shave."

He had no idea how close. My legs wouldn't obey me, and I had to be lifted onto the horse by the patient Johnnie. Cullen eased himself into the saddle with a hiss of pain. "Hold tightly around my waist," he said. "I'll try to keep the pace even for both of our sakes."

Then he dug in his heels and we were off. I wanted to cling on tightly, but I was afraid of hurting Cullen's wound. I tried to grab onto the saddle instead, but there was really nothing to hold onto. It was like sitting on a plank on the ocean, which I'd done as a girl.

"You will not fall off," I instructed myself.

Cullen took us through narrow back streets until city gave way to big houses set back from the road. Then he urged the horse into a canter. I stifled a cry as I was thrown up and down. I wanted to cling on tighter, and grabbed at Cullen's thigh as the one stable thing. After a while I began to feel the rhythm a bit better.

"Where are we going?" I asked.

"To a place where we can hide out for the night," he said.

"And after that?"

"We pray that there's a boat at the proper place and the proper time."

The last lights of the city were left behind and only open country was ahead of us. It was almost too dark to see anything, but we appeared to be in a narrow lane that climbed and wound up a hillside.

"Are we heading for the sea?" I asked.

"No, we're heading inland," he called back.

"But I thought you said something about a boat."

"I thought the roads to the water would be watched. They won't suspect we'd go this way. We can drop down to the coast later."

We rode on, passing the occasional hamlet with the warm light of lanterns glowing from windows, inviting with the promise of normal life and safety. Dogs barked from farmyards. At last we seemed to have reached an open area of heath. Cullen reined in the horse, and a great iron gate appeared ahead of us. It swung open when pushed, however, and we passed through, coming to a halt beside what seemed to be an old ruin.

"This is where we rest for a while," he said. "Can you dismount by yourself? I don't think I can help you."

I slid down in what was probably a most undignified manner, then I helped Cullen. He groaned as his feet touched the ground and would have collapsed if I hadn't been holding him.

"Where are we?" I asked.

"Safe for the night," he said, breathing heavily.

"Will there be someone who can do something for your wound?"

"No. There's nobody here but us." He led the horse forward, loosened the saddle girth then tied the reins to a post. "You'll have to make do like that until tomorrow, old chap." He slapped the horse's side, then turned to me. "This way."

The building that loomed out of the darkness looked like an old abbey, grim, windowless, made of rough stone. No welcoming lights shone from the windows. In fact, there were no lights to be seen, only the sigh of wind through dead bracken and bare branches. I shivered in the cold.

"What is this place?" I asked.

"It's an old chapel, no longer used."

"Why here?"

"Because nobody will find us, and it's an easy ride to the ocean from here."

He stumbled ahead of me to a side porch and turned a big iron knob on the door. It swung open with a creak. I followed him inside. It was pitch dark and smelled very old, musty, moldy, damp, and not at all appealing.

"I don't like it here," I said. "It has a bad feeling to it. Are you sure it's a chapel?"

"Decommissioned since the time of Henry VIII. And you're right about the bad feeling. I believe the Hell-Fire Club used to meet here a hundred years ago."

"Then for God's sake, let's go somewhere else."

I was truly shivering now.

Cullen turned to face me, putting a hand on my shoulder. "My dear girl, perhaps you don't realize, but all of Ireland will be out looking for us tonight and they'll have orders to shoot to kill. There are no other places where we can rest safely until the time to meet the boat."

"Then why is this one so safe?"

"Because it is on the Hyde-Borne's estate, and, as we know, Lord and Lady Ashburton are with their retinue in Dublin. That's why it's fine to leave Lord Ashburton's horse here. They'll know where to find him. Now let's find a dry corner and maybe something to lie on."

We blundered around, bumping into tables and benches, arranging several of the latter into a platform we could lie on.

"I wish we'd find some kind of light," I groaned as my shin met a bench for the tenth time.

"We couldn't risk using it if we did. We're on a hilltop here. A light shining out from a disused chapel would certainly be noticed. And seeing that it has associations with the Hell-Fire Club, rumors would fly."

"I'm cold and hungry and scared," I said, then felt terrible about saying it. At least I didn't have a bullet wound in my side. "If we had light I could maybe redress that wound."

"The moon will be up later, if it doesn't cloud over," he said.

I spread my cloak on the benches.

"Go ahead and lie down," I said. "I'll keep watch."

"A lot of good you'd do, keeping watch." Cullen managed a chuckle that turned to a cough. "Come and lie here beside me."

"The last time a man said that to me, it brought me nothing but trouble," I said, and he laughed.

"My dear, I promise you you're quite safe. I am in no fit state to do anything more than sleep, although on any other occasion I must admit that you would not have been safe from my impulses." He took my hand. "Come on, Molly. I'm cold and I'm hurting. I need your warmth beside me."

He groaned again as he tried to lie down. I helped him to get comfortable then I lay beside him and put my arm over him. He did feel very cold. I suppose we must have drifted to sleep because when I awoke the moon was shining in through a high window. Cullen's breathing sounded ragged. I got up and tucked the cloak around him. He opened his eyes.

"Are you still in pain?" I asked.

He nodded. "It hurts like the devil to breathe."

"If you come into the moonlight perhaps I can do something for you."

He shook his head. "I don't think there's anything you can do for me, except stay close to me. I need to feel you're here."

"I'm here," I said. I lay back beside him, and wrapped my arm over him again. "It won't be long now. We'll get down to that boat, and then they'll be able to remove that bullet and all will be fine."

"Molly," he said quietly, "I want you to listen to me. You're to leave here as soon as it's light enough to see the way. When you look out toward the east you'll see the little harbor down below. It's not used much any more, since they built the big port at Kingstown. Make your way straight down the hill to it. There will be a rowing boat with something green showing, a green hat or even a green handkerchief in the rower's pocket. He'll ask you if you'd like a trip out to the island, and you'll say yes. If he doesn't ask, don't go with him. It might be another trap. Hopefully our boat will have waited out the night on the far side of Dalkey Island."

"Why are you telling me all this? We'll be going together."

"I'm not sure that I'll make it," he said quietly.

"Don't be ridiculous, of course you're going to make it."

"I've lost a lot of blood, Molly. I'm awfully weak. And every breath feels as if I'm on fire."

I bent toward him and rested my cheek against his. "Just hang on, Cullen. Not much longer. You can't give up now, after all you've been through."

"I know. A stupid waste, isn't it? I had such grand ideas, Molly. Such splendid plans. An Irish Republic, ruling ourselves with dignity. Was that too much to ask?"

"Of course not. It will happen, Cullen."

"I wish I could believe it." He sighed. "The important thing now is that you save yourself. You're young. You deserve a happy life."

"I'm not going without you. I'll get you on that horse somehow, and we'll make it to the boat if it's the last thing I do."

"Dear Molly," he said, and lifted his hand to stroke my hair. "If things had been different—" He let the rest of the sentence hang. "That young man you have waiting for you at home . . ."

"Yes?"

"Treasure him, Molly. Don't let him out of your sight. If only I'd been sensible and not given up all hope of happiness for this stupid dream—for nothing."

"It wasn't for nothing, Cullen. Even if this raid didn't go as we planned, we've rattled them. And the Irish people will read of our boys being gunned down, and they'll start thinking that maybe they should do something too. You'll see. Small pebbles that start the landslide."

He sighed again. "Almost morning, Molly. Look, the moon's going down."

"Let me put a new dressing on that wound for you."

"And where would we find a new dressing?"

"I've still got my blouse and my knickers."

He gave a half cough, half laugh. "This must be the only time in my life that a girl has offered me her knickers and I haven't taken her up on the offer."

The laugh turned into a bout of coughing and I noticed the spittle that ran down his chin was dark. He was coughing up blood. I wiped it away with my sleeve.

"Don't try to talk any more. Save your strength for the ride. We should get going soon, don't you think?"

He didn't answer me.

I looked at him. His eyes were staring up at the ceiling, and I could no longer hear his breathing.

I don't know how long I sat beside him holding his cold hand in mine. I felt so helpless. I should have done more, I kept on thinking. I could have saved him if only I'd known what to do. Then it became clear to me that Cullen knew he wouldn't survive a journey like this. He had only done it to get me away to safety. Had he been alone, he could have gone underground and found someone to hide him in the city, I was sure of it. And maybe a doctor could have removed the bullet and stopped the bleeding and he need not have died. A deep and terrible sense of loss and anger engulfed me as tears ran down my cheeks and dropped onto his cold cheek below me.

"I don't want to leave you, Cullen," I whispered, but I forced myself to stand up. What good would it be to either of us if I allowed myself to be caught? I wrapped my cape around him, and folded his arms across his chest, then I tiptoed out into the gray dawn.

愛 Thirty-four 愛

Rooks were cawing in the little wood below the hill. I could make out the coastline and the gray expanse of sea beyond. A couple of miles, probably, but I certainly wasn't going to attempt to ride that horse. At very least I'd draw attention to myself, and at worst he'd bolt for his own stable or I'd fall off, break a bone, and be captured. No, my own two feet would have to serve me again. I looked back at the building. By daylight it was even more grim and formidable and I was half tempted to go back for Cullen and drag him into the open air rather than leave him there.

The horse looked up expectantly as he heard me coming, then followed me with his gaze as I went past. At least someone would be coming for him and would then find Cullen's body. I started down the hill, over springy turf and soon picked up a track that wound ever downward until I caught a whiff of sea tang ahead. The little town was just coming to life with a milkman delivering bottles to doorsteps and the shutters being raised at the bakery. The tantalizing smell of baking bread almost made me relent and buy a roll to keep me going, but I forced myself to walk past like a healthy young woman, out for a morning constitutional.

I came at last to the harbor. Men were working on nets on the harbor wall. A fishing boat was chugging out into the North Sea. I didn't see the rowing boat at first because it was tied up at the wall, but I heard a voice calling out as I strolled past.

"Like a trip out to the island, miss? Only tuppence."

I looked down at a sailor with a jaunty green scarf around his neck.

"All right," I said, and climbed down the ladder into the boat.

That's pretty much all there is to tell. We met the mother ship—a sturdy little steamer, in the lee of the offshore island and soon were sailing full speed ahead for France. On board were four of our lads, including Liam. Joseph had never made it. Liam and I hugged each other and wept. I told them about Cullen, and we all wept some more. I didn't notice Mr. Fitzpatrick on board and frankly I'd rather not know what happened to him. If I made it safely to New York, then Tommy Burke would hear the whole story.

We landed in Brittany the next day and a passage was booked on the French liner *L'Aquitaine* sailing out of Le Havre to the United States. As a precaution the group's forger had some lovely travel documents made for me in the name of Mary Delaney, so once again I'd be arriving in America under an alias.

We sailed out of Le Havre on a still, cold morning with the smoke from the funnels rising straight in the air. As we left the coast of France behind, it came to me that I could never go home again. Probably never see my brothers again. It was a sobering thought until I realized that America was now my home. I had loved ones waiting for me and an exciting life ahead. I couldn't wait to reach New York.

Historical Note

The attempted break-in at Kilmainham Gaol is fictional, although it represents the kind of skirmishes and actions against English rule that were going on at the time.

The Irish Republican Brotherhood was a forerunner of the IRA—a secret organization pledged to drive the English out of Ireland and to establish home rule.

The Daughters of Erin were as described: founded by actress Maude Gonne to promote the dignity and awareness of Irish womanhood.

Various true-life characters make cameo appearances and Grania Hyde-Borne is based on a real-life countess who gave up her position in society to fight for Irish freedom.

Most early battles in the war for independence were just as poorly planned and futile as the attack on Kilmainham Gaol. Even the Easter Uprising of 1916 was by most standards a fiasco. However, when the young men who took part in it were sentenced to death by firing squad, the Irish populace was stirred for the first time. With the whole population of Ireland now working to drive out the English, independence was finally achieved.